A Note from the Author

Dear Reader,

Ever since I was in high school and began nurturing the dream of becoming a writer, I toyed with different ideas for my nom de plume. Back then, my choice was Melissa Jill Barclay, and Melissa it remained for several years while I tried to break into publishing.

When my friend Sandra Canfield and I sold our first book to Silhouette, we had no choice but to take a pen name—Sandi Shane—combining her first name and my maiden name.

When I started my solo career, I picked Bay Matthews as my pseudonym (after my niece and nephew). Bay was different and catchy—hopefully *memorable*. It worked! Bay Matthews has published twelve titles, had several bestsellers and garnered an award or two.

If there's one thing I've learned about writing, it's that nothing stays the same. Trends come and go. Different elements creep into romance. Some books are easy; others are hard. The list goes on. One recent change is that Silhouette has graciously offered to let me be myself. Starting with *The Greatest Gift of All,* I will be writing for Silhouette under my real name of Penny Richards.

I'd like to take this opportunity to express my sincere thanks to the many readers who've written to Bay throughout the years. It's those letters of encouragement and thanks that make all the hours in front of the computer worth it. I hope all of you continue to enjoy my work as Penny Richards as much as I enjoy exploring the emotions, highs and lows of the characters I create.

Happy reading!

Penny Richards

Dear Reader,

Welcome to Silhouette **Special Edition**...welcome to romance.

Some of your favorite authors are prepared to create a veritable feast of romance for you as we enter the sometimes-hectic holiday season.

Our THAT SPECIAL WOMAN! title for November is *Mail Order Cowboy* by Patricia Coughlin. Feisty and determined Allie Halston finds she has a weakness for a certain cowboy as she strives to tame her own parcel of the open West.

We stay in the West for A RANCHING FAMILY, a new series from Victoria Pade. The Heller siblings—Linc, Beth and Jackson—have a reputation for lassoing the unlikeliest of hearts. This month, meet Linc Heller in *Cowboy's Kin*. Continuing in November is Lisa Jackson's LOVE LETTERS. In *B Is For Baby*, we discover sometimes all it takes is a letter of love to rebuild the past.

Also in store this month are *When Morning Comes* by Christine Flynn, *Let's Make It Legal* by Trisha Alexander, and *The Greatest Gift of All* by Penny Richards. Penny has long been part of the Silhouette family as Bay Matthews, and now writes under her own name.

I hope you enjoy this book, and all of the stories to come. Happy Thanksgiving Day—all of us at Silhouette would like to wish you a happy holiday season!

Sincerely,

Tara Gavin
Senior Editor

Please address questions and book requests to:
Silhouette Reader Service
U.S.: 3010 Walden Ave., P.O. Box 1325, Buffalo, NY 14269
Canadian: P.O. Box 609, Fort Erie, Ont. L2A 5X3

PENNY
RICHARDS
THE GREATEST GIFT OF ALL

SPECIAL EDITION®

Published by Silhouette Books
America's Publisher of Contemporary Romance

This book is for Heidi, who came up with the idea. And to think it sounded so simple—*NOT!* And for Kathey Burton, because *Hardhearted* should have been dedicated to you (the least I could do for coming up with the title), and I forgot!
Special thanks to Mike Walton, M.D., for answering all my medical questions.

 SILHOUETTE BOOKS

ISBN 0-373-09921-5

THE GREATEST GIFT OF ALL

Printed in U.S.A.

PENNY RICHARDS

is the "real" name of writer Bay Matthews, who has been writing for Silhouette for ten years. Claiming that *everything* interests her, she collects dolls, books and antiques. She has been a cosmetologist, an award-winning artist, and worked briefly as an interior decorator. She loves movies, reading, research, redoing old houses, learning how to do anything new, Jeff Bridges, music by Yanni, poetry by Rod McKuen, flea markets, yard sales and finding a good bargain. She lives in Louisiana, with her husband of more than thirty years, has three children and seven grandchildren, all whom she loves dearly. Always behind, Penny admits to procrastination and working better under pressure. She claims she's trying to simplify her life, but just decided to take up quilting and crocheting.

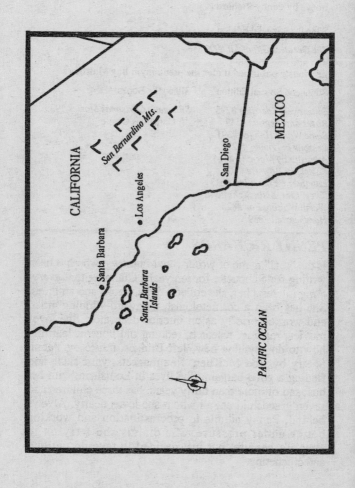

Chapter One

The trial run is only a formality. The job is yours. The soundless chant, born of his nervousness, reminded Baron Montgomery that his good fortune was real. He sat in the room that had been designated as his dressing room and sipped his cooling coffee, waiting for the makeup person who would ready him for his first stint in front of the camera since signing with the new syndicated talk show "The Edge!"

Price Weatherby, Chairman of the Board and CEO of the Los Angeles-based Weatherby Television Network—WTN, one of the most influential cable networks in the country—was impressed with Baron's ten-year career in Houston television. Impressed enough to believe Baron could charm, cajole and otherwise command viewers nationwide. Impressed enough that he offered the native Texan a five-year contract working with Delores SanAngelo, the first Hispanic woman to make really big waves in the world of network television.

Weatherby's decision to hire Baron was based on an unshakable feeling that the Texan's wit and good looks would lure in the feminine viewers, while his natural charisma and his ability to conduct a thought-provoking interview would draw in male watchers, as well.

Though weeks away from airing, "The Edge!" was already being touted as "on the cutting edge of what's happening in your world—now!" The daily, hour-long production would showcase a variety of services, advances and changes along with the people responsible for them, topics ranging from the most recent medical, scientific and socially relevant findings to the newest and hottest authors, artists, musicians and actors. WTN predicted that "The Edge!" would be every man's and every woman's show.

Though Baron had dreamed of moving into a more serious television setting—a Larry King-type interview show or maybe serious investigative reporting—Weatherby's proposition had come when Baron was recovering from an affair that had left him with a whole, but bruised heart and a severely battered ego.

Preoccupied with his inner reactions and impressions of the doomed affair, he had found the thought of change appealing; never mind that the money was better than excellent. Not one to act on impulse, he had analyzed his options with his usual clear logic and decided to accept WTN's offer. It was a move up any way he looked at it.

Though his newly purchased house in one of Houston's nicest neighborhoods was the first place he'd considered home since he moved out of his parents' house at the age of eighteen, thirty-four-year-old Baron nonetheless put his dream house on the market, packed up his belongings and moved to L.A. WTN had given him two weeks to settle in, and he'd spent the bulk of it exploring the city.

Today was his first day reporting to work, though he didn't consider doing what amounted to a screen test with Delores SanAngelo work. Unlike him, Delores was a tried-and-true addition to the show. She had been offered the job because her popularity among the viewers spanned age, race and social boundaries. Tom Madsen, newly come to WTN as head of the marketing department, felt that her spontaneous and often hilarious onscreen didoes would be a nice contrast to Baron's more serious persona. Baron thought of Delores SanAngelo as an unlikely combination of Charo and Barbara Walters.

The light knock on the dressing room door brought his thoughts to an abrupt halt. Before he could answer the summons, a tall, whipcord-thin woman pushed the door wide and stepped through, crossing to him in a smooth, long-legged stride that managed to look both slinky and feline. Baron recognized her as Thea Barlow, Price Weatherby's assistant, who he'd met on one other occasion. He rose in a gesture as automatic as breathing to a well-bred Texas boy.

"Hello, Baron," Thea said, extending a well-manicured hand, complete with a fuchsia, hundred-dollar nail job that matched the splash of color on her wide mouth.

Baron took her hand and was reminded, to his dismay, of her slack handshake. He didn't trust people with limp handshakes. It might be silly, but there it was. And he wasn't crazy about hairstyles that leaned toward the "wet head" look. Though Thea Barlow's short hairdo—

gelled and finger combed into an off-the-forehead-away-from-the-face style—was pure L.A. chic, Baron didn't find it particularly attractive. His personal preference—that his sister continually told him was sexist—was long, thick hair, enough to drown in.

He hoped his smile held enough warmth to camouflage his feelings. After all, Thea Barlow was his boss, second in command only to Price Weatherby himself. "Ms. Barlow," he said.

Thea's eyelashes swept up toward her brow bone that was shaded a delicate taupe color. "Thea, please."

"Thea, then," he said, hoping he was misinterpreting her coy look.

Thea's eyes made a lingering, scorching survey from the toes of his gleaming dress shoes to the impeccable knot of his paisley tie, her gaze coming to rest on his. In a spark of awareness, Baron realized how a woman must feel when some jerk gave her the once-over and followed up with a wolf whistle.

Thea smoothed a hand over his shoulder, as if to brush away a speck of lint, and let her fingers trail slowly down his arm. "You look very nice. Very professional."

"That's the intention, ma'am."

Grimacing, she stepped back. "For heaven's sake, don't call me 'ma'am'. I'm too young to be a ma'am, and I'm neither your mother nor your schoolmarm."

"I beg your pardon," Baron said, a bit surprised by the venom in her voice. "Manners usually impress, not irritate."

The displeasure disappeared from Thea's dark eyes. She shook her shapely head. "No, I beg *your* pardon. I'm a little testy because we have a major glitch in this morning's shooting." At the question in Baron's eyes, she continued. "Delores is a no-show."

"What!" Baron couldn't have been more shocked if she'd told him he was fired. He saw his new career crashing and burning, which was quite a feat considering that it hadn't even gotten off the ground. He was hardly a household word outside of Texas. Without Delores's "star" quality, what chance did "The Edge!" have of making it in the ruthless world of television?

"It seems she got a better offer from NTN."

"Didn't she sign a contract with WTN?" Baron asked, the implications of the situation whirling inside his head.

"Actually, no. Everything was still verbal. She and Price were still working out a few nitpicky details. It seems she's been playing us against NTN, holding out for the better offer."

"So what happens now?" Baron asked.

"Well, Price is thinking of suing. While he and his attorney put their heads together, we're calling in some other, lesser-known personalities who'd interviewed for the part before. Price is hell-bent on staying on schedule and budget—with or without Delores."

Baron felt his tension abate somewhat. He liked a man with determination and dedication.

"He's got a sample audience rounded up for this morning, this afternoon and tomorrow morning to do a trial show with each of the applicants. He wants some input from the audience and the marketing people to see which one of the ladies you have the best rapport with."

"Super." Baron began to pace the small room.

"Don't look so glum," Thea urged, catching his arm as he passed her. "All is *not* lost. One of the new candidates is Kathey Kramer—you know? From the hit morning radio show."

"Never heard of her."

Thea's laughter was low and throaty. "Then you aren't listening to the right radio station. Kathey is pretty, personable and quick-witted. Her face may not be familiar to the viewers, but her name is. Frankly, I'm not too sure she isn't better suited to 'The Edge!' than Delores."

Baron had to admit that she sounded promising. "Who else is in the running?"

"Paula Kingsley, a local newscaster with a decent following who's hoping to make a move up. And Mallory Ryan."

Baron's antennae went up when he heard no tag line. "And what's Ms. Ryan's claim to fame?"

"Like the others, she sent in her résumé and interviewed for Delores's part about three months ago. When we chose Delores, Price insisted that Personnel give Mallory a job."

Baron couldn't hide his astonishment.

"I know, I know, it didn't make sense to any of us, either, but she claimed she needed a steady job, and Price sent down the directive."

Baron's lips twisted. It was a scenario he was personally familiar with. It didn't take a genius to figure out that Price probably had more than a passing interest in Mallory Ryan.

Thea lifted her slim shoulders in another eloquent shrug. "Anyway, we hired her to work in our research department. As soon as word got out this morning that the part was up for grabs again, Mallory marched herself into Price's office, and the next thing I knew, Price informed me that Mallory was getting another shot at the job."

"Has she had any exposure in front of a camera?"

Thea looked irritated by the question. "Price Weatherby hasn't made it to the top by making stupid moves. He would never consider someone without any camera experience for a project as big as this. Mallory Ryan has been playing bit parts on the soaps for three or four years. Nothing steady, which was unfortunate, because she is talented."

Something in Thea's voice told Baron that it was hard for her to admit that Mallory Ryan was good at anything.

"She was always one of those throwaway characters," Thea mused. "She'd signed with 'Until Tomorrow Comes,' and it looked as if she was finally going to get a break—the audience loved her and her character—and then the show was canceled."

Baron shook his head and rolled his gaze heavenward in supplication. "Why me?" he asked an unseen deity.

"Don't worry about it," Thea said, running her hand up and down his arm in a gesture that was meant to be comforting. "Mallory doesn't stand much of a chance of landing the job. Letting her try for the part amounts to nothing more than satisfying Price's whimsy."

"So when do I have the pleasure of working with Ms. Ryan?"

"First thing tomorrow morning." Thea glanced down at the watch circling her narrow wrist. "I've got to go. Makeup should be here any minute." She headed for the door where she turned and flashed Baron a smile. "Break a leg."

Baron groaned. He wished she hadn't left him with the old stage adage. The way things were going, he probably would! He sat back down in the chair, his thoughts turning longingly to his house in Houston that, according to a message left on his machine the previous day, had sold to a young couple with a kid and a dog.

The realization that an honest-to-God family had bought his house led his musings to Karel, the most recent in a small coterie of women who'd made their way into his bed and his heart. Seeing Karel for what she was had hurt, but after six months, the pain had subsided to an occasional twinge. And more often than not, the twinge was one of irritation that he'd allowed himself to be taken in by her.

Fortunate enough to be born with good looks and brains, Baron had no illusions about himself. He knew he was just a kid from a hardworking, middle-class family who was lucky enough to pull the right genes from his parents' DNA pool. There had been a time or two when his looks had actually caused problems, times he'd been overpassed because some executive thought he was too good-looking to be taken seriously. And women thought that all the sexist discrimination was directed toward them!

He could have pushed, found a greedy attorney and sued, but that wasn't his style. He didn't want easy money or a position where he wouldn't be appreciated. He certainly didn't want to build a reputation for being anything other than what he was—damn good at his job.

When he'd gotten the offer from WTN, it looked as if his ability to persevere in the face of adversity—both in his personal life and when a good story was in the making—had stood him in good stead. And now, this...

He cursed the departed Delores and prayed that Kathey or Paula would blow the audience out of the water. Mallory, a soap ingenue who gave every appearance of using her closeness to the head of the company to boost her career, sounded like another Karel. Or another Thea. Dollars to doughnuts, Thea had used her feminine wiles and selective sleeping arrangements to get where she was, too.

Baron swore. Thea Barlow and Mallory Ryan were both the type of woman he despised. How could one guy get so lucky?

So that was Baron Montgomery, Mallory thought, sneaking a peek at the masculine half of the host duo for "The Edge!" All she'd heard the day before was Baron Montgomery this and Baron Montgomery that. He was *so* handsome. His Texas drawl was *so* cute. His body was to *die* for.

He was certainly handsome, Mallory thought, stealing another surreptitious look under the guise of checking the clipboard of papers she was carrying. It was understandable why every woman under ninety-nine seemed to have fallen under his spell. Unfortunately, Mallory herself had been cursed with a weakness for dark hair and blue eyes...not to mention wide shoulders and sexy mouths, two physical attributes Baron Montgomery had also been blessed with.

Cool your jets, Mal, she told herself. *The man's ability to raise your temperature and stir your hormones does not necessarily make him anything other than a good-looking jerk.*

As she sometimes found necessary, Mallory reminded herself that three-plus years in the unwedded state amounted to something close to a thousand long, lonely nights. Her reaction to any other good-looking man would no doubt be as strong.

She was stifling a sigh when Baron Montgomery looked up and caught her looking at him. There was nothing she could do but offer him a polite smile. The chilly look of dislike that crossed his features took her by surprise.

Her smile died an instant death, and her heart took a nosedive to the bottom of her stomach. In a state of utter confusion, she turned and started back toward the office she shared with three other WTN staff members. What on earth could she have possibly done to deserve a look like that? They hadn't even been introduced yet!

"Mallory!"

Thea Barlow's imperious voice caught Mallory up short. She turned. Thea was making tracks toward her, and Baron Montgomery was headed toward his dressing room. The look on Thea's face was unpleasant at best.

Lord, Mallory thought, the last thing she needed was to have a run-in with her boss. After hearing that Kathey Kramer had performed like a champ the day before, Mallory was already nervous about her upcoming camera session.

Mallory squared her shoulders and shrugged off her uneasiness. She wouldn't let Baron Montgomery or Thea Barlow intimidate her. She needed the money and security of Delores SanAngelo's job.

She pasted what she hoped was a pleasant look on her face. "Thea. Hi."

"I'd prefer you call me Ms. Barlow." Thea's smile didn't quite reach her eyes. "We aren't working on the same soap anymore, and I am your superior."

Before Mallory could stop herself, she said, "At least you haven't forgotten where you came from...*Ms*. Barlow."

Thea's eyes narrowed. "I haven't forgotten, but I don't intend to let where I came from keep me from getting where I want to be."

"I'm sure you won't," Mallory concurred. "Did you want me for something?"

"I don't want you for anything. Price does." Thea's insolent gaze traveled over Mallory from head to toe. "I can't imagine why."

Mallory stifled a small gasp. There was no mistaking the meaning of the words or the look. Guilt set her face aflame.

Another icy smile claimed Thea's lips. She gave Mallory a dismissive, run-along-now wave. "You'd better go do whatever you need to do to try and cinch the job," she said, and left Mallory standing there, fighting back the sting of angry tears.

Mallory turned toward Price's office, dashing away the moisture with her fingertips. She would not let the likes of Thea Barlow make her cry!

Inside the reception area, she told Abbie, Price's secretary, that she was there to see him and took a seat to wait, her anger simmering just beneath the surface.

Thea and Mallory had met when Mallory landed her first small soap role three years before...just after Mallory's husband, Mark, had packed up and moved out, claiming that he couldn't take the pressure of their child's heart condition day after day.

Back then, Thea had reveled in the success of her role as Vanessa Brandt, a villainess the viewers loved to hate...the Alexis Carrington of daytime's Emmy-winning "Friends and Lovers."

But Thea hadn't been happy with her success as an actress. She'd wanted more. So she'd made a move on the show's executive producer and effectively ended his marriage. Though she'd never gotten her prey to the altar, she did manage to get a toehold in the corporate end of the industry.

It had come as something of a surprise to everyone, including Mallory, that Thea was as sharp and savvy at business as she was a fine actress. And it was astounding how fast she'd moved up the ranks to her present position as head of WTN's creative development department.

Considering Mallory's own struggle to keep her head above the financial problems that went hand in hand with Cassie's heart condition, it was hard not to envy Thea's meteoric rise, at least on occasion. On those rare instances that the green-eyed monster reared its head, Mallory reminded herself that the end didn't always justify the means. She wasn't a Thea Barlow, and she couldn't do what Thea had done to get ahead. She had to rely on hard work and pray for good fortune.

The good fortune of Price Weatherby's advent into her life was uppermost on Mallory's mind when Abbie indicated that Mr. Weatherby was available to see her. Drawing a deep breath, Mallory entered the executive office.

Price, still fit and handsome at fifty-three, rose as she stepped through the doorway. "Good morning," he said with a slight smile.

"Good morning," Mallory replied.

He waved toward a chair upholstered in a bone colored leather. "Have a seat."

"Thanks." Mallory smoothed the skirt of the moss green double-breasted coatdress she wore and sank into the soft depths of the chair. Price seated himself behind his desk.

"Thea said you wanted to see me."

Avoiding her eyes, Price began to straighten the items on his desk. "I just wanted to wish you good luck and caution you not to be too disappointed if you don't get the position. The competition is tough."

"I know. But the difference is, I'm going to be the best because I need this job."

The determination in her voice brought his gaze to hers. "If you need more money, I can—"

"No!" Mallory's voice was sharper than she intended. She made a conscious effort to lower it. "I can't take anything more from you. You've done enough. More than enough."

"There's no way I can ever do enough, so more than that is impossible."

Mallory's troubled gaze found the desolation of his, and she shook her head, forbidding him to say anything else. She wasn't comfortable with Price's guilt. And in spite of all he'd done for her and Cassie, she wasn't sure she could trust him.

"I have to do this on my own, Price." Without warning, a mental picture of the house he'd provided for her and Cassie flashed through her mind, along with a reminder that he was responsible for her current job at WTN. Her lips curved in a wry smile. "More or less on my own, anyway."

"I suspected you'd say that. That's why I wanted to caution you about the outcome of your test shoot today. Kathey Kramer was pretty impressive yesterday, and you know I can't just hand you the position no matter how much I might want to."

"I know," Mallory said, horrified at the thought. "I never expected you to give me anything."

Price's smile held a hint of sorrow. "Maybe that's why I want to, but the network has a lot riding on the success of this show, and I owe it to the shareholders to put together the best group of people I can."

"I understand your position, but you need to understand mine, too. I have to try."

Price sighed and nodded.

Mallory rose, urging an unsteady smile to her lips. "Wish me luck?"

The corners of Price's green eyes crinkled in an attractive smile. He was a nice man, she thought. An incredibly easy man to love. "Always."

Thirty minutes later, a knock sounded on Mallory's door, and a familiar face appeared in the opening.

"Tom!" Mallory said, motioning for him to come in.

Tom Madsen was WTN's newest and most prized acquisition. Just a week after hiring Mallory, Price lured the successful advertising guru away from a major film studio to ensure that "The Edge!" made the biggest possible splash on the nation's viewers.

It didn't take long for Mallory to realize that his easygoing, self-effacing manner hid a quick, creative mind that could store and recall details with the efficiency of the most sophisticated computer. Taken with his boyish smile and unable to resist his friendly overtures, it wasn't long before Mallory found herself with an ally at WTN. More importantly, Tom had become a much-needed friend.

She watched him saunter through the door, his long limbs moving with an easy, almost shuffling nonchalance, a smile on his pleasant features. He pushed a swath of sable-colored hair from his forehead. "Nervous?"

"Petrified," she confessed. "I don't think our Texas star likes me."

"Why do you say that?" Tom asked with a frown.

"Because he looked at me a little while ago as if he hated me at first sight."

"Maybe he has PMS."

Mallory couldn't squelch the smile that twitched at the corners of her mouth. "PMS?"

"Pretty Mallory Syndrome," Tom said, his voice and manner dead serious. "You've never noticed? It usually happens when a man sees you for the first time. It's characterized by nervous fidgets, a dry mouth, worry about sounding like an idiot in the presence of a goddess, and in extreme cases, a feeling of such inferiority that it makes a poor bozo more than a little angry—thus the glaring look that is frequently mistaken for dislike."

Mallory couldn't help laughing.

"That's my girl," Tom said. "If you can remember to laugh at yourself, it makes getting through life a little easier."

Mallory dabbed at her eyes with a tissue. "Why hasn't some lucky woman snatched you up?"

Tom's smile faltered. For an instant, Mallory thought she saw the shadow of sorrow in his eyes. Then the glint of humor was back, and she decided that her imagination was working overtime.

"Not this cat," he said. "I'm far too clever to get sucked into the old marriage trap."

A sharp rap sounded on the door. "Five minutes, Mallory!" a disembodied voice called.

Mallory threw a panicked look at Tom who winked at her. Then she drew a deep breath and stood. This was her second chance, and she couldn't blow it. She squared her shoulders and headed for the set, letting Tom close the door behind them. She'd show Thea and Price and Kathey Kramer that she was a force to be reckoned with.

She was attractive. She was smart. She had plenty of experience in front of a camera.

Unexpectedly, the hum of a hundred conversations sounded from the area where the audience was seated. Mallory's stomach turned a double back flip. Of course, she didn't have any experience in front of a live audience, but it couldn't be that different—could it?

"Mallory!"

Thea's commanding voice again. Mallory turned toward the source of the sound and saw Thea standing next to Baron Montgomery.

"Come meet Baron."

Her heart racing, her palms sweating, Mallory started toward the handsome couple, careful to keep her gaze fastened somewhere in the vicinity of the third button of Baron Montgomery's white shirt.

Thea waved a beringed hand toward Mallory. "Baron, this is Mallory Ryan. Mallory, I'd like you to meet Baron Montgomery, a recent Texas transplant."

Mallory winced at Thea's choice of words. Thea had no way of knowing just how ill Cassie was, but still . . .

Despite her distress, Mallory extended her hand. Baron reached out and took it in a firm grip. She expected his hands to be smooth and well kept, but even though the nails were short and clean, she could feel the roughness of calluses on his palms. This small indication that there might just be more to Baron Montgomery than a pretty face was an unexpected surprise.

Without volition, Mallory's gaze lifted to his. Instead of the censure she expected, there was a question in his blue eyes. Eyes so blue, she could see herself reflected in them. Eyes so blue, she could drown in them.

"Nervous?" he asked.

She blinked and tried to smile. "Some. I never know what's worse—being the first to do something, or being the last."

"The competition is pretty stiff," Thea said.

Thanks so much for reminding me. "So I hear." Determined not to let either Baron or Thea upset her, Mallory asked, "What's the lineup?"

"We have a new mystery author, an M.D. with some astounding claims about chiropractic treatment, and Paolo Mancuso, the Italian film star, touting his first American release."

"Sounds varied...and interesting." Mallory cast a look at Baron, who was silent, noncommittal.

"Since it's a new show, we'd like for the first few minutes to deal with your personal lives—what you like and dislike, that sort of thing. Let the audience get to know you, let the two of you get to know each other. And, whenever it's possible, we'd like you to connect the guests or their products to incidents you've experienced or people you've come into contact with."

"Like my aunt Mary who sees a chiropractor on a regular basis and thinks they can raise the dead?" Mallory asked.

"Exactly," Thea said with a nod. "Or your cousin Ginny who had an affair with an Italian waiter—that kind of stuff. Just remember that the purpose of 'The Edge!' is to entertain. It isn't a soapbox for your personal feelings except in a broad sense. There are enough controversial shows out there. WTN feels that the viewing public is ready for a show that does more than exploit and encourage the worst in human nature." Thea gave one of her signature shrugs. "That's about it. Just let go, have fun and see what happens."

Mallory looked at Baron again. Another scowl marred his perfect features. Fun? she thought in dismay. She wasn't exactly a laugh a minute, and Baron didn't look as if there was a funny bone in his entire, gorgeous body....

Chapter Two

The huge screen faded to black, ending the scene that depicted the disillusionment and pain separating the estranged lovers. The house lights came up. The applause from the audience was deafening, proper homage and adulation for the star. Paolo Mancuso stood and directed elegant bows toward his public, a wide, white smile on his handsome face.

"Grazie!" he intoned in a deep, mellifluous voice. *"Grazie!"*

Baron clapped along with the rest. He had to admit that the guy was good. His acting was effortless, flawless. For those few celluloid moments, Paolo Mancuso *was* Vincent Scarpetti.

While the audience was quieting, Baron glanced at Mallory, fresh and attractive in her moss green coatdress. What was it about the woman that set his teeth on edge, anyway? After picking up on Thea's implications

about Mallory and Price Weatherby, Baron hadn't expected to like her much, but he'd been shocked by the
way his hackles rose the minute he set eyes on her. Instant antagonism was something he'd never dealt with
before. Logic told him that his reaction to Mallory was
ridiculous, but ridiculous or not, it was real. That same
logic made him concerned that his feelings might bleed
over into the show. He told himself that he was a professional, and he could handle it. He would. He had to.

Thank God, his earlier worries about Mallory Ryan's
qualifications—or lack thereof—were for nothing. They
were twenty minutes into the show, and so far, so good.
Mallory seemed a little wooden at first, but that was to
be expected. She was feeling her way, but she'd found a
certain rapport with the audience, occasionally directing her questions and comments to them as much as to
him. If their laughter and smiles were anything to go by,
they liked the format. A few times, someone had even
called out a comment to her. Unorthodox maybe, but
hey, this was a trial run.

The tender scene they'd just witnessed had left a look
of admiration for Paolo Mancuso in Mallory's eyes.
Baron felt his jaw tighten. The movie star and his cohost had hit it off from the first, and the actor, a known
ladies' man, had been flirting with Mallory since he'd
stepped onto the set, which, for some unknown reason
made Baron furious.

Paolo also had an irritating way of shutting Baron out
of the conversation. Obviously aware of what was happening, Mallory tossed him a question on occasion—like
a crumb from the master's table, Baron thought with
rising irritation. Damn it, they were supposed to be a
team. She wasn't supposed to hog the spotlight and use

the show to find herself a new man to use as a stepping stone to success.

"Wow," Mallory said now, smiling at Paolo as he sat back down. "What a powerful scene."

"Thank you." The actor's voice held the correct note of humility. He placed a well-manicured hand over his heart. "The emotions those two were experiencing just touched me deep inside, and of course Betina did a superb job with the role of Melisande," he said, ever the gracious star.

Baron crossed his arms over his chest. Paolo's line of b.s. was almost as perfect as his English. There was just enough of both to give women "the weak-kneed trembles," as his mama would say. It was pitifully obvious that Mallory had been taken in by him.

"Watching that scene makes me wonder if we ever know the people we love unless—or until—something happens and they show their true colors," Mallory commented. "And it also brought home how the innocent party always seems to wind up with the most pain."

"Oh, I agree," Paolo said. "Absolutely."

Yeah, and if she said the IRS was going to hand you over a ten-thousand dollar refund, you'd agree to that, too.

Tired of being ignored, Baron leapt into the fray. "You're waxing pretty philosophical, Mallory," he said. "Are you speaking from experience?"

The sarcastic tone of his voice ignited a flash of irritation in her eyes.

"Of course she is," Paolo piped up before Mallory could answer. "Can't you see the torment in those eyes? This is a woman who has suffered much in the name of love."

Baron saw the red of embarrassment rush into Mallory's cheeks. She batted her eyelashes at the camera. "That isn't pain," she quipped. "It's an eyelash."

The audience roared.

"Seriously," she said when they quieted, "I'm divorced, so I do know a lot about the pain in a failing relationship."

"Ah!" Paolo said, leaning toward her. "How long have you been alone?"

"A little over three years."

Paolo aimed a thousand-kilowatt smile at Mallory. "Ah! Perhaps your ex's loss is my gain. Is there a man in your life?"

From where Baron sat, it looked as if she swayed toward Paolo. She *did* cast a flirtatious look at the Italian from beneath her eyelashes. "Regrettably, no. Are you available?"

The audience hooted. Something twisted inside Baron. God, he thought. She was more obvious than Thea. Making a play for a man on a television show!

Paolo took Mallory's hand. "And if I said yes?"

Mallory laid a hand against her heart and feigned a swoon. The women in the audience went wild.

"Excuse me," Baron interrupted, thoroughly disgusted. "This isn't 'Love Connection.'"

"'Love Connection'?" Paolo asked. "What is this 'Love Connection'?"

"It's a game show that tries to match up single people on the off chance they'll fall in love. You know... hoping they'll make a love connection," Baron said. "I'm thinking of sending in Mallory's name."

The sarcasm passed right over Paolo's head. "What's the matter with the men in this city?" he lamented, throwing his hands up in the air. "She doesn't need a television show to find her love connection. She's an intelligent, beautiful woman. Don't you agree?''

The question was directed to both Baron and the audience, which cheered, clapped and whistled. Blushing again, Mallory thanked them.

Looking at her, Baron had to admit she was everything Paolo said—if you liked that type, which of course, Baron didn't. He liked busty brunettes with button noses. The only thing Mallory had going for her was her thick auburn hair. Enough hair you could bury yourself in.

"She's not my type," he said in a gruff, hard voice.

"You oughta get your eyes checked, Montgomery!" a male voice yelled from the audience.

Mallory looked at Baron as if he'd struck her, but she rallied quickly and waved at the unseen man. "Thank you, sir," she called. "It's a little hard for a girl to feel good about herself when there are two men prettier than she is sitting next to her."

"Your insecurities are showing, Mallory," Baron snapped. Before she could retaliate, he said, "Look, can we get this interview back on track? Paolo's here to pitch his new movie—not woo."

"What is to pitch woo?" Paolo said, casting a confused look from Baron to Mallory.

"Flirting," Mallory said with a sugary smile. "A pastime Mr. Montgomery indulges in with regular frequency, I'm sure."

My God! What was happening here? Baron thought, aware that he was fast losing command of his composure as well as the situation. It wasn't like him to lose control this way.

"I didn't mean anything personal," he said in an attempt to salvage the situation. "I just happen to have a penchant for brunettes."

As Paolo had done earlier, Mallory threw up her hands. "Well, that explains it, then."

"Explains what?"

"Why you're so stuck on yourself."

The crowd exploded into another frenzy of clapping and cheering.

My God! Baron thought again, as he searched his mind for a way out of the quagmire the show was fast sinking into. A movement in the wings caught his attention. Several of the crew stood there regarding them, expressions of horror etched on their faces. Thea was there, too. Not horrified. Furious. And Price. A stunned look on his face.

The collar of Baron's shirt suddenly seemed two sizes too small. Seeing the direction of his gaze, Mallory glanced to her left. She grew whiter than the tablecloth Baron's mother used for Sunday dinners.

Thea made a sign for a break. Mallory turned a sudden wide smile to the audience. "We've got to go to a commercial right now, but when my partner and I come back, we'll be talking to Dr. Josiah Helmond, a licensed M.D. who believes that the combined practice of chiropractic, homeopathic medicine and kinesiology can not only alleviate pain, but may actually cure many common medical problems."

Baron and Mallory surged to their feet. Paolo sat in stunned silence, as if he, too, was trying to figure out what had just transpired.

Baron grabbed Mallory's arm before she reached the privacy of the wings. The audience murmured among themselves, questioning what was going on.

"Who the hell put the burr under your saddle?" Baron demanded, propelling Mallory backstage and away from the curious spectators.

Mallory looked up at him with anger-bright eyes. "Sorry," she snapped. "I don't speak any foreign languages."

The dig at his Texan phraseology deepened Baron's own anger. "Don't play dumb with me. What the hell did you have in mind, mouthing off like that in front of the audience? You sabotaged the show—not to mention my career, damn you!"

"Me?" Mallory waved an arm toward Thea, who for perhaps the first time in her life, was speechless. "Thea said to have fun, to see what happened, which is what I was doing when you . . . *attacked* me with those tasteless remarks. All I did was try to hold my own against the—the crude comments you made. The way I see it, *you* jeopardized *my* one chance to have a career!"

She jerked her arm free of his hold and spun on her heel to face Price and Thea. "I'll be here first thing in the morning to clear out my desk and turn in my resignation."

Speechless, Baron watched her flee from the presence of her peers and the noise of the audience. Baron, too, was upset, so upset he didn't notice that the crowd's eager chant was "Mallory! Mallory! We want Mallory!"

An hour later, Baron, Thea and the marketing people, led by Tom Madsen, were crowded into Price's office to discuss the phenomenon they'd just witnessed. Though those in charge of "The Edge!" were horrified at the snipping and baiting that had transpired between Mallory and Baron during the show, the audience's reaction was completely different.

In an effort to get feedback from the people who would be watching "The Edge!" every day, the audience participants who watched Baron at work with each of the three women were asked to fill out a "Comments" sheet about the shows. The group in Price's office was busily pouring over the results.

"It was a fiasco!" Her arms crossed, a pungent European cigarette of some sort burning unsmoked between her fingertips, Thea paced the length of the room and back. "A complete and total disaster."

"That isn't what these papers say," Price said, picking up a sheet from the mound of papers littering his desk. "'Mallory Ryan is wonderful!'" he read. "'She's no phony baloney and can give Baron Montgomery a run for his money anyday.'"

"Listen to this one." Tom Madsen shot a smirk at Baron and began to read. "'Baron Montgomery is to die for. Absolutely the sexiest guy to ever come down the pike. He can put his shoes under my bed anytime.'"

Baron, who was content to listen without comment, slid down on his spine.

"'Mallory Ryan is a witch deluxe,'" Tom read on, "'but I *loved* the sparks flying between those two. If you hire Mallory Ryan, there won't be a dull day on 'The Edge!'—and I, for one, will be waiting in front of my TV set to see what those two are up to.'"

"How about this one?" Rick, a part-time college student asked. "'Mallory Ryan's performance stands head and shoulders above the other two candidates, but I had the distinct feeling these two weren't acting. They really hate each other, don't they? I love it! These are real people. They said what they thought and damned the consequences. I'm sick of the polished, perfect hosts who give the appearance of never having a bad hair day.

It's refreshing to know that there are celebrities out there who wake up and feel like growling instead of smiling. I'm sick of the same old format and the same old homogenized questions. Baron and Mallory will really spice up those dull afternoons.'"

Thea swore softly, and Rick gave her hand a comforting squeeze as she passed. Thea shot him a dirty look. The gesture took Baron by surprise. He shot a look at Price, whose impassive features hid whatever he was feeling. Tom's face was ruddy with suppressed fury.

The incident passed, and they got back to the problem at hand. They read more comments about Mallory and Baron, all in the same vein. Tom commented that while everyone seemed to favor Mallory over the other two women, the audience was clearly divided into two definite camps. The I-love-Baron bunch and the Don't-take-anything-off-him-Mallory group.

But even the women who pulled for Mallory agreed that Baron was handsome and excellent at what he did, and those who sided with Baron admitted that Mallory was sharp, pretty and quick-witted, which would be a plus for the show.

Tom laid down the last piece of paper and looked from Baron to Price to Thea. "I don't think you have a choice, Price," he said. "Mallory Ryan should get the job."

Baron felt that sick feeling in the pit of his stomach again.

"But she doesn't have any experience!" Thea cried, taking a deep drag from her cigarette.

"Obviously, she doesn't need any," Tom countered. "Sometimes talent is enough."

Thea looked daggers at him, then faced Price. "This is a mistake."

"I don't know, Thea...."

"They love her!" Tom said, hoping to shore up his case for Mallory. "Even the ones who hated her loved her. It would be stupid not to let her have it. Like the one woman said, the viewers are sick of the sameness on the talk shows. Other than 'Regis and Kathie Lee', all you've got is a bunch of copycats. If you miss the dysfunctional family or the criminal of the week on one show, all you have to do is catch them a couple of weeks later on another network."

Price gave a considering nod and looked at Baron. "What do you think, Baron? You're the guy who has to work with her."

Baron's smile was grim. "You mean you still want me?"

"Of course we do," Price assured him. "I'm not sure what happened out there, but whatever it was, it worked. The big question is do you hate her so much you can't work with her?"

Baron sat up straighter in his chair and rolled his shoulders in an attempt to alleviate the tension knotting them. "How the hell can I hate her? I don't even know the woman." He shook his head. "I don't know what got into me out there."

"Forget that. Can you work with her?" Price probed.

Baron considered a moment. He didn't want to work with her. He was afraid her inexperience would be a detriment, and he didn't like what Thea had insinuated about her and Price. Mallory was the kind of woman he did his best to steer clear of. But if the audience was that enamored of her, WTN would be downright crazy not to hire her—no matter what her relationship with Price Weatherby might be. He himself had given up a lot to take a chance on breaking into the big time. This show was his future. And God help him, it looked like Mallory Ryan was part of that future.

"I can work with anyone who will make the show a success," Baron said at last.

Price smiled in relief. "Well, that's a load off my mind."

"You know," Tom said, rubbing his chin thoughtfully, "we can make all this antagonism between the two of you work for us."

"What do you mean?" Price asked.

"Why not go with the premise that these two aren't crazy about each other? Let them bicker. Play it up, but give it definition. Let Mallory get her digs in about Baron being the handsome ladies' man, the man-about-town, and let Baron give her hell about the fact that there isn't a man in her life…that sort of thing. He could constantly be trying to fix her up. As long as they don't get too acerbic, it would be a scream. We can run some spats from the trial show as teasers."

Listening to Tom, Baron bade a silent farewell to his dream of becoming another Larry King. If "The Edge!" made it, he'd never be able to be a straight man again. There would be nothing left but stand-up comedy— "Saturday Night Live" if he was real lucky.

Price looked thoughtful.

"I think it stinks," Thea said, jabbing out her cigarette in a jade ashtray. "I think we should stay with the tried and true."

"You read the comments from the audience," Tom said with a wicked smile. "The viewers are sick of all that crap. Admit it, you're just ticked off because you wanted your cousin to get the part."

Thea's face flamed. "Kathey is qualified, and the audience liked her just fine until Mallory came along."

"Hear what you're saying, Thea," Tom said pointing his finger at her. "They liked Kathey *until* Mallory came along. But they love Mallory." He looked at Price. "What do you say, boss?"

"I want to sleep on it, but off the top of my head, I have to say that I think we'd be cutting our throats if we didn't give the job to Mallory."

There was a pleased expression on Price's face as he spoke the words. It made Baron wonder again if Thea was right, and Mallory and the aging executive had more going on between them than anyone could prove.

Considering how hard she was crying when she left the studio, Mallory wasn't sure how she drove home without getting involved in a major accident. Why did Baron Montgomery hate her so much?

Think, Mallory. What did you do?

She'd seen him with Thea, thought he was cute. He'd looked up, seen her, hated her on sight. What had she done to antagonize him, and why had he attacked her right there in front of the audience with that condescending remark about her waxing philosophical? The dig kicked her old feelings of low self-worth into high gear and her wall of defense had gone right up. Open mouth, insert foot, she thought with dismay. It was a frequent habit of hers. Still, it wasn't like her to be so hostile.

Could he have been upset over Paolo's flirting? She'd only gone along with it because Thea instructed them to go with what felt right, and the trial audience seemed to like it. Paolo *had* tended to ignore Baron, but she'd done what she could to include him in their conversation while still playing out her star-struck role. Baron's responses were brusque at best.

Mallory shrugged off the questions angrily. Now that she'd made a fool of herself in front of a few hundred people, none of it mattered, anyway. Her only consolation was that she'd never have to see the churlish Mr. Montgomery again.

The thought that she'd just lost the best job she'd had in three years was a depressing one. She'd heard that one of the soaps was looking for someone to play a hooker who eventually gets axed by a cop gone bad. She'd worked with the director before, and it had been a positive experience. Maybe she ought to give Darren a call. She had no problem with letting herself be killed off again. At least it would pay a few bills.

In the troublesome way it often did, her mind made a segue from the thought of bills to thoughts of Cassie. Mallory shook her head in disgust. What a terrible person she was to even think of Cassie and bills in the same breath!

But then again, how could she not? Money—or the lack thereof—had been a constant worry since Mark walked out on her and the child he had sired. Still, despite her illness and the constant worry, Cassie was the only good thing left in Mallory's life.

Mallory's lips tightened. Mark, and the havoc his leaving had wrought in her life, was another frequent, unwelcome subject of her thoughts.

When Cassie had been born with a heart murmur, there was the usual parental concern, but when that heart murmur was later diagnosed as hypertrophic obstructive cardiomyopathy, a condition that would only worsen, Mallory and Mark had been devastated.

The doctors had explained that the septum—the muscular division between the right and left ventricle—became enlarged and blocked the blood being pumped into the left ventricle, that gradually became stiff and resistant.

The disease was characterized by short-windedness with exertion, weakness and fatigue, dizziness and fainting spells, chest pains and palpitations—things that would go unnoticed in an infant but would become more pronounced as Cassie got older and became more active.

The symptoms could be alleviated with beta blockers and diuretics to help maintain fluid balance, but the bottom line was not promising. The best treatment was a transplant.

Shortly after they received the doctors' news, Mark quit his job as a croupier, left his wife and daughter alone in Las Vegas and filed for a divorce. Cassie was five months old, and Mallory had no one to fall back on but a kindly landlady.

Living with the idea that death was Cassie's closest companion was sometimes more than Mallory thought she could bear alone. Struggling to hold things together, needing some emotional support, Mallory had called her mother in L.A. and arranged to move in with her so that Betty could care for Cassie while Mallory worked. It wasn't an ideal situation, but Mallory soon learned that few were.

The end of Mark's job meant the end of his insurance, and when he picked up with a new company in a totally different line of work, they wouldn't cover Cassie's illness because it was preexisting. Mallory was forced to seek help at the university hospital, where cost was determined by the patient's ability to pay. It felt like charity, but she couldn't afford to let her pride get in the way. Instead, she took solace in the knowledge that Cassie's care was some of the best—after all, the university was where they trained the doctors who then went out and charged the exorbitant prices for their services.

Though she was extremely smart, Cassie's physical development was slow, and what most children would consider everyday childhood play was out of the question. Every illness was life-threatening. Even a case of the sniffles required constant care and a long period of recuperation.

For more than three years, Mallory had gone from one bit soap opera part to another, leaving Cassie in Betty's care, always cherishing the fragile hope that one day she'd get the big break. But when the big break had come, it was only as a result of her mother's death and in the unexpected form of Price Weatherby.

And now she'd blown even that, Mallory thought reliving those few moments at the studio.

Depression settled over her like a cold, damp blanket. L.A. might be a big place, but there was little doubt that what had happened on the set of "The Edge!" would be all over town in a few days, which would make finding another acting job that much harder.

Mallory took a fast-food napkin from the glove compartment and used it to wipe the moisture from her face. It would never do for Cassie to see her like this.

By the time she pulled into the driveway of the house Price owned near San Fernando, where she and Cassie had lived for the past four months, Mallory had her tears under control. She even managed a wisp of a smile for Carmen, the Mexican woman who had looked after Cassie since Betty's death.

Carmen shut the door behind Mallory, glanced at her watch and frowned. "What are you doing home so early?"

"The taping didn't exactly go as I'd hoped," Mallory said, looping the strap of her purse over a hook of the antique hall tree that had once belonged to her mother.

"What happened?"

"If you'll fix me a cup of tea while I change, I'll tell you all about it."

"I just had a cup, so the water's hot," Carmen said.

"Great. Where's Cassie?"

"She was in her room putting together a puzzle the last time I checked. She's having a good day."

"I'm glad one of us is," Mallory called over her shoulder as she started down the hallway.

She stopped by Cassie's utterly feminine bedroom on the way to her own room. Striped rose-and-white wallpaper served as a wainscoting. A wide paper border of teddy bears wearing fancy hats, furs and jewelry banded the room that boasted a Jenny Lind twin-size bed that Mallory had once slept in—complete with a rose-and-white polka dot comforter and striped dust ruffle.

Cassie was sitting at a child's table, the pieces of a one-hundred-piece puzzle spread out before her. To Mallory's surprise, her daughter had put together her first sixteen-piece puzzle before she was three, quickly graduating up the ranks. She was so good at figuring out the intricacies of puzzles that she grew bored with them after assembling them a time or two.

Before Mallory snared the researcher's job at WTN, Cassie's "habit" as Mallory jokingly called it, threatened to get out of hand, so Mallory had started picking up puzzles at rummage sales. She sighed. It looked like there would be a lot of cutting back again. Yard sales for Cassie's puzzles, and clothes for them both from Aardvarks, her favorite second-hand store. She didn't mind for herself, but Cassie deserved the best. She was the best.

Mallory regarded the child with a mixture of sorrow and pleasure. Strands of curly red hair had escaped her barrette, creating a fiery halo that framed her too-pale, too-thin, face. A spattering of whiskey-hued freckles danced across the bridge of her pug nose.

A swell of love so powerful it brought tears to her eyes surged through Mallory. Why Cassie? she wondered, blinking back the moisture. Why her baby? Almost as soon as the thought formed, Mallory rejected it. She wouldn't want to wish Cassie's condition on any child . . . any family.

As Mallory watched, Cassie's forehead puckered and the tip of her tongue peeked from her mouth as she struggled to make a piece of the puzzle fit.

"Having trouble?"

Cassie looked up, a smile of pure delight on her face. "Mommy!"

Mallory crossed the room and knelt at her daughter's side, giving her a kiss and a big squeeze. "Hi, Moppet. How's it going?"

"Fine." Cassie looked up at Mallory, her forehead puckered in concern. "Are you sick?"

"No, why?"

"You aren't supposed to be home till after Bullwinkle's over."

The child was altogether too smart, Mallory thought with a rueful twist of her lips. "Well, I thought I'd come home early so we could do something together. Something to celebrate."

The announcement drove the serious expression from Cassie's eyes. "What are we celebrating?"

"That we have a nice house and a wonderful person like Carmen to take care of you since Nana went to heaven. And that we have each other."

"Don't forget we have Price since Nana died, too," Cassie reminded.

A shaft of misery shot through Mallory. Oh, Lord! Cassie adored Price. Would what happened on the set of "The Edge!" affect his relationship with Cassie? Surely he wouldn't deliberately hurt the child.

Mallory hid her anxiety behind a smile. "Right!" she said in a too-cheerful voice. "We have Price."

Mallory popped the puzzle piece Cassie had been struggling with into its right spot. If only the pieces of her life were so easily put back into place.

"I'm going to change my clothes," she said. "Would you like to have a cup of chamomile tea with me and Carmen?"

"Can Matilda come?"

"*May* Matilda come," Mallory corrected. Cassie rolled her eyes and Mallory laughed.

"*May* Matilda come?" Cassie parroted.

Mallory looked at the battered bear that had been Cassie's favorite toy from the time she was born. "If she puts on her best party manners," Mallory said.

"She always has good manners," Cassie said. She gave her mother an impish grin. "And she's always *very* quiet."

"I've noticed that about Matilda," Mallory said with a nod, her smile still firmly in place. "Why don't you run on into the kitchen and tell Carmen you're joining us?"

Cassie got up and came to Mallory, hugging her around the knees. "I love you Mommy. I'm glad you came home for a celebration."

"I love you, too, Moppet."

Mallory watched as her daughter left the room and started down the hallway. Even though enthusiasm for the tea party shone in Cassie's green eyes, she didn't run. She never ran anymore.

Mallory's throat tightened. Her grandmother had always said that there was a reason for everything, that God had a plan. Intellectually, Mallory believed that, but her heart often questioned why a loving God would give her such a precious child, only to demand that she be given back.

"Price has lost his head over that little twit," Thea said as she and Baron exited the two-hour meeting. "I can't believe he's really going to give a no-name, no-experience soap actress a job that was supposed to belong to Delores SanAngelo! It doesn't make sense!"

Though Baron sensed Thea was talking as much to herself as to him, he said, "There isn't much we can do about it. We'll just have to hope for the best. My whole future is tied to the success or failure of 'The Edge!' "

Thea swung the door to her office wide and indicated that Baron go in. He stepped into the room, a spacious sunbathed area swathed in plush platinum-gray carpeting and splashed with massive Boston ferns, silver-framed artwork by Erté and pricey Art Deco art objects. He was too upset to be more than marginally impressed.

Thea gestured toward a fern-green brocade chair. Baron sat, crossing his legs ankle to knee, resting his elbows on the chair's arms and steepling his fingers together.

Thea settled herself behind the ebony desk with a gesture as graceful as it was sinuous. "I wouldn't be too worried about my future if I were you."

"That's easy for you to say." Baron regarded her over the tips of his fingers. "It isn't your career that's on the line."

Thea rested her forearm on the shining surface of the desk and leaned toward Baron with an earnest expression on her angular face. "Anything that affects WTN affects me, whether it's the success of a show or its failure. I can be axed as easily as you. *I* don't have any special relationship with Price—remember?"

Baron didn't care for the erotic picture of Mallory and Price that flashed into his mind.

"Stop frowning," Thea said. Baron's sharp gaze found hers. Her smile was slow, seductive. "You'll get wrinkles."

"So?"

"So you're an extremely handsome man, Baron. That face will take you as far as you want to go in this business."

Baron's frown deepened. If there was anything he hated, it was the implication that he'd gotten where he was by making the most of his physical attributes. He struggled to hide his irritation.

"Thanks—I think." His smile was crooked, stiff. "I'd like to think there's more to me than a pretty face."

"Oh, there's more than that, all right," Thea said with a lazy smile. "Much more."

Baron pretended not to notice the way her eyes moved over his body. Pretended he didn't hear the throb of hunger in her voice. He urged a smile forward.

"It's nice to know I'm appreciated for what really counts," he said with as much sincerity as he could muster. "It's amazing how seldom I get any credit for being good at what I do. I appreciate your noticing, Thea."

Thea looked taken aback for a second, then she smiled, a sort of vague, what's-going-on-here? smile.

It was all Baron could do to keep back a real grin. Dealing with women who made moves on him was nothing new. He had grown accustomed to putting them in their place, letting them know he wasn't an easy target.

But this was a different matter. Thea Barlow was his boss. Pretending that the hidden messages in her eyes were going over his head, pretending to misunderstand, was the only graceful way—the only safe way—out of the awkward position she seemed hell-bent on putting him in.

"Let's grab a bite of lunch," she said, trying a more direct approach.

"Thanks, but I have to record a radio spot in—" he glanced at his watch "—less than an hour."

"Maybe another time, then?" she said.

"Maybe." Baron stood and started for the door. "See you in the morning."

"Yeah. Sure." Thea's striking face wore a bemused expression, as if she were trying to get a handle on what had just transpired.

Baron gave her a jaunty wave and a famous Baron Montgomery smile and disappeared through the doorway. In the safety of the hallway, he dropped the pretense and released a deep sigh. Damn! Why couldn't he have one piece of good luck? Why did he have to have a boss whose interest in him went beyond what he could do for the show? Why couldn't he have the good fortune to meet a woman who was interested in someone besides herself? Was there one single, solitary woman out there who put other people's feelings ahead of her own wants and needs? One who wanted a man for who he was inside as opposed to what was on the outside?

A memory of Thea's confused look flashed through his mind. Baron swore beneath his breath. Maybe Thea hadn't been coming on to him, he thought, as he stepped out into the blistering heat and headed toward his metallic-teal pickup. Maybe he was reading too much into her behavior.

His recent fiasco with Karel had embittered him, no doubt about it. He was as angry at himself and his inability to gauge a woman's true measure as he was with his former fiancée for pulling the wool over his eyes. Maybe, as he'd been told many times before, he was just so conceited, he imagined every woman was after his body.

Maybe, but he didn't think so. Baron unlocked the door to the pickup. What was wrong with him? Between his breakup with Karel and the shake-up with Delores SanAngelo and WTN, his world and his confidence was at a low ebb. He was edgy. Spookier than a green-broke horse. A tad bitter. Paranoid, even.

All natural feelings under the circumstances, he reminded himself, feelings that would stand him in good stead in the long run. He promised himself that he would weather the storm at WTN and come out on top. He'd done it before. And as for women, he damn well wouldn't be taken in again. Not by the likes of Thea Barlow. Not by any woman.

No matter how much gorgeous auburn hair she had.

Tom watched Baron follow Thea into her office. His mouth tightened. Coming to work for WTN might not have been a smart move after all. Thea was as stubborn as she'd always been, and just as hell-bent on destruction.

He thought about the little byplay between her and Rick during the meeting and wondered if there was something going on between them. If there was, the poor boy was in for a rude awakening.

Chapter Three

Mallory would rather have stepped before a firing squad than through the doors of WTN the next morning. The feeling she'd experienced during her "celebration" with Cassie the night before, a conviction that things would be all right, had vanished the moment she'd opened her eyes. There was nothing like starting off your day with the sensation of impending doom hanging over your head.

Drawing a fortifying breath, she stepped through the doors and started for her office, glancing neither left nor right. She was too upset to recognize the curious and admiring looks that were aimed at her ramrod-straight back and the fetching picture she made in her Michael Bolton T-shirt and wash-faded, fanny-hugging jeans.

She'd decided against dressing for the job, since she'd promised Price her resignation. All she had to do was type the letter on her computer, print it out, clear out her desk and go home. The whole thing should take twenty minutes, tops.

Secure in the relative anonymity of the office she shared with two other researchers, she pulled off her sunglasses and dropped them in the cavernous depths of the huge straw bag that doubled as a purse. Then she assembled the storage box she'd bought at a discount store and began to empty the drawers of her desk, arranging the items neatly, making the most of the space. It didn't take long; she hadn't been employed at WTN long enough to gather a lot of extra stuff.

Cassie's picture was the last thing to pack. She looked at her daughter's smiling face—the sparkle in her green eyes, the dimples in her cheeks—and felt a quick rush of tears. How could she hide the fact that she didn't have a job from a child who was so quick to pick up on things?

Mallory crammed on the lid and secured the box with long strips of masking tape. As she affixed the box top, she vowed to have another job by Monday, even if it meant working on another soap and getting killed off in thirteen weeks by a bad cop. It would be better than no job at all. Darn it, she had to get control of her life!

Fighting the incipient tears, she switched on the computer and typed in the date followed by: *Dear Mr. Weatherby.* She paused. What could she say? *Thanks for doing what you could for me. Sorry I blew it.* Long moments passed as she tried to find the words to end her time at Weatherby Television.

Fifteen minutes later, she was still staring at the blue screen when there was a knock at her door and Tom Madsen sauntered in. Today, however, his cheerful smile failed to lighten her heart or her mood.

They had become good enough friends over the past several weeks that Mallory had trusted him with the story of her past. Tom was one of the few people who knew about Mark, and Betty and Cassie. He, of all people should understand that the mess she'd made of things on the set of "The Edge!" yesterday was a serious setback in her troubled life.

"Hey, Mal! How's it goin'?"

"Hi, Tom." Mallory's desultory greeting matched her smile. "As a matter of fact, it's not going very well. I'm typing my resignation. Or trying to," she amended.

"That's why I'm here. Price wants to see you in the boardroom ASAP."

"What about?"

"'The Edge!' of course."

Mallory waved her hand at the box she'd just filled. "I'm leaving. Crawling off with my tail tucked between my legs. What more can he possibly want? An apology? I gave him one. Blood? I don't—"

"He wants to offer you the job," Tom interjected.

Mallory's tirade came to an abrupt halt. "What?"

"You're getting Delores SanAngelo's job. You'd better get your pretty tush into the boardroom."

He disappeared before Mallory could do more than blink in surprise. She raised a trembling hand to her forehead. Was this someone's idea of a joke? If so, it was an unbelievably cruel one. Was it possible for such a dramatic change in luck to occur in so short a time? One minute she was typing a letter of resignation, the next she had a high-profile job, one that would put her in the national spotlight.

National spotlight.

The sudden realization that this was the opportunity she'd longed for hit her with the force of a tidal wave. If she hadn't been sitting down, she would have fallen.

Queasiness settled in her stomach. Excitement warred with apprehension. What if she blew it?

Remembering what Tom had said about hurrying, she jumped up and started for the boardroom, trying to prepare herself for the meeting that would change her life. She was outside the door when it dawned on her that, in her jeans and T-shirt, she was hardly dressed for success.

She put her hands on her hips in disgust. Why, when it was most important that she put her best foot forward, did she always mess up? Like being caught in jeans on the most important day of her life and her descent into idiocy in front of the camera the day before? So far in her twenty-seven years, she'd managed to botch just about everything in her life that mattered. Maybe it wasn't her fault, though. Maybe failure was programmed into her genes, like her auburn hair and brown eyes.

But to be offered Delores SanAngelo's job! A burst of optimism brought a smile to her lips. Maybe—just maybe—her luck had turned.

As she stepped through the door of WTN's small boardroom, she couldn't shake the feeling that she knew exactly how Daniel felt entering the lions' den. The whole marketing department was there, most of the public relations people, along with Thea, Price, Tom and Baron. Baron looked disturbingly attractive in pleated gray slacks, a long-sleeved lavender dress shirt and a floral tie that would have done Monet proud.

His shirtsleeves had been rolled up to reveal muscular forearms bearing a sprinkling of dark hair, and his tie had been loosened enough to guarantee a measure of comfort. His short, immaculately groomed hair looked as if he'd been plowing his long fingers through it.

Though his attire was casual compared to his polished appearance the day before, he still looked every inch the professional. In contrast, Mallory felt like a grubby child, a feeling that didn't do much for her flagging self-esteem.

From across the expanse of the large table, their eyes met. His scowl reminded her that nothing had changed since the day before, except his clothes.

"Come in, Mallory," Price said, his soft-spoken command yanking her attention back to the subject at hand. "We were wondering where you were."

"I was trying to convince myself that Tom was serious about the job," she said, as Tom pulled out a chair next to his. "After yesterday, it's a little hard to believe."

"Yesterday is the reason," Price said.

"You're saying I get the job because I screwed up?" she said in disbelief. "C'mon, Price. Pull the other one. It's got bells on it."

A titter of laughter rippled through the room.

"I'm not pulling your leg, I assure you," Price said. "After you left yesterday, we studied the comments from the audience. You were the overwhelming choice. They loved the way you and Baron took potshots at each other. Someone referred to you as 'Regis and Kathie Lee' with an *edge*." He grinned. "A little pun there."

Price went on to explain Tom's idea of how they could make the antagonism work for the show.

"Let me get this right," Mallory said, shooting a quick glance at her proposed cohost who didn't look any too happy about the situation. "You *want* me to put Baron down?"

"Exactly. And he'll do the same to you. As long as the two of you don't get too heavy-handed with it, Tom is convinced that it will work like a charm."

Mallory forced herself to meet Baron's brooding gaze. "How do you feel about this?"

The look in his blue eyes was cool as a mountain pool. "I'm willing to let bygones be bygones. I think everyone has been under a lot of stress since we heard about Delores."

It was as good an explanation as any Mallory could come up with for her own unusual behavior.

Price pushed a paper toward her. "This is a one-year contract. If all goes as we expect, we'll up your salary by twenty percent the following year."

Mallory listened with half an ear as she scanned the legal document. When she got to the paragraph that mentioned her salary, she looked up in surprise. It was more money than she'd ever dreamed of making.

"Do us a good job and there's no telling where this might take you," Price said.

There was an indulgent look on his face. Mallory couldn't stop the slow smile that claimed her lips. The look said he was happy for her, proud of her, that she could do it. Hers projected the message that she'd do her best.

The sound of someone clearing his throat intruded on the moment, and her gaze shifted unerringly from Price to Baron. If the look in his eyes was any indication, he had no intention of letting bygones be bygones after all.

Mallory looked away. Thea, who was inhaling a lungful of pungent smoke, let her insolent gaze move from Price to Mallory. The knowing gleam in the older woman's hazel eyes brought everything into sharp focus. Truth hit Mallory like the proverbial ton of bricks.

Thea believed that Price had given her the job because there was something going on between them. It was more probable than possible that everyone else at WTN—including Baron—believed it, too.

"Why don't you step into my office and give the contract a good read through?" Price said.

Mallory dragged her gaze away from Thea's and forced herself to concentrate on the situation at hand. "Fine."

She rose and crossed the room, aware that every eye followed her. She wanted to crawl in a hole and pull it in on top of her, wanted to run from the room and never come back. But she couldn't allow herself that bit of self-indulgence. She needed the money and security that came with this job, and she was going to take it, no matter what any of them thought. Numb with mortification, bolstered by determination, she stepped into Price's office and shut the door behind her.

Away from the prying eyes, she sank into a chair across from Price's and buried her face in her trembling hands. Pain, as sharp and acrid as Thea's cigarette smoke, pierced her. Why were people always inclined to think the worst? And why had it taken her so long to figure out what was going on? Oh, she'd intercepted an occasional speculative look when she'd left Price's office, but she'd assumed they were grounded in the usual curiosity that went hand in hand with a summons from the boss.

No, she amended, that wasn't exactly true. It had crossed her mind a time or two that, because of the way she'd been hired, her co-workers might think there was something going on between her and Price. But until a few moments ago it had been nothing more than a transient thought. She had too much on her mind to dwell on what other people thought of her.

She wished she could march herself out there and tell them the truth: Price Weatherby was her father, not her lover. But refuting the gossip was out of the question, no matter how bad the talk became. Her silence was one of the terms Price had set in exchange for his becoming a part of her and Cassie's lives. It wasn't that he didn't want to acknowledge them, but he had a wife and children he loved, and he didn't want them hurt by tangible reminders of a youthful indiscretion.

Her silence about the truth of their relationship seemed like a fair exchange for the security of a steady paycheck. Besides, Mallory knew firsthand how that sort of news could destroy a family, and she had no desire to infiltrate Price's life or to bring pain to anyone. She just wanted to take care of Cassie as best she could.

Signing the contract for "The Edge!" would be the first step in doing that, and no amount of gossip or speculation was going to stop her. She was reaching for the pen when a knock sounded on the door, and Thea stepped inside, flicking a disdainful look at Mallory as she headed for the desk.

Thea crushed out her cigarette in the crystal ashtray with short, staccato movements, her gaze as sharp as the glittering facets on the cut glass. "Price asked me to come see if there was a problem."

Mallory shook her head. "I was just thinking things through."

"Well, you'd better think hard and be damn sure you want the position, since Price is hell-bent on giving it to you."

There was no mistaking the malice behind the statement. Mallory felt her face flame.

"Don't be embarrassed." Thea's smile held all the satisfaction of a cat who'd just swallowed a very tasty canary. "Whatever is between you and Price is your business."

"There's nothing betw—" Mallory began.

"Spare me the explanations," Thea said with a dismissive wave of her hand, "and if you have a problem with the job offer, you'd better speak up right now."

Reminding herself again of how much she needed the job, Mallory swallowed back a sharp retort. "I'm just a little concerned about working with Baron after the fiasco yesterday," she improvised, pleased at the even tone of her voice.

"As well you should be. Price knows that I think adding you to 'The Edge!' is the kiss of death. Everyone thinks this sparring between you and Baron will be a big hit, but there's no substitute for experience."

"Well, thanks so much for that vote of confidence." Darn! She'd opened her smart mouth again!

Thea placed her hands on the gleaming desktop and leaned forward. "Look, let's just lay our cards on the table."

"Why, Thea! That's the best idea you've had since you snatched Glen Fletcher out from under his wife's nose and started your illustrious career as a TV executive." The comment flew from Mallory's lips before she could stop it. She cursed herself for her lack of control, even as her fury rose.

The release of Thea's pent-up breath sounded like the hissing of an angry cat. "You witch."

"It takes one to know one," Mallory snapped. *In for a penny, in for a pound.*

"You wouldn't be talking so big if you didn't have Price in your corner," Thea said. "Or is that *in your bed?*"

"You don't know what you're talking about, Thea. Give it a rest."

For a moment, Thea was too incensed to speak. "I know this," she said at last. "I know that you're interested in Baron Montgomery."

The charge took Mallory by complete surprise. "You're crazy!"

"Am I?" Thea challenged. "I saw the way you were looking at each other when you came into the boardroom. What were you doing, Mallory? Scoping out your next victim?"

For once, Mallory was too stunned to retaliate. The idea of her being interested in Baron Montgomery was ludicrous!

"Well, since we're laying our cards on the table, let me set you straight about Baron," Thea said. "He's mine, so you just keep your greedy little hands off. I may be second in command around here, but I've got enough clout to make your life a living hell."

With that, she turned on the heel of one stylish pump and stormed from the room.

For several seconds after she left, Mallory could do nothing but stare after her. Where did Thea get off, anyway? Accusing her of sleeping with Price and warning her off Baron Montgomery—as if she'd have the ill-tempered, conceited jerk!

Furious, determined, Mallory reached for the Mont Blanc pen lying on Price's desk. She'd show Thea Barlow. She'd show them all. She'd take this job and she'd be good at it. She'd make "The Edge!" a hit if it killed her!

Without another thought, she scrawled her name to the blank place marked with an *X*. The action drained her anger and left her with a hollow feeling. She dropped the pen and rubbed at her throbbing temples. What was she doing? Temper and her determination to spite Thea aside, working with people who believed a lie about her, people who looked down on her, would be miserable.

It will be miserable if you have to go out and find another job, too. Forget Baron and Thea and all the others. Their opinion doesn't matter. Cassie matters. This is the chance you've waited for. Don't let a bunch of narrow-minded hypocrites ruin it for you.

Taking her advice to heart, she squared her shoulders, picked up the contract and went back into the boardroom.

They were waiting for her.

Smiling, Price signed the contract and Thea and Tom served as witnesses. Price poured everyone a glass of champagne and they all raised their glasses in a toast.

"To 'The Edge!'" Price said. "May it rank high in the Neilsons and win us an Emmy!"

"Here, here!" There was the tinkling of a dozen glasses being clinked together before everyone raised the champagne to their lips. Laughing, they toasted WTN and Baron and Mallory. They toasted Price and the board. Tom toasted his crew. Then they got down to work.

"Assuming everything goes as planned, the show premieres November first," Price said. "That gives us plenty of time for media hype."

"Exactly what kind of prepublicity do you have in mind?" Baron asked, breaking the silence he'd held since Mallory arrived.

Tom consulted a list on his clipboard. "As of today, we have a mall and a new superstore bookstore for the two of you to dedicate, invitations to three celebrity shindigs to attend together, a massive radio campaign, a whole slew of billboards that will make your faces as familiar as Oprah's and a major TV blitz with bits and pieces from the trial show to give the viewers a taste of what the show's all about. There will also be pieces about what we're doing in *USA Today, Parade* and *Entertainment Weekly*. We're cultivating several other opportunities that aren't set yet."

"Pretty impressive," Baron said.

"We've worked our tails off," Tom told him. "Of course, since Delores is out of the picture, the scripts will have to be adjusted to reflect the new format we plan to use for you and Mallory, but I've got some talented writers, so it shouldn't be difficult." He glanced from Baron to Mallory and back again. "The two of you will be spending a lot of time together the next few weeks. Is that a problem?"

Mallory wanted to tell Tom that it was a huge problem, that she couldn't imagine working side by side with the arrogant Mr. Montgomery day after day. But she'd already pushed her luck with Thea, and she knew she couldn't allow herself the luxury of voicing her fears. The memory of Cassie strengthened her resolve to make the most of the opportunity God and Delores San-Angelo had dropped in her lap. Mallory sneaked a peak at Baron. The muscle in his jaw knotted. He was about as thrilled as she was.

"No problem for me," she said with as much enthusiasm as she could muster. "I'm ready to start anytime."

"Good."

Tom had just spoken when the cellular phone Mallory carried in her purse rang. Since there wasn't a phone in the boardroom, everyone looked around, trying to figure out where the sound was coming from.

"It's my phone," Mallory said, torn between embarrassment and apprehension. "I'll take it outside." She scooped up the bag and rose in one motion. Rummaging through the contents as she went, she scurried from the room.

Though the cellular phone was a strain to her budget, she felt it was necessary for Carmen to be able to reach her at any time and any place, just in case something happened to Cassie.

Her fingers closed around the small receiver that she unfolded and put to her ear. "Hello."

"Hi, Mallory," Carmen said. "I knew it would scare you if I called, but I forgot to remind you to pick up your cleaning and Cassie's prescription."

"Oh, thanks, Carmen. In all the commotion yesterday, it completely slipped my mind. By the way, I got the job."

"What!" Carmen yelped.

Mallory couldn't help the silly grin that leapt to her lips. "Yeah. I'll tell you about it when I get home."

Carmen expressed her pleasure, and, after saying their goodbyes they hung up. Mallory went back into the room, knowing that every eye would be on her.

She wasn't wrong. Like a ship seeking a safe port, her gaze sought Price's. Concern etched deep lines between his eyebrows.

"Is everything okay?"

Knowing their conversation was being monitored by a dozen people lent an unnatural stiffness to Mallory's voice. "Fine."

He relaxed visibly, and Mallory turned to Tom. "What did I miss?" she asked, hoping to divert attention from herself.

Tom launched into an overview of the past couple of minutes, and, though she appeared to give him her undivided attention, she was keenly aware of Thea's malevolent scrutiny and Baron's moody stare.

She allowed herself a small sigh. She might be on the road to success, but it looked as if the path were littered with obstacles.

By the time Baron left the meeting, he was mentally exhausted from trying to absorb and record everything he needed to know about his upcoming television debut. His head ached and his eyes burned from Thea's cigarette smoke. The scent of it lingered in his nostrils and no doubt clung to his clothes.

Though he was more than ready to go home and relax—or attempt to—he had to admit that the meeting had provided some valuable insights. After seeing them together, his gut instinct told him there was definitely something going on between Price and Mallory. They could carry on whole conversations without saying a word, and, when Mallory had returned from her phone call, there had been unconcealed worry on Price's face. What had caused him such concern?

Still, no matter what might be going on between them, Price Weatherby was a smart man, deserving of his success. And even though Baron was less than thrilled about working with Mallory, he had to give credit where credit was due: she was sharp. For that matter, so was Thea.

The realization that both women had more going for them than looks shouldn't have come as a surprise. The Thea Barlows and Mallory Ryans of the world got ahead by being smart enough to know which man to latch on to.

Which posed another thought. Was Thea's blatant dislike of Mallory based on the possibility that Mallory had come between Price and Thea? *Oh, what tangled webs we weave,* Baron thought with a bitter twist of his lips. And he was smack-dab in the middle of it.

"Baron!"

The sound of Price's voice halted Baron's nonstop course to the exit. He turned and saw Price approaching with his customary fast pace.

"I wanted to catch you before you left."

"What can I do for you?"

Uneasiness sat on Price's attractive features. "I wanted to ask if you'd have a talk with Mallory before we start with the preproduction campaign. An apology for what happened yesterday... an olive branch if you will." He smiled. "As a sign of goodwill."

Apologize! Price wanted him to apologize to Mallory?

"I couldn't help noticing that there's still a lot of tension between the two of you, and I think it will make for better working conditions if you openly discuss this antagonism you feel—whatever it is."

Baron shrugged. "Some people just rub you the wrong way—you know?"

"I know it happens," Price said with a nod. "But I can't imagine anyone feeling that way about Mallory. I don't know what got into her yesterday, but she's a wonderful person. Warm and giving..."

Yeah, I'll bet.

"I guess what I'm trying to say is that I want the two of you to give each other a chance, to reach some sort of harmony that will benefit the show."

The man had a point, Baron thought, but damn it, why did *he* have to be the one to apologize? Saying he was sorry was never easy for him, and being ordered to make amends was about as appealing as kissing Thea Barlow. But the success of the show was important. He'd burned his bridges in Texas, and there was nothing to do but go forward—into or over "The Edge!"

"I'll take care of it," Baron said, almost choking on the promise.

Price smiled and nodded. "I'll count on it."

Anger simmered inside Baron as he watched the older man walk away. This job would give him ulcers before it was over. He turned and started again for the exit. Halfway there, he muttered, "To hell with it," pivoted and directed his steps toward Mallory's office, the chip on his shoulder as big as his home state.

Her door was ajar, and her back was to him, her curvy derriere pointed at him as she riffled through some things in a box. Baron leaned one shoulder against the doorjamb and crossed one foot over the other, the toe of his stylish loafers buried in the carpet while he watched the play of soft flesh against worn denim and imagined Price Weatherby's hands cupping those supple curves.

His soft curse sent Mallory whirling around, an eight-by-ten photo clutched in her hands.

"What are you doing here?"

"Royal decree."

She set down the picture—a little girl with copper-hued curls and big dimples. There was no doubt the child was hers, even though her eyes were sea green instead of brown like Mallory's.

"I beg your pardon?"

"I have instructions to apologize for my boorish behavior yesterday."

"Instructions? From whom?" she asked, but the look in her eyes said she knew.

"Price, naturally." A telltale pink crept into her cheeks.

"I don't need Price Weatherby to fight my battles for me," she said with a lift of her chin. "And you know what you can do with your apology."

Baron lunged away from the doorframe and went to the desk, placing his palms on it and leaning toward her in much the same way Thea had earlier. "Look, why don't I just lay all my cards on the table?"

In perfect mimicry, she planted her palms on the desktop and leaned toward him, tilting her face upward and meeting his angry gaze with a candid look of her own. The curl of her lips was more a sneer than a smile.

"Well, why the hell not? Everyone else has."

Bewildered by her statement, he said, "The success of this show is very important to me, and I have no intention of letting you ruin it. I'm willing to go along with Tom's idea, but you just make damn sure you don't get off any cheap shots."

"If I recall correctly, you were the one who drew first blood."

"*You* were flirting with Paolo Mancuso!" Baron could hear his voice rising and made a conscious effort to tone it down. "*I* was trying to salvage the show, not to mention your dignity."

"Déjà vu."

Baron's handsome face wore a blank look. "What?"

"I think we've already had this conversation, Mr. Montgomery."

For long seconds, Baron and Mallory looked deep into each other's eyes. It didn't take them long to reach the same conclusion: they couldn't be in the same room five minutes without the conversation deteriorating into a duel of sharp-honed words. They realized something else: even with bickering as the cornerstone of the show's format, their inability to get along didn't bode well for an hour-long production.

Without another word, Baron straightened and left the room. He'd tried to apologize, but he wasn't any good at it. He should have told Price that up front.

Baron was unlocking his truck door when he heard Thea call his name. *What now?* The last thing he wanted or needed was to have a conversation with the barracuda. He turned.

"You're off for the day?" she said with a smile.

"Yeah."

Thea shielded her eyes from the sun with her hand as she looked up at him. "I just wanted to get your impression of how the meeting went."

"I think it went fine."

"Even though you'll be working with Mallory instead of Kathey?"

Baron figured he knew why Thea was questioning him about Mallory. If she could keep him stirred up about his working conditions, she could make Mallory's life miserable. He knew there was no love lost between the two, but he refused to let himself get caught in the middle of their particular war. A show that was filled with personal problems was a show that stood a good chance of failing, and God knew he'd have enough trouble controlling his own situation with Mallory.

A half smile hiked up one corner of his mouth, and he surprised himself by taking Mallory's side. "She's a smart lady, Thea. Give her a chance."

Thea reached out and brushed back the short hair that fell over Baron's forehead. He had to steel himself not to jerk away from her touch.

"You're too kind."

"I want to give this show a chance. Upheaval only creates problems."

"She's interested in you, you know," Thea said, catching hold of his tie and casting a flirty glance up at him.

"Yeah, right."

"She is."

"Well, like I said on the show the other day, she isn't my type."

"What is?"

Baron had no trouble stating what he liked in a woman; he just had trouble finding it. "A woman who's smart, sexy and secure in who and what she is. One who doesn't need a man but wants one."

Thea gave a throaty laugh. "Where do I send my application?"

Good Lord! Did Thea Barlow actually see herself as fitting that description? He bestowed a wistful smile on her. "Sorry, I'm not taking any applications right now. I'm still recovering from a broken heart."

"Someone in Texas?"

He nodded.

"I bet I can help you get over her."

Baron shrugged his wide shoulders. "Maybe. But I'm just not ready right now."

"Well, you can't blame a girl for trying," Thea said, a pout on her red lips.

"Nope," he said, unlocking the door of his truck. "Everybody's got to do what they've got to do."

* * *

From his vantage point just inside the front entrance, Tom saw the whole exchange. The way Thea touched Baron. The tenseness in Baron's stance. Disgusted, Tom sighed as Thea turned and headed back to the building.

"What do you think you're doing?" he snapped as she entered the door.

Thea's loose-limbed stride carried her past him without so much as a hello. "Talking to an employee—not that it's any of your business."

Tom fell into step beside her and, grabbing her arm, spun her around to face him. Her pointed look moved from his hurtful fingers to his angry gaze. Fury blazed in her eyes. "I think maybe you've forgotten who's the boss around here."

Tom's eyes narrowed. "I haven't forgotten, but maybe you have."

"What's that supposed to mean?"

"It means that 'The Edge!' has the earmarks of being a huge success. Price has a lot riding on it. Leave the stars alone, or you might find yourself out on your pretty butt."

Thea turned a cool gaze to his. "Are you insinuating that there's something between me and Baron?"

"If the shoe fits..." Tom said, letting the old cliché make the accusation for him. "I'm also concerned about the abominable way you treat Mallory."

Thea's eyes widened guilelessly. "Oh?"

"She's a friend."

"Hmm."

Repulsed by the cunning in her eyes, Tom released his hold on her arm sorrowfully. "I've told you before that you don't need to step on other people to get to the top,

Thea. All you've got to do is use the resources God gave you."

Thea gave him an innocent smile. "Oh, but that's exactly what I'm doing, Tom," she said and, without another word, walked away.

Mallory was going through the items in the box, trying to decide what she would need when she was moved from her office to her new dressing room, when Price came into her office ten minutes later.

"Hi," he said.

"Hi." Mallory's voice was cool.

"What's the matter?"

Mallory's eyes held reproach. "Did you ask Baron to apologize to me?"

"Yes."

She released a harsh breath. "Why?"

"Why? Because I'm not crazy about the way he's treated you." Price met her anguished gaze and raised his palms in a helpless gesture. "There isn't much I can do for you, Mallory, you know that. But I like to try and make your life easier whenever I can."

She felt the sting of tears beneath her eyelids and wondered if they were tears of weariness, disillusionment or anger. "I know you mean well, but you need to stop and think about what you're doing."

"What do you mean?"

"Ask yourself how your actions are going to affect things. You. Me. Everyone. You must know that there has been a lot of talk about us ever since you insisted that I be given a job. But now, with your giving me Delores's position . . . well, frankly, it's raised a lot of eyebrows."

"I don't see how. I didn't *give* you the job. It wasn't just my decision. Everyone agreed that you were the best person for the job. All I did was make it official."

"I know that, but—"

"I think you're imagining things."

She wanted to tell him about Thea's accusation, but she didn't want to worry him. "I'm not imagining things," she insisted. "For both our sakes, I want you to... to not act so... interested in me and my life. Like when I got the call today."

"I was afraid something was wrong with Cassie."

"I know, and as Cassie's mother, I appreciate it. But an employer just doesn't show that much concern over an employee's personal calls. Your curiosity just drew attention to us."

Pain shadowed Price's green eyes. He nodded. "I see what you're getting at. I'll try to watch it."

"I'm thinking about you as much as I am myself."

"I know," Price told her. "And I appreciate it."

Mallory watched as he left the room. As usual, she was filled with an indefinable sorrow and troubled by conflicting thoughts and emotions.

Belated empathy for her mother and a genuine understanding of how Betty had fallen in love with Price.

Anger at her mother and Price for acting on those feelings even though Price was married and had children.

And gratitude for all he was doing for her, the daughter he hadn't even known existed until five months ago.

Chapter Four

Over the next four weeks, the set of "The Edge!" was modified and refined. A kitchen was added to showcase new appliances and a fireplace was built to give the set a homey feel. As Tom predicted, Mallory and Baron were almost inseparable. True to his projection, WTN saw to it that the new duo was available for anything and everything that put their names or faces in front of the public.

They filmed TV ads and made radio commercials together and separately. They were interviewed by magazines with national distribution as well as by local press and periodicals. Their story was available for print through UPI and AP wire services, and picked up by papers throughout the country. There was interest in every facet of their lives, from their backgrounds to what movies they liked to watch and what they liked on their pizza.

Their pictures were taken while they were busy at work and as they went about their everyday lives. They were on the cover of *People, Entertainment Weekly* and the *National Enquirer*, whose cover story, "The Truth Behind Mallory and Baron's Bickering" claimed that the real reason the two snipped at each other was that they'd been star-crossed lovers in a former life.

Mallory had been mortified. Baron was philosophical. Tom loved it. Publicity was publicity.

A choice few of the people from the test audience were filmed giving their impression of the sparks that flew between Mallory and Baron. The teasers from the test show were aired and the feedback was phenomenal. The show was talked about, talked up and put down by a few skeptics who joined the Thea Barlow ranks.

Tom's dream materialized as Mallory's and Baron's faces became as familiar as any television celebrity's ever hoped to be. He was, he claimed with a wide smile, a marketing genius.

By the end of the month, all the taping was done and Baron and Mallory started making themselves available for public appearances. Like hounds on the scent, the paparazzi dogged them as they made themselves visible to the movers and shakers of Tinseltown.

Rubbing his hands together in glee, Tom claimed that the show was as awaited as the Second Coming. If it didn't fly, if—God forbid—it sank into ratings obscurity, at least it would go down with the same fanfare and notoriety that surrounded the *Titanic*.

Other than the fact that the hectic pace meant far too much time away from Cassie, Mallory had to admit that the hours she spent with Baron were more pleasant than she ever dreamed they could be. Though she was still in awe of the easy way he romanced the camera and his intuitive knack for saying the right thing at the right time, he seemed less inclined to put on his sparring gloves as he had those first few days. And, though she caught an occasional mocking glance and perceived an infrequent condescension in his attitude, she could only guess that, like her, he had decided that the show's success should take precedence over whatever ill feelings they had for each other.

Which was exactly what Baron had done. As his mama had often said during his youth, there was no sense cutting off his nose to spite his face. He needed "The Edge!"—and he was willing to give Mallory Ryan the benefit of the doubt, at least for now.

Thea, too, backed off from both Baron and Mallory. She wasn't above pulling rank on Mallory, but she wasn't stupid. She knew who buttered her bread. She knew Price wouldn't stand for any overt moves against Mallory. Since Baron refused to cooperate, Thea had no choice but to lie low until Mallory fouled up again.

"A little closer to Baron, Mallory." Brad Murphy, the photographer who was doing the photos for a magazine interview, gestured inward with his outstretched hand.

Mallory took a step nearer her cohost who sat in one of the overstuffed chairs from the set. Wearing a black tuxedo, Baron was drop-dead gorgeous. His long legs were crossed, and his hands, which somehow looked both strong and elegant, were curved over the edge of the rounded, heavily padded arms of the chair.

"No, no, stand in back of him a bit, Mallory," Brad said, peering through the viewfinder.

Mallory moved another step and caught a whiff of some peppery, masculine cologne.

Brad looked up, his brow knitted into a frown. "Relax, for cryin' out loud."

"I *hate* having my picture taken," Mallory fumed, rolling her shoulders to ease the tension.

"Well, you'd better learn to like it, 'cause you're gonna be doing a lot of it," Brad said. He stepped out from behind the tripod, placed his hands on his hips and surveyed the situation.

"Baron, why don't you cross your left leg over your right? Mallory, sit on the arm of the chair and rest your right arm along the back. And try to look like you aren't sitting next to Jack the Ripper, okay?"

Taking short steps—all that the tight, floor-length gown she was wearing would allow—Mallory moved around to the side of the chair and eased herself into place. She hesitated. Putting her arm along the back of the chair meant leaning closer to Baron, so close she could see the beginnings of a five o'clock shadow, even though it was closer to noon.

"Mallory!" Brad called, a hint of annoyance in his voice. "Sometime this century, okay, sweetheart?"

Baron glanced up at her, his customary frown in place, his whisker-shrouded face evoking an aura of danger. "I don't bite," he said, his voice low and, like Brad's, a bit irritated.

"No?" Mallory said with a lift of her eyebrows. "You could have fooled me."

Wriggling her hips, she inched nearer to him and slid her arm along the back of the chair behind him. They were so close that the side of her breast touched his shoulder. So near that she imagined she could feel the heat rising from his body.

"Okay, now, lean in a little more...put your face closer to his. Baron, look up at her."

He did, and Mallory's heart took a nosedive.

"Baron, give me another of those scowls. The women will love it. Mallory, let's see some sparkle, some sass!"

To cover the fact that she was suddenly and uncomfortably aware of Baron as a man, Mallory held up two fingers up in a vee behind Baron's head—devil's horns as Cassie called them.

Brad chortled and snapped away. "That's it! Let him have it. Good! Great!"

Much to Mallory's chagrin, the shot—with Baron looking diabolically handsome even with the devil horns and her with an impish grin—would later be used on the cover of the magazine.

By the time they were finished posing for the indefatigable Brad, Mallory was bushed and irritable. She knew the crankiness went hand in hand with her unexpected awareness of a man who didn't even pretend to like her. An attraction to Baron Montgomery was out of the question. Not even a mild fascination was permissible. Liking his shadowy beard was unacceptable. Loving the scent of his cologne was taboo.

She knew his type. He was a leaver, not a lover, and considering her track record, she'd had enough of that kind of man to last her a lifetime. . . .

Finished with the shoot, Baron escaped to his dressing room, glad the day was over. He needed some time and space away from Mallory to take inventory of his thoughts and feelings, both of which had undergone some major changes of late—especially today, while they were mugging it up in front of the camera.

Through some silent, mutual agreement, things between them had settled into an amiable working relationship, for a couple of reasons that Baron could think

of: First, maintaining an active dislike was too draining, considering he and Mallory had been spending more
than eight hours a day with each other for the past several weeks. Second, enmity wasn't good for the show,
and making "The Edge!" a success took precedence
over everything else, including their common animos-
ity.

He would be the first to admit that working with
Mallory hadn't been the ordeal he expected. Congenial
working conditions were fine, but today, something unexpected had happened. Though they'd posed together
countless times, today, for the first time, he was acutely
aware of Mallory's nearness and more than a little startled to realize that his vexing cohost was a beautiful, desirable woman.

Hell, it was hard not to be aware of her when she was
so close he was drowning in the exotic fragrance of some
sexy perfume. And the creamy swell of her breasts, revealed to best advantage by the push-up bra she wore,
would be distracting—and alluring—even to a saint,
which he'd never claimed to be.

He banished the recalcitrant thought and made a
concerted effort to put Mallory out of his mind. Instead, a vision of her mouth flashed into his thoughts.
Until the photographer instructed him to turn toward
her, Baron had managed to disregard the fact that her
shapely mouth had one of those full, bee-stung lower
lips, the kind designed for a man to nibble on....

As luck would have it, her mouth wasn't the only
thing shapely about her. On some level, he'd known that
her figure was decent, but he'd never realized just how
perfect her fanny was until she walked into the studio
sheathed in the sequined, midnight blue gown. His pulse

leapt at the memory, and he cursed himself for noticing.

He didn't want to be aware of Mallory Ryan as an attractive, desirable woman. He didn't want to be aware of her as anything but the enemy. She was Price's woman, he reminded himself. The kind of woman he hated.

Unfortunately, the prompting didn't have much effect on his heart rate or his maverick thoughts. All he could do was hope that the awareness would pass and that, until it did, he could keep his thoughts a secret.

She was on the cover of another magazine. He couldn't believe that she was so beautiful and about to become one of the most successful women in television. Not that he didn't believe she had it in her, but... somehow he'd never expected it. He was proud of her. Prouder than he'd ever thought it was possible to be. Mallory. His daughter. Maybe he should call and tell her. He reached for the phone and put it down. No. He couldn't call her. He'd set the rules. He had to live by them.

The traffic was horrendous. Even though they were still a block from the theater where the premiere of *Wild Hearts,* starring two of Hollywood's most promising young stars, would make its debut, the limo carrying Mallory and Baron had slowed to a crawl.

At least the jumble of vehicles postponed the moment they would be forced into a performance of their own. Dressed to the nines—Baron in the same black tux he'd worn a week ago, Mallory in a gold lamé gown that was falsely demure—Mallory felt like a farce.

The gown was a simple form-hugging sheath with a halter top that was secured at her nape by a single rhinestone button and an off-center slit in the front that revealed a tantalizing portion of thigh. The back of the long dress left her bare to the dip in her spine just below her waist. Her only jewelry was a pair of gold-beaded earrings that brushed the curve of her jaw when she turned her head. Her hair was upswept into a casual jumble of curls that tumbled onto her forehead; a few had escaped the beaded clasp to tickle her cheeks and nape.

She clenched her hands in her lap and sneaked a glance at Baron, who lounged beside her, calm and apparently at ease. Exhaling a small sigh, she forced her thoughts to the panorama unfolding before her.

A burgundy canopy flowed from the entrance of the theater out to the curb where stretch limos deposited their occupants as fast as they could disembark. Thick gold cable stretched between brass posts cordoned off the area. With the help of a regiment of security people, the roped-off section kept the steady influx of arriving celebrities separated from the hordes of fans who had assembled outside the auditorium on the off chance of spotting their favorite star.

Excitement and expensive perfumes mingled in the air. Voices blended with the muted sounds of traffic. Cameras flashed. Spotlights chased each other across the night-lighted sky, like bright beacons flashing danger warnings to unsuspecting travelers. The only risk Mallory could see was possible blindness from staring at the ocean of sequin-spangled gowns without the protection of sunglasses. As much in awe as any star-struck fan, she voiced the comment to her companion.

"Your first premiere?" Baron asked.

The forced intimacy of the car had been a surprisingly pleasant experience so far. Ever since the limo had picked her up in front of her house, Baron had been politeness personified.

She nodded. "How about you?"

"I went to a premiere in Houston a few years ago. A local, small-time independent, convinced he'd filmed the next Cannes winner." His lopsided smile was evident, even in the semidarkness of the limousine. "Believe me, it was a far cry from the pomp and ceremony we're seeing tonight."

"How did the film do?" Mallory asked.

"Direct to video," he said, aiming his first genuine smile at her.

Being the recipient of a stun gun blast couldn't have paralyzed Mallory any more than Baron's million-megawatt smile. She was sure her heart stopped beating—at least for a second or two—and the interior of the limo not only shrank, it was suddenly devoid of oxygen. She sent up a silent prayer to whatever patron saint was in charge of foolish hearts, asking that hers be put on top of his—or her—list.

The limousine glided to a smooth stop in front of the canopy, saving Mallory the necessity of contributing another sparkling gem to the conversation.

"We're here," she said, the inane comment a testimony to the deterioration of her mental faculties, a condition she blamed on his devastating smile.

"Nervous?" Baron asked, as the chauffeur got out and rounded the long hood.

She nodded.

"Me, too."

She looked at him in surprise. "You're scared?"

"Petrified," Baron confessed. "Tom has either created two of the most popular TV personalities of the decade—no mean feat since 'The Edge!' hasn't even aired yet—or two of the biggest flops of the century."

"I don't know about you, but I can't afford a flop," Mallory said, unaware of the desperation in her voice.

"Me, either."

The chauffeur swung the door wide, and Baron stepped out, reaching in and offering Mallory his hand. She placed her hand in his and stood, aware as she did so of some high-pitched, excited voice squealing, "Oh my God! It's Baron Montgomery and Mallory Ryan!"

Startled, Mallory looked up at Baron, who slid his arm around her in an automatic, protective gesture. Side by side, they started up the wine-hued runner to the doors.

"Hey! I thought you two hated each other!" some man called from the crowd.

Before Mallory knew what Baron was up to, he stepped behind her, clamping a hand on either shoulder. His voice was a teasing rumble over her head. "I only brought her along to shield me from the crazed women."

For a moment, the crowd went wild, and then another celebrity alighted and the moment passed. Mallory felt herself being swept along on a tide of expensive perfumes and oversize egos. Safe inside the packed lobby, she looked up at Baron again. They shared their first smile.

"Quick thinking, partner."

"Thanks," he said, taking her elbow in a firm grip.

"They knew who we were, and they didn't throw rotten tomatoes at us," she observed as he propelled her though the crowd.

His smile was quick, pleased. "I guess we can tell Tom, 'So far, so good.'"

It had been ten days since Mallory had attended the *Wild Hearts* premiere with Baron. Ten agonizing days since she'd arrived home and found Cassie feverish and coughing, the victim of some virus that lingered and lingered, determined to rob the frail child of what small reserves of strength she had left.

Mallory was thankful that most of her day work was finished for now. A majority of the things she was slated to attend with Baron were scheduled at night. Price had insisted on hiring an R.N. to stay at Cassie's bedside twenty-four hours a day. It wasn't that he didn't trust Carmen; it was just that he wanted his grandchild monitored every minute.

No matter where she went, Mallory's cellular phone was her constant companion. She demanded on being apprised of the smallest change in Cassie's condition. At home, she spent every minute at the child's side, talking to her, reading her stories, watching her sleep—and praying. She had prayed so much that she was afraid she might burn up the lines of communication between her and God.

Nights were spent on a cot by Cassie's bed, awake for the most part, afraid to fall asleep in case her baby started coughing and choked, or—God forbid—drew her last shallow breath while resting in the dark arms of Morpheus.

After a week, the worry and lack of sleep began to manifest themselves in dark circles beneath Mallory's eyes, pale features and irrational bursts of anger. She didn't care. Cassie came first.

The crisis passed as she'd prayed it would, but it remained to be seen just how much damage had been done.

When the doctor had finished a thorough examination of Cassie, Mallory ushered her daughter to the waiting room where Carmen sat working on her cross-stitch.

"Dr. DeBorde wants to see me in his office a minute," Mallory said to Carmen. She lifted Cassie—who seemed lighter every day—into the chair next to her sitter's. "I shouldn't be long."

Carmen nodded and took a book from a canvas bag for Cassie to look at.

Mallory knelt by her daughter's chair and cupped her face with a gentle palm. "Mommy will be right back, sweetie, okay?"

Cassie smiled. "Okay."

Mallory kissed Cassie's cheek. Forcing back tears of weariness and sorrow, she left the room.

Dr. DeBorde, six and a half feet tall and all elbows and knees, greeted her with a wan smile. "Have a seat."

Mallory sat on the edge of the comfortable-looking chair, her knees clamped together, her hands clenched in her lap.

"I saw an ad for your new television show the other night. It looks interesting."

Her smile of thanks was quick, brittle. "Thank you. We have high hopes for it." Then, because there was no sense beating around the bush, Mallory blurted, "She isn't doing very well, is she?"

Dan DeBorde shook his head. "I'm not going to lie to you, Mallory. Cassie is past the crisis and on the mend, but we both know she isn't a robust child, and this last bug took its toll."

Mallory's nails dug into her palms. Two of the tears she'd made such a valiant effort to control rolled in silence down cheeks that were as waxen as her daughter's. She tried to smile and failed. "I feel like that kid in 'Peanuts'—you know, the one with the black cloud hanging over him all the time?"

The doctor was silent, knowing instinctively that she needed to vent her feelings.

She drew in a deep breath that snagged on a sob. "No matter how hard I try," she said, instigating a methodical shredding of the tissue clutched in her fingers, "I can't seem to get my life in order. Ever since Mark left, I've had a constant worry over money. Then my mother died, and I had to hire Carmen, and that meant more money. I thought when I got the job as cohost of 'The Edge!' all my worries would be over."

She shook her head. "Well, not over. There was always Cassie, but I guess I thought things would level out, that I'd get a break. And now—" Her voice broke. She looked into the doctor's kindly, lined face. His image blurred and wavered. "I don't think I can take this, Dr. DeBorde."

"You have to put up a good front. For Cassie."

"Cassie knows more than I like to think she does." Mallory couldn't help the bitterness and frustration that spilled over into her voice.

"Most terminally ill kids do."

Mallory winced at his choice of words. "You don't believe in pulling any punches, do you?"

"Pretending things are all right never works for very long. It's best to face the truth and start coping with it."

"Isn't there any chance of finding a donor before—" she sniffed "—before it's too late?"

"Of course there's always that chance," the physician said. "But realistically, I wouldn't pin my hopes on it if I were you."

Despite Dan DeBorde's prognosis, Cassie grew a little stronger every day during the next week. The nurse was dismissed, and Cassie began to take interest in her puzzles again. Seeing the color return to her cheeks and her dimples make a reappearance made it easy for Mallory to relegate the doctor's hateful words to the back of her mind and pretend things were normal . . . whatever *that* was.

Though they were less than twenty-four hours from taping the first show, Mallory and Baron were scheduled as part of a panel of judges for a local beauty pageant.

Because they were considered one vote, Mallory found herself squeezed into a small area next to Baron. She would have preferred voting separate from him, because reaching an agreement meant they would literally have to put their heads together—an unsettling proposition at best. No doubt about it, the Baron Montgomery she had gone to the premiere with, the one who smiled and treated her as a real human being, was a hard man to resist.

It was the longest three hours Mallory ever sat through. Even though she scooted as far away from Baron as the limited space permitted, the hardness of his thigh pressing against hers was a constant source of awareness. And as they leaned close to confer about the scores they would give each contestant, there was no denying that he smelled deliciously male or that the serious look on his face was as compelling as his smile.

Lord, Mallory thought, suppressing a shiver, it had been an eternity since she'd been close to a man whose nearness disturbed her on such an elemental level. Of course there hadn't been a lot of men in her life the past few years. There was Price, who didn't count, and more recently Tom, who could never be anything more than a good friend.

It came as a bit of a shock to realize that she hadn't had a date since Mark left her. Even if she hadn't been busy worrying about Cassie and trying to keep body and soul together, she'd had neither the inclination nor the time for a relationship. Up until now, the lack of male companionship in her life hadn't been a concern.

It was distressing that when she did find herself responding to a man, it was one who barely tolerated her. She only hoped she could keep her wayward feelings under wraps. If Baron guessed what effect his nearness had on her, she would die of humiliation.

By the time the winner of the beauty pageant was announced, Mallory was a bundle of nerves. The whole event had taken longer than she anticipated, and she and Baron were obligated to at least make an appearance at a postpageant party held at a nearby hotel. With shooting of the first live showing of "The Edge!" scheduled for the following day, all she wanted to do was go home and try to get some sleep.

While the auditorium emptied and Baron was chatting with various other judges, Mallory threaded her way through the pack of people to the bank of pay phones in the lobby. She was anxious to see how Cassie had fared during the evening and had accidentally left her cellular phone at home in the excitement of her departure. Unfortunately, several other people had the same idea, and Mallory was forced to wait her turn to use the phone.

A quick call home satisfied Mallory that Cassie was doing fine. Mallory hung up with a relieved sigh. An easy mind would make the time she spent at the party pass much faster. And it would make the first day of filming much easier.

Her clip-on earring in hand, she turned and saw that the crowd had more or less dispersed. A movement drew her gaze to the far side of the lobby. Baron stood there, leaning against the wall, his arms folded over his chest, one leg crossed over the other, the gleaming toe of his black dress shoe resting against the glossy marble floor— a pose reminiscent of his stance the day some six weeks before, when he'd come to her office to "apologize." There had been anger on his face that day, and belligerence. She saw none of that now. There was a quiet, waiting quality about him, and a look of mild curiosity in his dark blue eyes.

Feeling as if she'd been caught doing something she shouldn't and not knowing exactly why, she clipped on the earring and stepped away from the phone booth, feeling awkward and uncoordinated.

"I'm sorry I kept you waiting."

Baron straightened from the wall and eased his hands into his pockets. He ambled toward her, meeting her in the middle of the foyer. "You didn't keep me waiting. Is something the matter?"

"No!" Her denial was quick, sharp. "I had to call and check on my daughter. She's been sick ... some kind of flu virus."

She purposely didn't mention Cassie's heart condition. The fewer who knew about her personal life, the better. She didn't need or want anyone's pity.

"How is she?" Baron asked.

Mallory blinked. "What?"

He shrugged, as if he'd tried to figure out her train of thought and, failing, given up. "How is she? Your daughter?"

His genuine interest caught Mallory off guard. Since few outsiders knew her situation, concern from anyone except those few people she was close to was rare.

"Oh!" Mallory's smile was fleeting, uncomfortable. "She's fine."

"Good."

"Are you ready to go?" she asked, eager to change the subject to something more impersonal. "The driver is probably pacing the sidewalk."

"I told him to go home," Baron said. "My ego hasn't gotten so inflated I can't ride in a cab. How about yours?"

She saw the glint of humor in his eyes. "Not yet," she replied with a hesitant smile of her own. "Actually, the hotel is only about four blocks away. We could walk . . . blow away the cobwebs, release a little night-before-the-first-show tension.

"Are you nervous?" he asked as they started toward the door.

"Scared spitless," she said, glancing over at him. "Aren't you?"

"A little. I have to admit it's going to take some doing to live up to the hype, but I think we're up to it."

She gave him a keen, sideways look. "You do?"

"We'd better be." He glanced down at her feet, encased in glittery high heels and stopped in his tracks.

Mallory came to a halt beside him. "What?"

"Can you walk four blocks in those?" he asked.

"If I can't, I'll take them off."

"And ruin your stockings?"

"I'm a television celebrity," she said with an imperious lift of her eyebrows. "I can afford a pair of ruined panty hose."

"Ah!" Baron said, falling into the banter with his customary ease, "I forgot." He stuck out his elbow and made a sweeping gesture toward the door with his free hand. "Shall we?"

Mallory hooked her hand through his arm and they stepped out into the night together. The sidewalks were scattered with strolling couples. The temperature was perfect and a slight breeze riffled the leaves of the palm trees. It might have been Mallory's imagination but even the air seemed fresh and smog-free.

At the end of the first block, Baron asked, "How old is your little girl?"

Mallory looked up at him in surprise. "Four."

"Are you divorced? Married? What?"

"Why do you ask?"

"It occurred to me that we've spent more than eight hours a day together for the past six weeks, and we don't know anything about each other's personal lives."

"There isn't much to tell," Mallory said. "I'm twenty-seven. I got married at twenty-one and was divorced at twenty-three. I got the only good thing that came out of the marriage—Cassie."

"You sound bitter. Was it another woman?"

"No," Mallory said. "Mark had a small problem with the parts of the wedding vows that deal with 'poorer,' 'worse' and 'sickness,'" she said, without looking at Baron. "What about you?"

"I've never been married. I almost made the big leap, but things fell apart at the last minute."

"What happened?"

Baron looked down at her. "She found someone with a bigger wallet and more clout, who just happened to be a good friend of mine. I decided it was time to move on...in more ways than one. That's why I accepted this job with WTN."

"A new city, a new woman, huh?"

"I'm not looking for a new woman."

Mallory would have liked to ask about Thea, but decided that there was no sense rocking the boat. So far, it had been a pleasant evening.

They walked the last block in a companionable silence. Outside the hotel, Baron said, "You made it— heels and all."

"I'm tough."

"Yeah," he said, with a curious look in his eyes, "you are."

Smiling slightly, he ushered her through the elegant foyer and into the hotel elevator. They heard the sounds of the party as soon as the doors swished open. Inside the room, they were caught up in a round of introductions, a flurry of handshakes and a shower of good-luck wishes for the success of their show.

They were separated within minutes, and Mallory soon escaped to a small balcony, her only companion a glass of expensive champagne. It didn't matter that she'd been left alone; she preferred it that way. She had too much on her mind to care about mingling. Pretending to be on top of the world was taxing when her own world was so shaky.

Tomorrow, the waiting would be over—thank God. By tomorrow evening they'd know if Tom's massive publicity campaign had worked...or more specifically, if the concept of her and Baron as a team worked. She'd know if she had a future with "The Edge!" and whether or not her and Cassie's future was secure . . . at least for a few years.

Mallory lifted the glass to her lips and was surprised to see that she'd finished the champagne. She could already feel it working its subtle magic, easing the tension binding her and relaxing her taut muscles. She didn't hold any liquor well, but figuring a second drink would make her sleep better, she scooped up another glass from a silver tray that was being passed around by a waiter with a white jacket and a whiter smile.

She spotted Baron across the room, surrounded by a bevy of women, all of whom were looking up at him in varying degrees of adoration.

No wonder. He was an incredibly handsome man, and an incredibly nice one when the mood struck him. The walk from the auditorium to the hotel had been enjoyable, and what little she'd learned about his past gave her a deeper insight to him as a person.

Mallory took a sip from her bell-shaped glass and was surprised to find it empty, too. With a sigh, she set it on a small wrought-iron table. Grasping the balcony railing, she lifted her head to the slight breeze and looked out over the lights of the city. She wondered what Price and Tom and Thea were doing and if they were as tense as she was about tomorrow.

"Would you care for something to drink, ma'am?"

The polite question sent Mallory spinning around. Her head whirled and the lights did a crazy pirouette. Without considering the wisdom of her actions, she favored the young waiter with a brilliant smile, picked up another glass of champagne and raised it in a toasting gesture. "Thank you."

"You're welcome." The waiter disappeared, leaving her to the night and her thoughts that wandered willy-nilly back to Baron and her undeniable physical attraction to him. Like it or not—like *him* or not—her body reacted to him in ways that were unsettling, to say the least.

"What are you doing out here by yourself?"

Mallory turned toward the voice, careful to move more slowly. The object of her thoughts stood framed in the doorway, silhouetted in the light spilling out from the room behind him.

"Drinking champagne," she announced with an airy wave of her hand.

"Alone? You should never drink champagne alone," he said.

A soft giggle erupted from Mallory's lips. "*I* should never drink champagne. Or anything else, for that matter," she added as an afterthought.

"Have a problem holding your drink, do you?" He sauntered toward her, his hands in his trouser pockets, a slight smile curving his lips.

She held up her thumb and forefinger with a scant inch of space between them. "Just a small one."

"Good God!" Baron said in mock horror. "You're tipsy."

"I'm relaxed," Mallory corrected, an indignant look on her face.

"Relaxed? Yeah, well, if you were any more relaxed, you'd be laid out on the floor." He took one hand out of his pocket and held it out to her. "Come on. Let's get you home. We've got a big day tomorrow."

"That's why I needed to relax," Mallory explained, taking an unsteady step toward him and putting her hand in his. She swayed, and Baron released her hand and slid his arm around her shoulders.

Keeping her clamped close to his side, he bade their goodbyes and he helped her out to the street where he whistled down a nearby taxi.

Ensconced in the back seat, Mallory gave Baron her address and leaned her head against the battered upholstery, letting the pleasant dizziness wash over her. The ride to her home had a dreamlike quality. She was aware of motion, of stops and starts, of city sounds. She was aware of Baron sitting close to her. She heard the cabbie honk, swear, and felt the leap of the cab as he pressed on the gas. A sigh fluttered from her lips.

"Are you awake?"

Mallory lifted leaden eyelids and looked up at Baron's face, shrouded by shadows, dappled by the glow of neon streaking past. "More or less."

His smile flashed in the dim interior of the cab. "Mostly less, I'd say. We're almost there."

"Good," she said around a yawn she tried to smother with her hand. "I'm really tired."

She started to sit up straighter, but the taxi driver chose that moment to practice his stunt driving, taking the corner sharply and throwing Mallory against Baron.

His arms closed around her protectively, pulling her against his chest and holding her there while the driver wrestled the car under control. The alcohol and Baron's nearness left Mallory feeling too safe to be afraid.

"You got a death wish, buddy?" Baron asked.

"Sorry about that," the driver said. "I'm about to go off shift. I'm anxious to get home, I guess."

"So am I—preferably in one piece."

The brief exchange couldn't budge Mallory from the languor that left her docile and clinging. Her open palm rested beneath Baron's jacket, against his hard middle. The starched stiffness of his shirt was smooth against her

cheek. She breathed in the clean scent and listened to the
beating of his heart. How long had it been since she'd
heard a man's heart racing against her ear? How long
since she'd felt this secure? Since before Mark left?
Ever?

She felt Baron ease his hold on her and drew back to
look up at him. His face swam before her—handsome,
frowning...almost angry. He made a sound, something between a groan and a curse, and gripping her upper arms, leaned toward her and lowered his mouth to
hers.

His lips touched hers once, twice...three times, in
quick, hungry succession. Unsuspecting, Mallory was
helpless to do anything but clutch his shoulders and return the soft urgency of his kisses.

How could a man's lips be so firm and yet so soft? He
slid his fingers through her loose hair and cupped the
back of her head, opening his mouth over hers and
deepening the kiss. A headiness, far more intoxicating
than the champagne she'd consumed, left her feeling
dizzy and weak. And eager for more.

She touched his jaw with her fingertips and encountered the exciting prickle of whiskers, those whiskers that
gave him a dangerous pirate look.

Danger. Danger. Danger. Her heart pounded out the
word. The truth of the message was grave, sobering.
She'd known from the first moment she'd set eyes on
Baron that she was attracted to him, just as she'd known
from that moment that he despised her....

He pushed her away so abruptly that she wondered if
he'd read her mind. Shame seized her, and she suddenly
felt sober. She moved across the seat away from him and
closed her eyes, as if shutting out the sight of him would
erase the memory of what they'd done.

Dear, sweet God! What was she thinking, letting Baron kiss her that way!

She opened her eyes to sneak a glance at him. He was staring out his window, a stony set to his features.

"Number 222 Devon," the cabbie said, pulling over to the curb in front of Mallory's house. As soon as the car was fully stopped, she wrenched open the door and bolted up the sidewalk, mortification nipping at her heels, her heart beating out the message: *Fool. Fool. Fool.*

Chapter Five

Mallory was breathing heavily when she pushed through the front door. She locked it behind her and leaned her forehead on the cool enamel, while she tried to gather her shredded emotions. Through the leaded glass of the front door window, she saw the lights of the cab flash by as it pulled away from the curb.

The tears she'd denied herself while she was in Baron's presence stung her eyes. She shook her head in a mute denial of what she'd allowed to happen. What had she been thinking? How could she have jeopardized her future that way? And with a man who'd given every indication of disliking her—a lot.

She could blame it on the champagne. Or a libido in revolt. But even sexual deprivation was no excuse for what had happened, not when the person it had happened with was Baron Montgomery.

Mallory moaned out loud. How could she face him tomorrow—in front of a studio audience, no less? How could she keep her mind on the guests and the verbal sparring Tom and Price expected of her when she knew that every time she looked at Baron, all she would think of was the way his mouth tasted, the way his arms felt . . . the way his kisses had made her feel?

"Mallory? Is that you?" Tom's voice came out of the darkness.

Mallory brushed away the tears with her fingertips and cleared her throat. "Yeah."

The hall light came on, and she found herself face-to-face with the man who'd managed to become a valued friend—and occasional baby-sitter—in spite of her determination to keep him at arm's length.

"You've been crying. What happened?" Tom demanded, placing a knuckle beneath her chin and lifting her gaze to his.

"I just made a fool of myself with Baron Montgomery, that's all," she said, breaking free and pushing herself away from the door. She stepped out of her green satin pumps.

"Want to talk about it?"

"I let Baron kiss me—okay?" Mallory said, uncertain whether her anger was directed at Baron for taking advantage of her weakness, herself for letting him or Tom for being so nosy.

Tom frowned. "An interesting development since the world in general is convinced that the two of you don't get along."

"We don't," Mallory said with a shake of her head. "Didn't," she corrected. Then she shrugged. "We have been, lately. Sort of."

"So the guy kissed you. Why are you crying?"

"Because he really doesn't like me, and it was my fault. I had too much champagne, and he'll think I'm . . . easy or something."

"Mallory," Tom said, putting his arms around her and drawing her into a comforting embrace, "a little kissing hasn't made a woman easy since the Dark Ages, and you aren't solely to blame. I've seen the way the guy looks at you."

The amusement in Tom's voice made Mallory look sharply up at him.

"You know those sparks that fly between you two?" Tom said, ushering her into the living room and forcing her to sit. Mallory nodded. Tom plopped down beside her. "Those are sexual sparks."

Sexual sparks? The idea was ludicrous. "Wrong. It's dislike. Baron thinks there's something going on between me and Price—just like everyone else at WTN."

It was the first time Mallory had mentioned her dilemma at work to anyone other than Carmen.

"So tell him the truth," Tom urged in a placating tone. "Tell everyone at WTN that Price is your father."

Mallory gasped. How had Tom found out? Other than Price, no one knew except her and Carmen and Cassie. "What makes you think that?"

Tom laughed and took Mallory's hand in his. "I'm a very smart man. It's clear to anyone who takes the trouble to look beyond the obvious."

"It is?"

"Of course it is. You're not a cheating kind of woman. There's also a strong resemblance between the two of you, but when you start comparing Cassie's picture to Price, the likeness gets downright uncanny—she's got his green eyes and the dimples." Tom's grin was unrepentant.

So much for secrecy, Mallory thought with a small sigh.

"And then there's the fact that Cassie spilled the beans tonight."

"She didn't!" Mallory wailed.

Tom gave her hand a comforting squeeze. "Don't blame her. She's just a kid. They don't usually keep secrets well. Want to tell me about it?"

The urge to share her secret was strong. The need to have an ally at WTN was stronger. "I can't. I promised Price."

"Price Weatherby has no guts," Tom said. "If he did, he'd do the manly thing and own up to his past."

She looked at him, her eyes troubled, her resolve wavering.

"Look, it doesn't take a rocket scientist to figure out that there was something between Price and your mother," Tom said. "It isn't fair for him to make you bear the brunt of all this when he's the person to blame." Tom gave her hand a brotherly pat. "So come on and get it off your chest. I guarantee you'll feel a lot better."

Mallory shook her head, uncertain whether or not she was able to talk about the painful subject, even after almost eight months.

"It might take a while."

"We've got all night," Tom said. "Come on, tell me."

Mallory took one look at the concern on his face and launched into the tale of her mother's deathbed confession a few short months ago, Betty's final attempt to clear her conscience before going to meet her maker....

"Your real father is Price Weatherby." Betty's features were haggard and pinched with pain.

"Price Weatherby? WTN's Price Weatherby?" Mallory said, shocked.

"Yes."

Mallory listened with growing disbelief as Betty explained that she was just off the bus from Peoria, a green eighteen-year-old farmer's daughter when she and Price had met and she'd fallen in love. The affair was brief, no longer than a month or two. Betty had soon discovered she was pregnant. Without telling Price about the baby, she had urged him to leave his wife and marry her. He had refused because of his religious beliefs.

Brokenhearted, Betty had bade him goodbye and lost herself in the sea of people who lived and worked in L.A. She'd confessed her plight to her roommate, who had urged her to call Kevin Damian and fall in love— fast! Kevin, whose fast-food roast beef chain was just getting off the ground had made no secret about being crazy about Betty. He was thrilled that she'd decided to go out with him. Following Frances's advice, Betty had wasted little time in going to bed with Kevin and eventually passed off Mallory as his child.

"I'm not proud of what I did," Betty said in a tear-thick voice, "but back then, it seemed like the only thing to do. I was only eighteen. I didn't have a steady job and no family to speak of."

"So you lied to Daddy and ruined his life."

Betty's already pale face blanched at the cruelty of Mallory's statement. "I didn't ruin his life. I was a good wife. A faithful wife. Whether or not you believe me, I learned to love Kevin, and I never gave him any reason to be dissatisfied with me as a wife."

"Then why did he divorce you and disown me?"

Betty plucked at the light blanket on her bed with fingers that had grown bony the past few weeks. It was obvious that their talk was draining her small reserves of energy.

"You know the old Biblical saying about your sins finding you out? Well that's exactly what happened. Kevin found out that he wasn't your father."

"How?"

"The summer you were seventeen and had that car wreck, we needed blood donors. I couldn't give you any, because our types didn't match. Kevin said he'd give. I told him not to bother, that we'd use the blood bank, but he went ahead without my knowing it. Needless to say, when his type wasn't a match to yours, he was furious."

The pain and anger Mallory had experienced ten years ago rushed back in frightening intensity. "Needless to say."

"I don't blame him for hating me," Betty choked out. "But to take out his anger on you the way he did when it was none of your doing... It took me a long time to forgive him for that."

"And Dad never knew Price was my father?"

"No. I wouldn't tell him. I suppose I should have told you and Price back then," Betty said thoughtfully, "but I didn't want Kevin to know, and I didn't think you could deal with any other problems just then."

She exhaled harshly. "God, Mallory, we were all so devastated. Our lives were in ruins. I couldn't see the sense in disrupting Price's life, too. There was nothing he could do after so long. Besides, causing someone else pain never eases your own."

"And later?" Mallory prodded, recalling all the times she'd begged Betty to tell her the name of the man who fathered her and Betty's insistence that she didn't want to talk about it.

"Later, you went off to school, and married Mark and moved away. I just assumed—hoped—that with your new life, my mistakes weren't so important anymore. I figured you'd gotten over the hurt."

Mallory swallowed the emotion knotted in her throat. Forgotten the hurt? How could she ever forget the hurt of learning that the mother she idolized had an affair with a married man and lied to the man Mallory had thought was her father for seventeen years?

But even the blazing anger she'd felt toward Betty couldn't hold a candle to the pain and disillusionment she felt when the man she called "Daddy," the man who raised her and doted on her had cut her out of his life and his will with the calculated deliberation of a surgeon determined to rid a patient of a malevolent malignancy.

"Why did you decide to tell me now?" she demanded. "My God, Mother, it's been ten years since Kevin walked out on us."

"I know, but now..." Betty's voice faltered "...now that I know I'm...dying, it seemed right to try and straighten things out."

"So you've told him? You've told Price Weatherby?" Betty nodded. "Oh, Mother!" Mallory cried, rising and going to the hospital window.

"I'm sorry if you're angry, but it occurred to me that Price might like knowing he has a daughter and a granddaughter."

"I'll bet he was as thrilled as Kevin to find out the truth," Mallory said, turning to face her mother again.

"He was shocked, of course."

"No kidding! A man like Price Weatherby probably considers himself an easy target for a scam. I'm surprised he believed you."

Betty met Mallory's angry gaze steadily. "He had no reason not to believe me. I was a virgin when we met."

Mallory let the implications of her mother's confession settle in her mind. She was angry with Betty all over again, and it wasn't a feeling she liked—or one she was proud of. As an adult, she knew people had weaknesses and faults; her intellect told her that she had plenty of her own. But her heart was smarting, the way it had when she'd first learned of Betty's youthful affair.

Mallory shook her head and pinned her mother with a hard gaze. "I hope you feel better getting this off your chest, Mother, but you may as well know that I have no intention of contacting Price Weatherby. It's a little late to try and establish a father/daughter relationship after twenty-seven years."

"That's between you and Price," Betty said, the look in her eyes unrepentant. "But I still wanted you both to know."

"And I meant it," Mallory told Tom, ending her story. "As far as I was concerned, Price Weatherby was nothing but a sperm donor. It had been twenty-seven years, Tom. I couldn't see myself contacting him and setting myself up for another letdown. Kevin and Mark both claimed to love me, but their behavior proved otherwise. I couldn't expect undying love from Price, could I?"

"Does it still hurt?"

"About Kevin, you mean? It will always hurt," Mallory confessed. "He was my father. I still don't understand how he could just put me out of his life, as close as we were, but as an adult I understand the depth of his hurt and the feelings of betrayal he must have felt."

"I imagine his ego was involved to a certain extent," Tom said. "After all, no man likes thinking he's been taken in by a woman—especially for seventeen years."

"That cuts both ways, friend," Mallory said, elbowing him in the ribs.

"Touché," Tom said with a laugh. "So how did the job at WTN come about?"

"I hadn't counted on Price taking the initiative. He called one day out of the blue and asked to see me and Cassie. I was surprised, but he sounded so nice, so... humble, it seemed churlish to refuse."

"And you were curious," Tom said with a grin. "Admit it."

"You're right," Mallory affirmed. "I was. So I asked him over, and wouldn't you know it! My ice maker went on the fritz that day. I couldn't even offer him a glass of ice tea."

Tom smiled in sympathy.

"Price didn't seem to mind, though. He was very interested in me and Cassie, who took to him like a duck to water. I figured if he passed that test, he couldn't be all bad."

"Kids are pretty good judges of character."

"So they say." Mallory sighed. "Price told me his side of the story, which pretty much jelled with Mother's. She'd told Price about Cassie's illness and Mark leaving us. Price wanted to know what he could do. He seemed disappointed when I told him I didn't need or want anything from him."

"I imagine the whole thing was as awkward for him as it was for you."

"Probably," Mallory admitted grudgingly. "The next day, an armload of toys arrived for Cassie, along with a new refrigerator for me. I called WTN and told Price in no uncertain terms that I couldn't accept the gifts. He told me to have Goodwill pick them up, then—he had no use for them."

Her lips twisted in a wry smile. "I may be stubborn, but I'm not stupid. Needless to say, I didn't call Goodwill."

Tom smiled with her.

"Then Price told me that even if I wasn't interested in forging a relationship, he'd like to be a part of Cassie's life, since she had no active grandparents. But he made it clear from the beginning that he didn't want his family finding out about me and Cassie."

"Like I said, no guts."

"Yeah, well, it didn't make any difference to me." Mallory's eyes begged Tom to understand. "Cassie really took to him, Tom. Knowing how tentative her hold on life is and how few childhood pleasures she can experience, I agreed. That was my first mistake."

"What do you mean?"

"Give Price an inch and he takes a mile. After a couple of weeks, he insisted that we move into this house. It's a rental house of his. I told him I couldn't afford it, and he said I could live here for nothing. I declined."

"Pride?"

"Darn right. But Price can be stubborn, too. He told me that even though I had no desire to become his daughter, he felt beholden and he wanted to help me help Cassie. He said it was the least he could do." She smiled wryly. "He knew what buttons to push. I told him if he really wanted to help, he could give me a job, not presents. That's when he told me he was looking for someone to share the host duties of a new talk show in the works."

"Aha!" Tom said. "The plot thickens."

"I auditioned for the show and lost out to Delores SanAngelo, but Price did insist that I get a job on WTN's research team. I don't think either of us realized how the tongues would wag."

"Why don't you insist that he come clean to everyone?" Tom said again.

Mallory shook her head. "Price has his stipulations, and I agreed to them. It's an awkward situation, but my life has gotten easier, and if 'The Edge!' goes over the way you think it will, things will be really good. That's why I can't afford to alienate Price, Baron or Thea."

Tom nodded. "I don't think you have anything to worry about with Price or Baron, and I can handle Thea."

"You can?"

"I've done it before."

Mallory didn't miss the red that crept into Tom's face. "There's something between you and Thea, isn't there?"

"There used to be."

"Want to talk about it?"

Tom pushed himself to his feet and helped Mallory to hers. "Another time. It's late and we've got a big day tomorrow."

"Thanks for baby-sitting," she said, preceding him to the door.

"Anytime."

He smiled. "Feel better?"

"Yeah," she said, "I do."

"Good." Tom leaned over and kissed her on the cheek. "See you tomorrow. Good night."

"Good night." Mallory watched his retreating form thoughtfully. "Tom!" she called when he was halfway to the curb.

He turned.

"What makes you think that this—" she waved her hand in a vague gesture "—whatever it is between me and Baron is sexual?"

Tom grinned. "My aunt Lora told me once that anytime there's an instant, unexplained dislike between two people, it's usually triggered by an instant, unwanted attraction. My aunt Lora was a very wise woman. Besides, I recognize it because it's still there between me and Thea, whether she likes or acknowledges it or not."

Mallory smiled and shook her head. "Life!"

"Yeah, well, it's better than the alternative," Tom said with a final wave.

Mallory waited until his car disappeared down the street before she turned off the porch light and went to Cassie's room. The soft glow of a night-light was sufficient to show that she was sound asleep. Mallory leaned over and pressed her lips to Cassie's cheek, murmuring a silent prayer of thanks that she was better.

There was a certain relief in sharing her secret with Tom and knowing he didn't condemn her for taking the position she had with Price. There were days she felt as if she were prostituting herself by taking what he offered, and there were days she agreed with his feeling that helping financially was the very least he could do.

Since Price had come into their lives with the house and the job, both she and Cassie were under less strain. And there was the added benefit of having more time to spend with her daughter. On the days Mallory's guilt rose up to haunt her, she reminded herself that the improvement in Cassie's condition was worth it all. Cassie's welfare was the bottom line; never mind the damage to her own self-esteem.

For a long time after the man who'd raised her had turned his back on her, Mallory had labored under the certainty that she was lacking in some way, a feeling Mark had fostered when he left her. Apparently, it was easy for some men to jump ship when things got tough, easy for them to turn off their feelings and move on, to put the burden on someone else and not worry about the consequences—as Tom maintained Price was doing with her.

She wasn't a man hater—far from it. One of her fondest wishes was to live happily ever after with some nice dependable guy who would love her and Cassie to distraction. What it did mean, however, was that she was darn careful in her dealings with the men she came in contact with.

After tonight, she would have to be very careful about how she interacted with Baron. She didn't need the problem of any more friction between them at work, and she certainly didn't need the complication of having him or any other man in her life just now. She had enough on her plate with Cassie's illness.

Tucking the light blanket around her daughter's shoulders, Mallory went to her own room. Suddenly exhausted, she creamed off her makeup in record time, removed her evening wear and slipped a silky satin gown over her head. She was beneath the covers in a matter of minutes. In spite of her agitation over Baron's kisses, Mallory knew she would have no trouble falling asleep.

She was drifting on the shores of slumber when the telephone rang. Irritated, groggy, she groped for the receiver and drew it to her ear. "Hello," she mumbled.

There was no answer.

"Hello?"

Still no answer. A wrong number or a crank call, she thought, slamming the receiver onto its base. She rolled to her side with a mighty yawn and prayed it wasn't the latter.

Baron was still savoring the memory of the taste of Mallory's mouth when the cabdriver pulled up in front of his condo. He cursed himself for succumbing to the temptation of her lips. Dear God! What had prompted him to kiss her—the easy camaraderie they'd shared during the evening or the presumption that their shared personal histories had edged their relationship across some imaginary boundary from impersonal to intimate?

Most likely, the fetching picture Mallory made in her emerald green moiré dress, the alluring smoothness of her shoulders and the way the short, tiered skirt exposed the shapely length of her legs had a lot to do with it.

And possibly it had something to do with the ache that clutched his heart when he'd seen her standing alone on the balcony and sensed in some deep part of him that loneliness was something she'd grown accustomed to.

It could have been the teasing light in her eyes as she'd confessed that she shouldn't drink, or the ripple of desire he experienced when she'd giggled, a sound so unexpected, so unlike the Mallory he'd grown accustomed to, that it came as a shock and a pleasant surprise.

And maybe he was fooling himself. His awareness of her didn't have to be generated by anything but the lengthy, self-imposed celibacy he'd sworn to after he and Karel split. Whatever it was, he'd been a fool to give in to it, and for more reasons than one.

First, he wasn't ready to rush into another relationship with anyone. Second, even if he were ready, Mallory Ryan wasn't a likely candidate. He had learned years ago that mixing business with pleasure wasn't a smart thing to do. And third, even if he and Mallory weren't working together, it was apparent that she had something going with Price Weatherby, which put her in the same category as Thea and Karel and automatically put her out of bounds. Too bad it didn't lessen her desirability.

With a curse, Baron opened the door to his condo. He was shedding his tuxedo jacket when the phone rang. He pushed back his shirt cuff and glanced at his watch. One-thirty. Who on earth would be calling at such an ungodly hour?

Muttering an oath, he grabbed the receiver and dragged it to his ear, barking a sharp "Hello!" into the mouthpiece.

"Uh-oh . . . you're cranky," a sultry voice said.

Baron suppressed another curse. "Thea?"

"Uh-huh."

Wonderful. A heart-to-heart with his boss who had the hots for him was just what he needed after the little scenario with Mallory.

"Just get home?" she asked.

"Yeah. What are you doing up so late?" *Why the hell are you calling me so late?*

"I'm sorry if I'm disturbing you, but I couldn't sleep—nerves, I guess—so I thought I'd check and see how the pageant went."

"Fine." Maybe if he was uncommunicative, she'd get the idea and hang up.

"And the party afterward?"

"If you've been to one of those things, you've been to them all," he said, unhooking his bow tie and working free the buttons of his pleated shirt.

"Not necessarily. You can have a good time if the person you're with is someone special."

Baron had a sneaking suspicion he knew where this conversation was leading. He removed his gold cuff links and pulled the shirt free of his dark pants.

"I'll bet I'd have had a good time if I'd gone with you."

Baron grimaced. *Yeah, but would I?* He shrugged out of his shirt and started to toss it onto the sofa. A whiff of Mallory's perfume wafted upward. He lifted the shirt to his nose and inhaled. Of their own volition, his eyes closed. He could see the look on her face as she sat, looking up at him in the cab, her gaze slightly out of focus, her hair windblown, her lips parted. God, her lips...

"Baron? Are you there?"

Torn between trying to recall what Thea had just said and fury at himself for letting memories of Mallory infringe on his thoughts, he threw down his shirt and forced himself to concentrate on getting rid of Thea.

"Yeah, I'm here."

"You sound distracted." Was that curiosity in her voice or censure? "Are you alone?"

That's really none of your business.

"I was trying to undo my tie," he lied. "And thanks for the compliment, but I'm really not much of a party animal."

"Now that's a surprise."

"Is it? Why?"

"A man with your looks... I don't know, I just had you figured for a guy who lived for the nightlife. One who liked to go places and check out the girls."

"Actually, my idea of a good time is a bowl of popcorn, a bottle of beer and a good video."

Thea laughed. "You're *so* funny."

"At the moment, I'm exhausted," he said, taking a chance on angering her.

"I guess that's a hint that you want me to let you go to bed, huh?" She didn't bother disguising the disappointment in her voice.

"You should get your beauty sleep, too. We've got a big day ahead of us," he reminded.

"Ah, yes. The day we've all been waiting for. The virgin voyage of 'The Edge!'—complete with her ship of fools."

The unkind remark that Baron knew was an oblique reference to Mallory, rankled, though Baron didn't know why. "Present company excluded, I hope," he kidded.

"Definitely." He heard her stifle a yawn. "I *am* tired. I suppose I should let you go to bed."

"In the morning, we'll both be happy you did."

"I'd be happier if I had someone to give me a good rubdown first. I'm all tense and uptight."

God, didn't the woman ever give up? "Try a snifter of brandy," Baron suggested.

"I already have. A couple, actually."

"Give it time."

"Yeah." He heard another sigh. "Time. Do you ever get the feeling time is running out?" An unmistakable note of loneliness overlaid the question.

"No," he said, but as soon as the word left his lips, he knew it wasn't true.

Thea gave a lusty sigh. "Well, since I'm getting no sympathy from you, and I can't talk you into coming over and giving me a massage, I'll let you go."

"I'll see you tomorrow," Baron said.

"Tomorrow." The phone clicked in his ear, and Baron replaced the receiver with a prayer of gratitude. He stripped down to his pale blue briefs and fell onto his king-size bed. He hadn't lied to Thea. He was tired. Overtired actually. The publicity merry-go-round he and Mallory had been on was an exhausting experience. He was glad that the bulk of it was over. No doubt Mallory was, too. She'd looked tired lately, with dark circles beneath her brown eyes.

Baron drew the sheet over him, his thoughts turning to the question Thea had posed. He did feel as if time were running out. But if he were forced to put those feelings into words, it would be the devil to explain. All he knew for certain was that seeing Karel for what she was and knowing she'd pulled the wool over his eyes had been one of the biggest disappointments of his life.

His disillusionment with her and women of her ilk had somehow magnified the weakness in every area of his life. He had no solid relationship and he had nothing tangible to show for his years in front of a camera. Even his Houston-based show, while being popular in Texas, was a far cry from what he'd hoped for when he'd gone into communications.

To try to remedy the situation, he'd bought a house, hoping that the purchase, tactile proof of his success, would give his self-esteem a boost. The ink was hardly dry on the real-estate contract when Price had called and dangled the carrot of "The Edge!" in front of his nose.

With emptiness gnawing at him, he knew he needed something to fill the void in his life, and he'd convinced himself that the higher-profile job at WTN would do it. Well, he was wrong. The hectic pace of the past few weeks had filled the empty hours of his life, but it hadn't begun to pervade the hollow chambers of his heart.

His mother claimed that he needed a good woman, needed to start a family. The older he got, he could see the merit in having someone to come home to, someone with whom to share the ups and downs. Someone who would love him like crazy and put an end to the groupies and gropeys and Thea Barlows that had cluttered up his life.

Unfortunately, his luck in locating one of those rare creatures was pretty bad. He couldn't count the times he'd played the fool by believing a woman cared for him when all she really wanted was to use his contacts to further her own career.

Well, he'd played the fool again tonight by allowing Mallory to get under his skin. He'd have to be more careful in the future. His ego couldn't take another blow, and his career didn't need any setbacks, either. And that's just what would happen if Price Weatherby caught him messing around with his woman.

Chapter Six

Mallory hadn't been at the studio for more than ten minutes the following morning when a knock sounded at her dressing room door. When she opened it and saw Baron standing there, she felt the blood drain from her face.

"We need to talk," he said, shouldering his way inside. While she shut the door behind him, he surveyed the small room. She could see him taking stock of the things she'd done to ensure that her small domain bore the stamp of her personality—from the floral love seat and glass-topped table to the prints hanging on the wall to the myriad bottles of creams and lotions and the hot curlers on the dressing table.

She caught her own reflection in the mirror and felt like crying. Not that it mattered, but she looked like death. Her hair was caught up in a ponytail to keep it out of her face. The haunted look in her eyes was a silent testimony to the strain that had her stomach tied in knots.

Baron plunged his hands into the pockets of his slacks. "I want to apologize for last night." His wide shoulders moved in a negligent shrug. "Blame it on circumstance and the fact that you're a very beautiful woman."

Mallory felt her face flame at the compliment and shook her head. "No need for the gallantry. It's my fault. I can't seem to learn not to drink more than one glass of champagne. I'm sorry if I embarrassed you."

"You didn't. I just don't want *you* to be uncomfortable when we start shooting."

Ah, she thought with a flash of insight. His concern wasn't as much for her as it was for the success of the show. Well, if the truth were known, so was hers. "I'll do my best."

"See you later, then."

She nodded, and he exited the room, leaving her there, her heart beating like a hummingbird in her throat, her hands trembling. And that, she thought with a bit of dismay, was that.

The first person Baron saw as he stepped into the hallway was Price. Baron didn't miss the surprise that transfigured his employer's face when he realized Baron had been in Mallory's dressing room. The older man turned away, but not before Baron saw the look mutate to one of serious reflection.

He wondered what Price would think about the kisses he and Mallory had shared the night before. And he wondered if she would catch any flak from Price for having another man in her dressing room.

Baron had barely reached the privacy of his own room when Thea knocked and pushed her way inside with a smile and a twist of her hips. The inevitable cigarette wreathed her in a cloud of smoke.

"Mornin', cowboy," she drawled.

Baron held his irritation at bay—barely. He urged a tight smile to his lips. "Hi. Did you get any sleep?"

"Finally!" she said with a self-satisfied little grin. "Once I'd reassured myself that you were all tucked in and ready for a good night's sleep yourself."

Baron wanted to ask when that had become a concern of hers but, of course, didn't.

"I was too tired not to sleep well," he assured her. "That schedule Tom's had us on has been a killer."

Thea blew a stream of smoke toward the ceiling. "Maybe, but Tom is very good at what he does."

From what he'd discerned about the man the past few weeks, Baron had to agree, but he had no desire to discuss Tom's merits with Thea. He needed some time alone to gather himself and focus on the upcoming show. He glanced pointedly at his watch. "What can I do for you, boss?"

Thea took another hard pull from the cigarette and exhaled, regarding him through the silvery tendrils of smoke. "Boss. Hmm. I never think of our relationship as employer/employee. I always think of us as being more . . . personally involved, don't you?"

Baron bestowed one of his charming, almost teasing, smiles on her. "I told you, Thea, I try not to get personally involved with my superiors. It can be really bad for business."

Thea took a step closer and raised her left hand, stroking the line of his hard jaw with her taloned fingers. The muscle in Baron's cheek clenched beneath her touch. Mistaking the act of aversion for one of a man seeking control, she smiled. She made no attempt to hide the desire in her eyes.

With the infinite care of a blind person, she trailed her fingertips over his lips, tracing the shape of his mouth. "I can make your business very, very good," she said in a husky voice. The look in her eyes implied that she could do great things for him if only he would treat her right.

Baron reached out and grasped her shoulders, intending to put as much space between them as possible—as *fast* as possible. A light tapping on his door held him motionless. Before he could call out a greeting, Mallory came barreling in. The sight she beheld stopped her just inside the door.

Baron knew how it must look, him standing with his hands on Thea's shoulders, her fingers against his lips. A wave of humiliation, greater than anything he'd experienced since childhood, swept through him. Mallory was embarrassed, too. He could see it in the way her eyes refused to meet his. Feeling guilty and not knowing why, he released his hold on Thea. She turned to face the newcomer, standing as close to Baron as she could get.

"What can I do for you, Mallory?" he asked.

"I, uh...thought I'd come and see if you had any ideas to start off the dialogue, but I can see you're busy."

"We were discussing some career strategy," Thea said, a Cheshirelike smile on her wide mouth, "but Baron and I can talk later. I don't want to hold up the show." Thea turned back to Baron. "Later, hmm?" she said.

Baron didn't answer. He was too busy watching Mallory's retreating back, too caught up in his own remorse to see the hard light enter Thea's eyes at his obvious lack of interest.

"How about lunch after the show?" she asked, grinding out her cigarette with sharp, staccato motions.

"I don't think—"

The smile on her lips didn't jibe with the coldness in her eyes. "Ah! Ah! Ah!" she said, tapping his chest with a long nail. "Boss's orders."

It was nothing short of blackmail. While he stood staring at her with a considering gaze and doing his best to figure out just what made her tick, she turned and left him standing there without another word or a backward glance.

Swearing, Baron scrubbed his lips with the back of his hand. How in hell did he manage to get himself into these predicaments, anyway?

When Thea emerged from Baron's dressing room, Tom was just exiting his office across the hall. Their eyes clashed; hackles rose. Without a word, Thea turned her back on him and headed for the canteen.

She was drinking a diet soda over ice and smoking a cigarette when Tom arrived a few moments later. From the look on his face, she had a sinking feeling that her period of grace had just come to an end.

She watched warily as he lowered his lanky frame into the chair across from her and pushed the forever-errant lock of hair from his forehead. She watched in silence as he reached for her drink and downed a healthy swallow.

Since Thea had made staying away from Tom a lifetime goal, she hadn't been pleased about his coming on board at WTN; nevertheless, she was professional enough not to let her personal feelings interfere in Price's vision. She had no qualms, however, about making her feelings clear to Tom.

"Get your own soda," she snapped. "Don't you ever think of germs?"

The dangerous glitter in Tom's blue eyes intensified as he slid the glass toward her. "Thea, my love, after all we've been to each other, all we've...sampled and tasted of life and love together, your concern over getting any of my germs is sort of like closing the gate after all the cows got out, wouldn't you say?"

"You're so crude, Tom," Thea said, taking a drag from her cigarette. "But then you always were." She deliberately blew the smoke in his direction.

Undaunted, Tom leaned back in his chair, folded his arms across his chest and regarded her through the lenses of his wire-rimmed aviator glasses. "You used to like it," he reminded her, a wicked smile on a face that was saved from mediocrity by a smile that Thea had always considered startlingly beautiful.

She pushed the thought away. "I used to like a lot of things—like real butter and red meat. When I realized they weren't good for me, I cut them out of my life." She pushed the glass back toward him.

"I'm not so easily done away with."

"Apparently not."

"Why don't you give it a rest, Thea?"

"Give what a rest?"

"Your pursuit of Baron Montgomery. It's obvious the man isn't interested, and your behavior is downright demeaning."

Thea's face colored. "Why don't you mind your own business?"

"This is my business," Tom reminded her with a grim smile. "I'm paid to help promote hit shows. Like I've told you before, I don't need you screwing with my people's lives."

"And like *I've* told *you*—I'm the boss . . . just in case you've forgotten."

Tom's gaze raked her from head to toe. The look—part angry, part hungry . . . and totally disturbing—was one she remembered well. In the past it had usually preceded an argument and making up in bed. It still had the power to send her blood screaming through her veins.

"I haven't forgotten anything about you, *Ms*. Barlow—word or deed. You know, Thea," he said in a thoughtful tone, "your problem is that you never learned that power and responsibility go hand in hand."

"Are you into psychology now, Tom?"

He shook his head. "Just truth. What did you think when you heard Price had hired me? That the television gods hated you?"

"You flatter yourself. I don't think about you at all." Even as she spoke the words, she knew it was a lie. She thought of Tom often . . . usually when she was feeling lonely. . . .

"Liar."

Fury flared through her. Was it that he'd hit on the truth or was it his attitude, so smug and condescending? Her smile was taut, humorless. "You always did have a high opinion of yourself and your capabilities."

"And despite your ambitions and your success, your opinion of yourself and your capabilities was never high enough . . . which is why you think you have to thwart every other woman's career and wrap every man you meet around your little finger. All to make your career more secure."

The barbed observation struck a sore spot. Eyes smarting, Thea scrubbed out her cigarette. "Who made you the all-seeing, all-knowing god?"

He shook his head. "It doesn't take omniscience to know that you're still on the same reckless course you've been on for the past six years—if not for your entire life."

Thea couldn't stop the shaft of pain that penetrated the heart she'd been hardening since she was twelve. Tom didn't have to spell it out. He was talking about her walking out on him to pursue Glen Fletcher. When Glen had dropped her, she had wanted nothing more than to crawl back to Tom, but pride and that debilitating lack of self-worth had stopped her. Instead of going back, she'd gone ahead . . . the best way she'd known how.

"What are you implying?" she asked.

"How did you come to work for WTN?"

Her eyes narrowed. "Price needed an assistant and someone to head Creative Development. I was qualified."

Tom nodded. "Are you as . . . creative with him as we were together?"

"Go to hell," she said, pushing herself to her feet with the intention of putting as much distance between herself and Tom as possible. Thea had never been into pain—her own, anyway.

Before she could take more than a step, Tom grabbed her wrist in a bruising grip. "I've been there," he said in a sorrowful voice.

Staring into his eyes, Thea felt the faint stirring of a feeling she thought she'd buried beneath half a dozen years and a veneer of hardness. A sea of memories she thought she'd banished forever washed unwanted through her mind.

"We were good together," Tom said. "I was good for you, but you were too blinded by the glitter of the big guys and the lure of fool's gold to see that we had the real thing.''

She forced the painful recollections away, all too aware that too much water had gone under the legendary bridge and that no matter how attractive the memory of old times might be, there was no going back to what they'd had.

"Let me go, Tom." It was a plea for release in more ways than one.

He let her go so abruptly she almost lost her balance. As she gripped the edge of the table to steady herself, he got up and walked away, leaving her there with a stinging wrist and a smarting heart.

Thea sat back down, stoked up another cigarette and took a sip of her watery drink in an effort to calm her tattered nerves. Tom had always been able to get to her she thought, rubbing her aching arm. No one but Tom could make her feel so low; no one but Tom could make her feel so good.

She'd known him for more than six years, ever since they'd lived together as friends and roommates while he studied film at UCLA and she worked at getting her fledgling acting career off the ground.

Like her, Tom was aggressive and ambitious. His acumen was evident, even back then. Because they were so much alike, their scant year together had been filled with the hope of the eager, the expectations of the untried and the bitter quarrels of two different approaches to success. Tom had approved of her talent but disapproved of her methods.

She was a brilliant actress; why did she constantly undermine her fellow cast members? She was pretty enough to have any man; why did she involve herself in affairs with men who had no intention of jeopardizing their position for her? She was intelligent; why did she pursue her own secret agendas when it would be easier to let her capabilities speak for themselves?

It was during one of their incessant quarrels that she'd struck out at him. Tom had pinned her arms behind her back and punished the transgression with a bruising kiss. Before either of them knew exactly how, they found themselves on the bed, kissing each other in a frenzy of need that had as much to do with anger as it did desire. In a matter of moments, they went from friends to lovers.

They stayed together for another three months, alternately making love and fighting—Tom trying to make Thea see the error of her ways, she trying to dominate him in and out of the bedroom. Thea had never met a man she couldn't wrap around her finger.

Tom was different. Tom was strong. And full of pride. When he found out about her and Glen, he'd accused her of cheapening not only herself, but their love. He had packed his things and moved out, saying that he couldn't—wouldn't—live with a woman who would prostitute herself for the sake of her career.

Pushing the hateful memories aside, Thea cursed both Tom and Price Weatherby. Though she knew Price had no way of knowing about her past relationship with Tom, she blamed her boss for putting her in the position of having to work with her former lover on a daily basis.

Maybe, she thought, as she drew on the cigarette, Tom was right. Maybe the television gods really did hate her.

Baron was nervous. Scared, even, though he did his utmost not to show it. They were almost ten minutes into the show, and Mallory had about as much sparkle to her as the marble stars scattered along Hollywood's Walk of Fame.

There was none of the snapping and snipping they'd done during the trial show, more than seven weeks before. She answered him when he directed a question to her, added comments only when it was necessary.

He knew she was tense; hell, so was he, but her anxiety was based on more than the fact that it was their first show. She was recalling their kiss, brooding on it. Baron's jaw tightened. If something didn't happen soon, this show would be their last.

Thankfully they broke away for a commercial. He leaned toward her. "What's wrong?" he asked softly.

She looked surprised. "Nothing."

"Don't give me that. You're about as animated as a rock."

"Thanks ever so much," she bit out with a false, bright smile she hoped deceived the audience.

Seeing the flash of irritation in her eyes sparked a bit of inspiration. "Just stating facts, ma'am," Baron told her. The bluntness of his delivery was as deliberate as his words. "And it's also a fact that this show is fast going down the tubes, thanks to you."

"What do you mean?"

Baron was encouraged by the flash of anger in her brown eyes. "We're supposed to be cohosts—remember?" His voice was goading. "But I'm doing all the work while you sit there looking pretty."

He glanced up and saw that the director was indicating that it was time to get back to the show. He turned back to the camera with a smooth flawlessness, as if he'd been waiting for just that moment to turn on the charm instead of chewing out his partner between segments.

Smiling into the camera with enough warmth to melt an iceberg, he said, "Hi. I'm Baron Montgomery, and if you're just joining us, this is the debut of 'The Edge!'—the show that's on the cutting edge of what's happening in *your* world right now! And speaking of that, how do you feel this morning after the beauty pageant, Mallory?"

A slight frown puckered her forehead. "I feel fine, why?"

Baron looked directly into the camera, leaned forward as if about to share a secret of utmost importance. Shielding one side of his mouth with the back of his hand, he said, "She had a little too much champagne last night."

A titter ran through the audience.

Mallory's mouth fell open. "I can't believe you said that on national television!" she cried, her distress obvious and sincere. "I only had a couple of glasses."

With a lift of his eyebrows, Baron held up three fingers to the viewers, who laughed again. Then he leveled a benign gaze at Mallory. "I only mentioned it because I thought our viewers might want to know why you aren't your sharp and snappy self this morning."

Like a chameleon, he shifted his attention back to the audience. "She was sharp and snappy last night, though. As a matter of fact, she was an animal."

"What!" Mallory exploded, almost coming out of her chair.

He motioned for her to sit. "The woman is so desperate for a date, she was even coming on to *me.*" He aimed a finger at his chest. "Me! Can you believe it?"

The audience roared with laughter. Their mirth only served to make Mallory's voice more chilly. "In your dreams."

Without thinking, she, too, looked into the camera. "Might I remind you that these accusations come from a man whose little black book could double for the Los Angeles telephone directory."

It was Mallory's turn to garner a round of laughter. The sound was like someone turning on a light switch inside her head. Baron knew the instant understanding dawned. It was in the thankful gaze she bestowed on him.

He smiled, a smarmy grin that told the audience she was crazy. "At least I have a little black book. How about you, Mal?"

She looked at him with feigned innocence. "I don't need one. I'm a little choosier than you. I believe in quality over quantity. I'd never make a move on one man if I had another in the wings."

Baron knew she was referring to the fact that he'd kissed her and then she'd caught him with Thea in what looked like a compromising situation. Of course, he could put the ball right back in her court. Hadn't she kissed him back, even though Price was waiting in the wings?

Taking a cue from the director, Baron said, "As much as I'd like to continue this little discussion, I need to remind you that we have a guest coming up."

"Oh, sure!" Mallory said with a lofty wave of her hand. "Change the subject. That's the same as an admission of guilt, you know."

"Guilt! What do I have to be guilty about?" He smiled into the camera. "We're going to take a commercial break right now, but when we come back, we'll be hearing the sounds of Grand Slam Jam, the newest and hottest group on America's college campuses."

"Guilt," Mallory said, pointing a finger at him.

"By the way," he said smoothly, "I'd like to warn those of you watching—don't try this at home. Verbal sparring can be extremely dangerous to your ego, not to mention your relationships. Mallory and I are trained adversaries with years of experience—which is why we're so darn good at it."

"Why, Baron! A compliment?" Mallory gushed.

He winked into the camera. "Back in a minute with Grand Slam Jam and their smash hit, 'Cool, Bitchin' Love.'"

He made a slashing gesture across his throat, and, as the camera cut away to a commercial, he leaned back in his swivel chair, wearing a pleased expression that was mirrored in Mallory's eyes.

Smiling, he raised his hand in a high five. Laughing, Mallory lifted her hand and gave his a hard smack. If the noise of the audience was anything to go by, Grand Slam Jam didn't have a thing on "The Edge!"

No doubt about it, Mallory thought, as she changed from her camel-hued suit and into the jeans she favored, Baron had saved not only the day, but the show and both of their futures, as well. She couldn't believe she'd almost blown it. Finding Thea in his dressing room had been as unexpected as her own reaction to his kisses the night before.

It wasn't that she imagined there was—or could be— anything between herself and Baron, but seeing Baron and Thea standing so close together, witnessing her possessiveness had lent credence to Thea's claim that Baron was hers. Mallory had hoped Baron would be made of stronger stuff, that he would be more discriminating, that he'd be able to defend himself from the blatant advances Thea bestowed on every man at WTN—whatever their rank or station.

Apparently, Mallory thought, men weren't as discerning as women about these things, and her disappointment at discovering that important fact had left her feeling somehow betrayed and inhibited during the first part of the show.

Thank God Baron had figured out a way to snap her out of her doldrums. She'd been furious at his attack until she realized there was a method to his madness. Then, she'd wanted to jump up and kiss him. Her lips twitched at the memory of their latest on-screen antics.

That initial scrapping session had set the tone, and the show had progressed smoothly from there, filled with digs and zingers and sly innuendo. Though it was too early for official feedback, if the reactions of the studio audience was any measure of their success, the debut of "The Edge!" had been a rousing triumph.

Eat your heart out, Delores SanAngelo.

And Thea Barlow.

Tom sat in his Southwestern-style den and nursed a glass of Chivas Regal, wondering why he was so depressed. If the initial reaction of the studio audience was anything to go by, the first airing of "The Edge!" had been an unqualified success, even though it had gotten off to a rocky start. For the moment, he was the fair-haired boy around WTN, and everyone's future looked rosy. So what was wrong with him? Why wasn't he out celebrating with the rest of the crew instead of sitting at home drinking alone?

Stupid question, Madsen.

He didn't have to look any further than his conversation with Thea that morning to know what was eating at him. As he'd known she had done, he'd deliberately stayed away from her since coming to work at Weatherby Television. Seeing her daily, watching her flirt with every man at the studio was hard enough. He didn't need to deliberately search out heartbreak by striking up a conversation with her and stirring up the ashes of a dead romance.

He wasn't sure why he'd followed her into the canteen, but as he'd known it would, seeing her had brought back a plethora of memories, both good and bad.

Despite their different approaches to life, and before the advent of Glen into their lives, they'd had some good times. To Tom's never-ending surprise, Thea had a genuine liking for children, and together they'd spent countless Saturdays at the park, watching kids play, swinging them in their swings, pitching balls to aspiring Major Leaguers.

When he had questioned her about the unusual way she spent her weekends, she'd grown quiet and, with a distant look in her hazel eyes, claimed she missed her brothers and sisters who lived in the Oklahoma hills.

He'd tried to talk to her about her past, her family, hoping to glean some tidbit of information that would give him a clearer understanding of what drove her, but she refused to give him any details of her life before she came to L.A.

Tom was smart enough to know that some man had hurt her. Some boyfriend, lover or ex-husband had done something to make her hate men. Though she would never admit it, Tom knew it wasn't a genuine liking for the male species that had Thea vying for a spot in their beds and hearts. It was a deep-rooted need to best them at their own game.

He also knew that the problem with their relationship had been that Thea had never been able to get him under her thumb. Her inability to dominate him had undermined her sense of self-worth in some way he couldn't fathom, and to balance the scales in her favor, she'd struck out at him however she could.

Tom sipped at his drink and smiled grimly at the room. She had no way of knowing that his fortitude was rooted in the sure knowledge that he had to be immovable if he ever hoped to make her see her potential as an actress, as a person, as well as a force to be reckoned with in the television industry. He'd known he had to stand his ground if he ever hoped to convince her that he loved her not just in spite of her zeal for success, but because of it.

A lot of good it had done him, Tom thought, reaching for the bottle and refilling his glass. She'd ditched him for Glen Fletcher without a qualm. She was nothing but a power-hungry, class-A witch. Why couldn't he just forget her the way she seemed to have forgotten him?

Strangely enough, during the past two years, he'd convinced himself that he had, but the minute Price Weatherby had asked him to come to work for WTN, Tom's heart had taken a plunge to the bottom of his soul, and he'd known he was only fooling himself.

He still loved Thea. Loved her gutsiness. Her dedication. Her determination. Her ambition.

Thea Barlow was a lot of things . . . including conniving and manipulative. Unfortunately, she was the only woman he'd met who spoke to his soul.

After that first day, the show was off and running. It was the talk of every deejay on the airwaves, the subject of a lively segment on "Entertainment Tonight" and was reviewed in all the papers.

Tom was hot property. His praises were sung by any and all who roamed the hallowed halls of television. Kevin Costner approached him about doing the publicity for an upcoming movie, and Paramount all but begged him to launch the ad campaign for the upcoming Selena Davis, Zachary Lamonte release. Price was worried that he might lose him. Thea was grudgingly impressed, and Baron and Mallory drew sighs of relief. For a while, at least, their futures looked secure.

It was Friday night of the second week of the show, and, for the first time since moving to L.A. Baron found himself at loose ends. At first he'd been busy settling in, and after that, he'd been occupied with promoting the show. The past two weeks had been spent working out the few remaining kinks and finessing the overall production.

Tonight was the first night of a work-free weekend, the first night in aeons he hadn't had to be somewhere. He was happy for the reprieve, but the prospect of sitting home alone wasn't very appealing.

He'd gone for a run, just to kill some time, and was now flipping through the channels, trying to find something worth watching, when his phone rang. He picked it up, figuring it was his mother's weekly call. "Hey!" he said by way of a greeting, "I was waiting for you to call."

"Now that's the most encouraging thing I've heard lately."

Thea. As attractive as it was, her husky contralto grated on his nerves. Since the first showing of "The Edge!" she'd stepped up her campaign to insinuate herself into his private life. A day hadn't passed that she didn't make some sly observations about his looks or his body. She was about as subtle as a bulldozer, and he found it harder and harder to deflect the comments by pretending to misunderstand or divert the overt sexual comments with teasing remarks.

Baron sank onto the sofa and scraped a hand through his short hair. "Sorry, Thea. I thought you were my mother. She usually calls about this time on Fridays."

"Your mother!" she said with a laugh. "Hardly. I thought I'd call and see if you had plans for the evening. I'm doing chateaubriand and thought you might like to join me."

"You cook?" Baron asked, not bothering to hide his incredulity.

"Of course I cook. Is that so surprising?"

"Yeah, I guess it is. A lot of career women don't these days—not chateaubriand, anyway," he said.

"Well, maybe you've been hanging out with the wrong women," she said in a suggestive tone.

"Maybe I have."

"So?" she said in her most cajoling tone. "How about dinner? It should be ready about eight-thirty."

Baron gave the invitation serious consideration. Dinner with Thea was preferable to sitting at home with a frozen TV dinner, but he had a strong suspicion that Thea's idea of dessert would ruin the evening.

He'd once heard his sister Merry talk about a date she called "the octopus" because the guy seemed to have eight hands. Baron had listened to her story and laughed. In retrospect, after being subjected to Thea's body brushing against his and her hands forever touching him here and there, it wasn't so funny.

As much as he longed for company, having dinner with her would set a dangerous precedence, and Baron was pretty sure he wanted their relationship to stay a professional one.

"I'd like to," he said, which wasn't exactly a lie, "but to tell you the truth, I've had a raging headache since early this afternoon." An out-and-out lie. "I think I'm just gonna have a sandwich and a couple of aspirin and turn in early."

"Why do I get the idea that you're trying to give me the brush-off?"

The question was asked in a voice so frigid, Baron felt a chill rush over him. Damn! He'd made her mad. It was getting harder and harder to retain his integrity and his job and still stay free of Thea's clutches.

He forced his most coaxing tone. "Look, Thea, I'm not trying to play hard to get. I certainly don't want to antagonize you, but I've tried to make it very clear that I'm not ready for a romantic involvement."

"Who says it has to be romantic?"

Striving for a gallantry he didn't feel and hoping to salve the obvious blow his refusal had made to her ego, he said, "With a woman like you, how could it be anything else?"

There was a long silence and then he heard a short burst of laughter. "You silver-tongued devil! Okay! You win. I'll give you a little longer to recover from your broken heart, and then it's no-holds-barred."

"I've told you how I feel about that, Thea. We have a professional association to maintain."

"I'm glad you haven't forgotten that."

Even though she delivered the statement in a voice as smooth as cream, it sounded like a warning, as if his decision not to see her on a personal level might affect his professional status. And he'd never taken threats—idle or not—in stride.

"C'mon, now," he teased even though he wanted to throttle her, "don't hang up mad." *Just hang up.*

"I don't get mad, Baron. I get even."

"Damn, Thea," he said in a light tone, "that sounded like a threat."

"No, darling," she purred. "Just a statement of fact. Now you go take those aspirin for your headache, and while you're at it, see if you can't find something for that broken heart, hmm? See you Monday."

The receiver clicked in his ear and he pressed the Off button of his cordless. He pushed down the antenna and tossed the phone onto the sofa, resting his elbows on his bare knees and burying his face in his hands.

What was he going to do about Thea? He'd done everything except tell her to get lost, a move that would be tantamount to committing professional suicide. As Thea was fond of pointing out, she was his boss, and the time was fast approaching when she wouldn't accept any of his excuses. What kind of world was it when a person's future hung on whether or not they played footsie with the boss?

The same old world it's always been, Montgomery.

The difference was, that until the past few years, only women found themselves in the position he now found himself in. A wry smile curved his lips. Damned if he wasn't a victim of sexual harassment! Wasn't that a hoot?

Yeah, about as funny as being left with a busted leg in a dusty draw filled with a nest of rattlesnakes, he thought. He picked up a small cushion and threw it across the room. It landed with a harmless plop.

He laughed softly, the humorless sound gaining strength as he realized his efforts to dissuade Thea were about as effective as venting his anger with a throw pillow. What could he do? Get an attorney and file a harassment suit? Oh, yeah. The publicity would really do his career a lot of good.

He supposed he could have a talk with Price.

"Uh, gee, boss, I got this little problem with Thea. She makes these lewd comments to me, and she's always, uh... touching me—you know? She's even implied that if I don't agree to see her socially, she'll have my job."

He laughed aloud. No matter how true they might be, the accusations against a little feminine-looking woman like Thea would seem ridiculous coming from a macho-looking guy who stood six-foot-two and weighed in at two hundred ten pounds. Price Weatherby would laugh him out of the station.

Baron stood and headed for the bathroom. Whatever happened, he had defused the situation for the present, and he'd be damned if he'd let Thea Barlow ruin a weekend that was already the pits. He took a shower and popped a couple of aspirin for the headache that had developed during his conversation with her.

Desperate for companionship, he got out his little black book—the same one Mallory had guessed he had—and skimmed through the pages. Contrary to what she'd said during the show, the pickings were pretty slim.

Maybe he'd call a girl he'd met at the Laundromat, a sexy brunette with a big smile whose nose crinkled cutely when she laughed. She'd seemed a little young, but he wasn't in the mood to be choosy.

He punched out her number, and she picked up on the second ring. "Lorrie? Hi," he said when she answered.

"This is Baron Montgomery. We met at Suds and Duds. You remember? Great. You liked the show? That's good, too." He laughed. "Yeah. Really? I'll be sure to tell her."

After promising to tell Mallory that Lorrie knew the perfect guy for her—a fitness trainer at a health club at the Beverly Center—Baron got to the point and asked her out. Unfortunately, since they'd met three weeks ago over piles of dirty laundry, Lorrie had not only met a guy, they were dating steadily. Baron enthused over her good fortune, wished her the best of luck and hung up.

Now what? he wondered, going to the refrigerator for a beer. He could go to a singles' bar, but that had never been his thing. He could rent a movie—there were several good ones he hadn't seen. He could sit here and twiddle his thumbs.

Without reason or warning, he found his thoughts wandering to Mallory. What did she do on Friday nights? Did she spend them with her daughter, trying to make up for the time she spent working? Or did she and Price rendezvous in some secret hideaway? The thought curdled the beer in his stomach.

Feeling a little queasy, he dumped the remainder of the beer down the drain and went back into the living room. Disturbing scenario aside, the more he got to know Mallory and Price, the less likely it seemed that they were involved.

From what Thea had said—and from a few things he had observed—he could make a case for it, but somehow, she just didn't seem like the kind of woman who would break up a marriage. From what he could see, Mallory was a smart, hardworking lady who gave her employer the best that was in her, which had to be difficult, since she was a single mom.

Baron cursed his wishy-washy attitude, which wasn't like him at all. Rationalization wasn't his modus operandi. He was good at assembling facts and figures, at adding up all the pros and cons and arriving at a clear solution based on logic, except when that logic, or the lack of same, involved his cohost.

He found himself wondering what Mallory's little girl was like—what was her name? Cassie? Yeah. Was she ornery and rowdy like his brother Bobby's little girl, or was she sweet and shy like his niece, Mandy?

Baron felt the sudden urge to find out. Why couldn't he just get in the truck and drive over to Mallory's house? If it looked as if she were at home, maybe he'd stop by and visit a minute on some pretext or another that had to do with the show. Maybe he'd get lucky and they'd invite him in for a hamburger or pizza.

And maybe Thea would give up the chase on Monday.

Well, whether or not he got invited in or even stopped, he wasn't going to sit around the rest of the evening. He'd just take a drive over that way and go from there.

After talking to Baron, Thea pitched the phone across the room. It landed on the far sofa with a muted sound. Who did he think he was? Didn't he know that she wielded a lot of power at WTN? She fumed for an hour, weighing her options for how to spend a lonely evening.

She supposed she could eat alone, but that held no appeal. She could call Rick from the station to join her. No. He was getting a little cocky lately—as if he thought he owned her because she'd flirted with him.

There was Bobby, the hunk who worked in the parking garage...and Lance, of course. A satisfied smile tilted the corners of her mouth. Lance was a young art student who supported himself as a part-time doorman for the building. He was a wonderful specimen of masculinity if she ever saw one.

They'd carried on a lighthearted flirtation for months, and during that time they'd compared notes on their favorite eating establishments and music and art. He was personable, intelligent and, more importantly, he looked at her with undeniable hunger in his eyes.

Yes, Lance would do quite nicely. He would love sharing chateaubriand and a bottle of wine with her, she was sure. They could play some music, talk... get to know one another, and just see where the evening led.

The street looked different in the fading light of day than Baron remembered it looking at night. While the houses were well maintained, they were definitely middle-class suburban, ranch types for the most part. There were the requisite cactus gardens and daisies ornamenting the front lawns and the customary date trees scattered throughout the neighborhood.

The backyards were fenced, tall wooden fences designed to keep troublesome children in and prying eyes out. Kids played in the yards and in the streets; any traffic in this neighborhood was just a parent coming in from work.

Baron wondered if he'd ever have another house in the suburbs. Wondered if he'd ever have a kid to play in the backyard waiting for him to come home.

He pushed the troublesome thoughts aside and turned onto Devon Street. Wondering about the future was too depressing. Right now, he had to concentrate on getting through the evening. He couldn't be worried about the rest of his life.

He spied a house he thought was Mallory's. A Span-
ish-design stucco, it was set apart from its neighbors by
buttresses and massive double doors in front that Baron
assumed led to an inner courtyard. Her Taurus sat inside the open garage. A strange car sat behind hers. He
whistled. Who did she know who drove a Lincoln?

The thought was barely formed when the front door
opened and Mallory stepped outside. She was wearing
shorts and a T-shirt, and her hair was caught back in a
ponytail that brushed her shoulders. Baron's heart faltered, stopped and began to race. Lord, she was beautiful. And she had the longest, prettiest legs he'd ever
seen.

While he was drinking in the sight of Mallory's legs,
a man exited the house, carrying a child.

Baron's runaway heart stumbled again. This time
when it recovered, it started beating with a slow, tortured rhythm. There was little doubt that the child in the
man's arms was Cassie.

And no doubt at all that the man himself was Price
Weatherby.

Chapter Seven

Mallory faced the camera. "Our first guest this morning will be Dr. Jamison Redman, a seventy-two-year-old physician married to a twenty-seven-year-old model. Dr. Redman is the father of a two-month-old son. He'll be sharing his knowledge and experiences, both as an M.D. and a layman about the physical and emotional challenges as well as the pleasures connected with a May-December romance."

"You'd better listen up, Mal," Baron said. "You might save yourself a lot of grief."

"My, my, you're as surly as a bear whose honey pot just went dry," she replied. "What's the matter, *Bear*-on, bad weekend?"

"Bad pun. But if you must know, I've had better." The admission was hardly more than a growl.

Mallory looked into the camera with a lift of her eyebrows that seemed to say that maybe she'd better tread easy around her cohost today. "Want to tell us about it?" she asked in her most solicitous, come-tell-Mommy-what's-wrong tone.

Baron shrugged. He knew his dialogue with Mallory had been a little stilted during the first few minutes of the show, a holdover from his anger and disappointment at seeing Price at her house on Friday evening.

"I was feeling a little homesick for Houston this weekend."

A collective "Ahhh" went up from the audience.

"Poor baby," Mallory murmured.

"I was bored and missing my family—okay?" Baron said defensively. "So I took a drive around town, around the 'burbs. People-watching, I guess you could say. You know, it's absolutely amazing how many May-December romances there actually are these days."

"I never noticed."

Obviously she didn't get the gist of his comment. He looked out at the crowd. "How about y'all? Have you ever seen so many old guys with young chicks in your life?"

The crowd answered with a round of applause and whistles.

"What's wrong with that?" came a challenging voice from the audience, which—according to the newest trend among the viewers—was divided into the Mallory section on her side of the stage, and the Baron bunch on his. Though the question came from Baron's side, it was asked by a man somewhat advanced in years.

"Nothing's wrong with it," Baron said, "if you can keep up—you know what I mean?"

"That depends on the woman," the man called, and the crowd roared.

Baron grimaced. "I think it's time to move on," he said to Mallory. The angle of his chin challenged. "How about you? Anything exciting happen this weekend?"

"No," she said with a shake of her head. "The same old weekend stuff. Laundry. Grocery shopping. Yard work."

Liar. "Oh, I meant to tell you that a girl I met at the Laundromat says she has the perfect guy for you. A trainer at this gym downtown."

"A muscle man!" Mallory said, aghast.

"According to Lorrie, this is a very sensitive guy, not to mention sexy. She—and he—thinks you're too uptight, too prim and proper. In her words, she says that if you had the right man to scratch your itch, you'd mellow out a little."

The comment brought another round of laughter from the crowd and several offers from guys who'd be glad to scratch Mallory's itch.

"I don't have any itches that need scratching, thank you very much. And I'm as mellow as I'm likely to get."

"That's what we're all worried about, Mal," Baron said, patting her hand in a concerned manner. The director gave the signal to cut for a commercial, and Baron flashed his famous smile. "Stay tuned. We'll have more about Mallory's nonexistent love life later, but right now we're going to take a commercial break. When we come back, we'll talk to Dr. Jamison Redman—physician and septuagenarian extraordinaire!"

"Listen up, kids," Tom said as he and Thea burst through the door of the boardroom where Baron, Mallory and the rest of Tom's team sat. Price was out for a couple of hours. Baron and Mallory had just finished shooting the show, and Thea had called the brief meeting, that both she and Tom thought was very important.

Tom flung his lanky frame into a chair and pushed his glasses up on the bridge of his nose. "Thea and I have come up with a couple of new opportunities to build our public image."

"Hell, Tom," Baron said testily, "if our image improves any more, we won't be able to hold up our inflated heads."

Even before he snapped at Tom, Mallory could tell Baron was in a bad mood, even though he'd done a good job hiding the fact on the show with his usual sharp-witted banter. She wondered what had happened to him over the weekend to put him in such a foul mood.

"That's where you're wrong, my man," Tom said, shooting down Baron's claim as he aimed the point of his pen in Baron's direction. "It's a jungle out there. The competition never lets up, and we can't afford to rest on our laurels or sit on our butts. In case you haven't noticed, Katy Couric and Tom Brokaw have started doing a little teasing, a little verbal sparring on occasion. Coincidence, you say? Nah. They're trying to cash in on the Baron/Mallory phenomenon."

"Okay, okay," Baron groused. "What's up?"

"First, the city fathers are putting on this big celebrity auction. Up-and-coming actors, actresses, popular radio and TV personalities, rich, eligible bachelors and bachelorettes—any single person who's in the public eye and will donate two nights. One for the actual auction. The other for the date or whatever you call it. The wealthy residents of our fair city will bid on the chance to spend an evening with the celeb of his or her choice."

"What's the money being used for?" Mallory asked.

"Half of the money you bring in will go to the charity of your choice. The other half goes into city funds to be used for a new clinic down in the barrio. I think it would be great if the two of you could find it in your hearts to help."

"You can count me out," Baron said flatly. "Spending a Saturday night with some groupie who's a total stranger isn't my idea of a good time."

"Surely you have a favorite charity," Thea said.

"Of course I do," Baron said, "but I'll just give them part of my check, thanks."

"Okay," Tom said with a shrug, "but I think it would be great publicity *and* a way to show L.A. what a nice guy you really are."

"I'll have my next publicity shot taken with my dog."

"I'll do it," Mallory said. "It sounds like fun and I can stand a groupie for a couple of hours."

"Great!" Tom said, rubbing his hands together. "I'll let Thea tell you about the other gig. It's her baby."

Mallory thought Thea grimaced, but couldn't be sure.

"As you probably know, the university hospital has been working on a new children's wing the past couple of years. Well, it's nearing completion and the dedication is set for two weeks from last Friday.

"WTN will be doing an in-depth documentary on the wing—its funding, facilities, its staff, what they hope to do for the underprivileged children of the area. It seems only fitting that the two of you attend the ribbon-cutting ceremonies and then distribute gifts from WTN to the children."

At the mention of sick children, of *visiting* sick children, Mallory felt the old familiar nausea churning in her stomach. She had no problem with letting herself be "sold" on the auction block, but she couldn't go into a place filled with ailing children, children who might be dying. She couldn't put on a happy face and pretend that everything was okay, that they would be okay, when she knew that many of them wouldn't.

"That sounds like a good deal," Baron said with a nod. "I think it's good PR for WTN to show itself as a friend of the community."

"I'm not interested," Mallory said with the same finality Baron had used to nix the celebrity auction. "Let Baron do the hospital, and I'll do the auction. I hate hospitals."

The look in Thea's eyes hardened. "I imagine the children in those hospitals hate them, too, Mallory," she said in a cold voice. "But they don't have a choice about being there, and neither do you."

Mallory felt her hackles rising. She cast a pleading look at Tom. "Why? If Baron can reject the auction, why don't I have the same privilege with the hospital?"

"Good point, Thea," Tom said, the only one in the room who knew what prompted Mallory's refusal.

"Because WTN is getting behind the hospital in a big way," Thea said. "Look, I go to the hospital all the time," she said in a cajoling tone. "It's not so bad once you realize what these kids are going through and how much they need to see a kind and caring face."

Mallory couldn't imagine Thea visiting sick children in her spare time, but there was no denying the sincerity in the other woman's eyes. Maybe she had a redeeming quality or two, after all.

"I'd really rather not."

"I'm afraid I must insist."

The flinty look was back in Thea's eyes, and Mallory knew that she had no choice but to do as her boss commanded. "Fine," she said. "I'll be there." She stood.

"If that's it, I'm outta here. I have a couple of things to do before I go home."

"That's it," Thea said with a smug smile.

Mallory headed for the door without so much as a goodbye. She couldn't get out of the room fast enough.

Baron watched as Mallory left the room and, excusing himself, followed. His dressing room was quiet, peaceful, a refuge from the emotions that seethed beneath the surface workings of WTN.

Thea's refusal to free Mallory from the duties of the hospital dedication smacked of despotism, and any fool could see that Mallory was genuinely upset over Thea's dictate—more upset than the situation warranted, in his opinion. He wasn't crazy about hospitals, either, but Mallory had overreacted.

He hadn't missed her silent plea to Tom. Baron wondered suddenly if there was more going on between them than met the eye, and laughed at himself for even thinking such a thing. Good Lord! Was he so jealous that he imagined her having an affair with every man at the station.

Jealous.

The word stuck in his mind, as tenacious and painful as the stickers that had worked their way into his bare feet when he had played in his granddad's pasture as a kid.

He was jealous. Jealous of Price. Jealous of Tom. And he didn't like it one little bit. Jealousy implied a deeper commitment of feeling than Baron was prepared to admit.

What did he feel for Mallory? He couldn't deny that there was something there or that he'd felt that something from the first moment he set eyes on her.

Okay, he thought with a short expulsion of air, he'd admit it. Why not? He wanted Mallory Ryan. Wanted her so badly that whenever he thought about the way her breasts had pressed up against him in the cab, whenever he recalled the way her mouth had parted beneath his, his body responded like that of some oversexed youth.

Which is why you were so furious when Thea told you her suspicions about Mallory and Price. Which is why you've treated her so badly all these weeks. You were jealous!

So what?

So that wanting and the jealousy were getting in the way of everything. He didn't want to date anyone else, didn't want Mallory to date anyone. His feelings were interfering not only with his personal life, but were beginning to infringe on his working hours, as well.

It went without saying that it had to stop. But what would it take to end it? The only way he knew to terminate his misery was to stop fighting his feelings and get Mallory out of his system. He had to do whatever it took to get his life back in order. All was fair in love and war, wasn't it? Besides, Price Weatherby was married.

You need this job, Montgomery. Mess with Price's woman and your brief and glorious stint as the talk-show host of the most popular show on TV is history.

He couldn't do it. Price had been fair to him, and besides, cold-blooded, methodic seduction wasn't his style. Except for the time they spent working together, he'd just have to keep his distance from Mallory. That decided, he left his dressing room and headed down the hall toward hers.

She answered his knock with a sharp "Come in."

Their eyes met in the mirror that reflected back her image, her hair slicked back with a headband, her face cleansed of the heavy makeup she'd worn for the show.

Baron felt the impact of her beauty like a fist in the gut. He shoved his hands into his pockets to still their trembling. How was it possible for her to be more beautiful without the enhancement of cosmetics than she was with it?

"What's up?" she asked.

"You seemed upset over the hospital gig," he said truthfully. "I thought I'd come and see if you were all right."

Mallory swiveled the vanity chair to face him. Was it his imagination or had her face lost some of its color? "I'm fine. I'm afraid I overreacted."

"There's usually a reason," Baron said. "I'm willing to listen if you want to tell me."

Indecision shadowed her eyes. "My daughter has been sick a lot," she said at last. "We both have an aversion to doctors and hospitals."

Baron sensed there was more, but he knew her well enough by now to know that she wouldn't tell him. "That's understandable, then."

He went to the dressing table and picked up the picture of Cassie that sat among the bottles and jars of cosmetics. She was a pretty little thing with those green eyes, dimples and that mop of curly auburn hair so much like Mallory's. "She's a cute kid."

Mallory's smile was wistful, almost sad. "Thank you. She's a sweetheart."

"I bet she is." Baron set down the photo, shoved his hands back into his pockets and bestowed a crooked grin on Mallory. "Look, I have an aversion to selling myself—even for charity. But I came to tell you that it's only fair for me to do the auction since you have to do the hospital dedication.''

He could see that the gesture took her off guard.

''You don't have to do that.''

''I know. But I don't want you telling the world tomorrow morning that I'm not carrying my load. It wouldn't be good for my image.''

Mallory laughed, and the sound touched a chord deep inside him. Her eyes held deep gratitude. ''It will be nice to have some support. Thanks, Baron.''

''Sure. Anytime. I'll see you tomorrow.''

Mallory nodded and he left her sitting in front of the mirror, a bemused expression on her face.

As he stepped through the door, he almost knocked down Price. Blue eyes met green in mutual surprise. Baron recovered first, though something in Price's steady gaze troubled him.

''Hi,'' Baron said. ''When did you get in?''

''A few minutes ago,'' Price said. ''I just spoke with Tom and Thea about the hospital dedication and the auction.''

''If you see Thea again, tell her I've reconsidered. I'll do the auction.''

''Good.'' Price's wide smile brought a deep set of dimples into play. ''You ought to fetch a fair price.'' He pushed back the sleeve of his shirt and glanced at his watch. ''I wish I could chat some more, but I have an appointment in less than an hour, and I really need to speak to Mallory.''

''No problem,'' Baron said, but he couldn't stop the spark of jealousy that burst through him. ''See you later.''

Price smiled, revealing those dimples again. As Baron watched the older man knock on the door of Mallory's dressing room, a sudden recognition flared, and he understood what had been nagging at him ever since he'd run into the older man.

The green eyes looking at him out of Price's face were the same green eyes he'd just seen in Cassie's photograph. The dimples that flashed so enticingly in her cheeks might have been cloned from Price's. The most logical reason for the striking resemblance settled in the pit of Baron's stomach like a wad of undercooked sourdough bread.

Dear God! Was Price Cassie's father?

"Price!" Mallory said as he entered the room.

"Hi!" he said with a smile. "Did you have a good day?"

"Fair," she said with a lift of her shoulders. "Baron was a little out of sorts during the first few minutes of the show, but we got everything smoothed out."

"I understand Thea laid down the law about your doing the hospital dedication."

Mallory's gaze slid from his. "It's all right," she said uneasily.

"No, it isn't," Price said in an adamant tone. "I know how much you hate being around sickness, so I made it very clear to her that you didn't have to take part if you didn't want to."

"Oh, Price, you didn't!" Mallory cried, rising. She could only imagine what Thea must have thought about that!

The look of self-satisfaction on Price's face changed to one of disbelief and surprise. "What did I do wrong, now?" he demanded loudly, throwing his hands into the air. "I thought I was doing you a favor!"

Mallory was very conscious that this was their first real argument since they'd found each other. Even while she knew that differences of opinion were normal in any relationship, the thought saddened her. She made a concerted effort to lower her voice to a normal level, and didn't quite manage it.

"Your running interference for me with everyone at WTN is just another way to draw attention to us. Thea is probably salivating over this juicy little tidbit even as we speak."

"You're too sensitive about this."

"I'm not!" she cried. "I've told you before that I don't need you to fight my battles for me. I don't want you interfering in my life. I know you mean well, but it's got to stop!"

He was furious. His face had that same shut-up look Cassie's got when she was put out.

"Fine," he said coldly. "You've made it very clear that you're an independent woman, that you don't want me or need me. You want me to butt out of your life, Mallory? Well, you've got it."

Turning on his heel, Price jerked open the door and left. The room shook with the force of the door's slamming. Remorse rose in Mallory in strong waves. She hadn't meant to hurt or anger him. Not wanting to leave things this way, she yanked open the door.

"Price!" she called to his retreating form. He never looked back.

She sighed in defeat and started to close the door behind her. A movement at the end of the hall caught her attention. Thea and Rick, who was standing very close to his boss, were outside her office. The look on Thea's face was definitely smug.

Controlling the urge to slam the door herself, Mallory stepped back inside and shut it quietly, leaning back against it in defeat. Her lips twisted in a wry smile. If Price's taking up for her had added fuel to the fire that there was something going on between them, she herself had just fanned the flames by making their argument public.

Out of all the people who worked at WTN, why did it have to be Thea who'd observed her argument with Price?

"What was all the commotion a while ago?" Baron asked when he joined Thea and Tom half an hour later. "I heard somebody's door slamming all the way in the studio."

Thea looked like the cat who'd not only swallowed the canary, but lapped up all the spilt cream, as well. "It seems Mallory and Price have had a love spat. He walked out on her."

Tom gave Thea a look of pure disgust. "Love spat? Are you crazy?"

"Crazy like a fox," she purred. "There's something going on between those two, and I'll bet a week's paycheck that it's a lot more than employer/employee."

"Yeah?" Tom said, surprising Baron by coming to Mallory's defense. "Don't judge everyone's moral fiber by your own. Did you ever consider the possibility that whatever is between them might be friendship and mutual respect, or are those emotions too highbrow for you?"

"Don't get smart, Tom," Thea snapped. "I can have your job, anytime."

With his chin jutting out in defiance, Tom leaned down until he was almost nose to nose with Thea. "In your dreams," he said in a soft, caressing voice. "In your dreams."

Without another word, he straightened and left the room.

Uncertain what to say to Thea after Tom's parting shot, Baron followed. He caught up with Tom just outside his office. "Hey, what's with you two?"

Tom didn't stop until they reached the canteen where he sat down in one of the chairs and lifted his Reebok-shod feet to the tabletop. "You mean between me and Thea?"

"Yeah. She's your boss. How can you get away with talking like that to her?"

The cocky grin on Tom's face didn't go well with the despair in his eyes. "Thea and I go way back," he confessed. "I guess you could say that we used to be more than friends."

Baron couldn't hide his astonishment. "You and the barracuda? How'd a nice guy like you wind up with her?"

"I didn't wind up with her," Tom said. "As you can see, we're both footloose and fancy-free."

"You know what I mean."

Tom dropped any pretense of humor. "Yeah," he said, "I do. All I can say is that I've seen a different, softer side of Thea Barlow. Unfortunately, it doesn't manifest itself often." He shook his head. "I don't know, something inside me says it's worth cultivating."

Baron wondered. All he'd seen of Thea since coming to work for Weatherby Television proclaimed her to be power-hungry, self-centered and egotistical. "If you say so."

Tom smiled. "I know. It's hard to believe, isn't it?" He sighed. "There's something deep inside her that's made her the way she is, and if she'd just confront it and get it out in the open, she'd be a lot happier person.''

Baron couldn't imagine Thea any way but the way she was.

"She's hitting on you pretty hard, isn't she?" Tom said.

Baron glanced up sharply. "You noticed?"

"How could I not notice?" Tom asked, offering Baron what was supposed to pass for a smile. "She wants you because you're unattainable. It's her M.O."

"I can handle Thea," Baron said, and added, "I think. What really bothers me is why she hates Mallory so much."

"It isn't just Mallory," Tom said. "Thea targets anyone who's a threat to her in any way. It's pretty obvious that Mallory has the inside track with Price, and somehow that undermines Thea's sense of power. She knows she can threaten Mallory, but if push comes to shove, she can't hurt her position here at WTN."

"So you think there's something going on between Mallory and Price, too."

Tom shook his head. "I suppose Thea planted that particular seed, right?" When Baron nodded, Tom said, "Actually I don't. I think just what I said in Thea's office. You know what a softy Price is. He could never resist someone with a background as wretched as Mallory's."

Baron frowned. "What do you mean? What kind of background?"

"You don't know about her daughter?"

"I know she has one, that she's been sick a lot. That's about it."

"Sick a lot." Tom shook his head. "That sounds like Mallory." He met Baron's questioning gaze. "Mallory's daughter isn't just sick. She was born with a heart condition—hypertrophic obstructive cardiomyopathy.''

Baron's own heart took a jolt. Even the official-sounding name sounded grave. ''It sounds pretty serious,'' Baron said, unable to imagine that there was anything wrong with the beautiful child in the picture in Mallory's dressing room. ''What does that translate to in English?''

Tom's eyes held a bleakness as cold as a windy winter day. He lowered his feet to the floor. ''A heart transplant,'' he said, brutally. ''Assuming they can find one before it's too late.''

Tom's words stayed with Baron the rest of the day. After dropping the bomb about Cassie's health problem, Tom had expounded on more of Mallory's background—from her parents' divorce and her discovery at the age of seventeen that Kevin Damian wasn't her father, to her husband's abandonment when he realized that Cassie was going to get worse, not better. Tom omitted the part about Price being Mallory's father. Mallory would kill him for telling Baron so much.

According to Tom, Mallory had spent the time before coming to work at WTN just doing her best to keep body and soul together while caring for her daughter. Finding a full-time job had been a dream come true, and snaring the cohost's position on ''The Edge!'' was the next best thing to winning the lottery.

Baron thought of Mallory's persistence in trying to land the job and her determination to make the show a success. It all made sense now.

What about the resemblance between Price and Cassie?

Coincidence, pure and simple, Baron told himself. Tom seemed sincere in his belief that nothing was going on between Price and Mallory. God knew, Baron wanted to believe him.

Cassie seemed worse. It wasn't anything Mallory could put her finger on, but she sensed a more pronounced lethargy than usual, and Cassie seemed more interested in lying in bed and watching television than playing with any of her toys. Dr. DeBorde examined her and just looked at Mallory, a helpless expression in his dark eyes.

The awareness that her daughter was slipping away from her day by day...minute by minute didn't make the prospect of the children's wing dedication any easier to bear. She found herself wishing that she hadn't been so darn independent and that she'd accepted Price's intervention with Thea with a graceful thank-you.

But no. She'd had to assert her self-sufficiency, and here she was, surrounded by a pack of reporters who persistently stuck microphones in her face and bombarded her with questions—both about her personal and professional life.

Her only consolation was that Baron was beside her and seemed to be acutely attuned to her state of mind. More often than not, he came up with a quip or comment that would draw the attention from her and save her the necessity of coming up with a witty reply. His presence was comforting, especially since she hadn't spoken to Price on a personal level in more than two weeks.

Price was polite, businesslike, but he was keeping his distance. Mallory told herself she didn't mind for herself, but he hadn't called to check on Cassie since the day of the argument. Cassie was starting to ask questions. Mallory was angry with him for letting his irritation at her interfere with his and Cassie's relationship—a situation that paralleled her relationship with Kevin Damian. She knew that she would soon have to approach Price about it, even if it meant eating crow.

On the other hand, her relationship with Baron had undergone another of those subtle, imperceptible changes. His behavior the past two weeks was almost...friendly. Whether or not the new truce lasted, she was thankful for his support.

When the dedication ceremony began, Mallory and Baron listened politely to the speeches of the mayor, the hospital chief of staff and the president of the chamber of commerce. Then, smiling the smiles that wowed and wooed hundreds of thousands of viewers a day, they cut the ribbon that led into the ultramodern hospital facility.

The media followed them inside. Sensing Mallory's trepidation Baron took her elbow as they entered the large common room where the children who were well enough were allowed to congregate to watch television, play games and mingle with one another. She gave him a wan, grateful smile.

The children, who ranged from toddlers to preteens, were, for the most part, laughing and having a good time, even though they were wearing casts, IVs and bandages. Mallory drew in a shaky breath. Thea was right. This wasn't so bad. She could do it.

"You okay?" Baron asked in a low voice.

Her smile was quick, relieved. She nodded.

During the next few minutes, she and Baron passed out gifts and chatted with the children, teasing them and making their smiles reappear. After a few minutes, the media got its fill and went on to other stories.

She was beginning to be glad she'd agreed to come when a nurse approached them, requesting their presence in the rooms of the patients who were confined to their beds. Apprehension spread through her like a dark, terrifying fog, but Mallory knew she couldn't refuse. After all, this was why they'd come.

She looked up at Baron, who gave her an encouraging smile. Urging a reciprocal smile—albeit a weak one—to her own lips, she followed the nurse down the hall.

The first stop was to see a little boy who'd suffered multiple fractures in a car accident and was confined to his room because both legs were in traction. Mallory managed to laugh, managed to get him to laugh.

In the second bed was another little boy who'd had his tonsils and adenoids removed just hours before. Mallory fed him ice cream and a steady line of jokes.

The third child was an eleven-year-old girl who was trying to kick an alcohol addiction. Mallory's smile faltered along with her courage.

She was so busy trying to hang on to her composure that she lost track after that, though a few of the children stood out in her memory, their faces indelibly imprinted in her mind.

There was a twelve-year-old girl who should have been at home jumping rope or listening to music, a victim of incest, who'd just given birth.

A ten-month-old baby with a broken collarbone and cigarette burns whose anguished brown eyes left a bruise the size of California on Mallory's soul.

As they headed toward the last patient, the nurse explained that the little girl—Cassie's age—had just undergone her third round of chemotherapy.

"She's in pretty good spirits, considering," the nurse said outside the room.

"What's wrong?" Baron asked.

"Leukemia. It's pretty obvious that this Christmas will be her last . . . if she makes it that long."

As they entered the room and saw the child lying there, so pale and still, bald except for a few wisps of fair hair, Mallory felt the room sway. She wasn't aware of grabbing Baron's hand, but she was aware of the strength that seemed to flow from him to her, and of the way he took control of the conversation, how he made the little girl smile.

It seemed to Mallory that Cassie's face was transposed onto the features of the frail child. Mallory felt herself growing hot, then cold. Her head began to spin, and the room dipped. Baron's arm went around her shoulders and he pulled her against the solidness of his body.

The next thing she knew, she was being hustled out of the room and down the hallway to an empty waiting area. As Baron folded her into a close embrace, the fleeting dizziness passed, to be replaced with an anguish and despair that tore at her with vicious claws.

Mallory held on to him as if she would never—could never—let him go. Her harsh, racking sobs tore at her throat and Baron's heart.

"Cassie." The name was a groan of desperation. A wail of hopelessness. A sigh of resignation. "Cassie . . ."

Chapter Eight

Baron didn't know what happened to the nurse. He didn't care. All he cared about was easing Mallory's pain. All he was sure of was that he would never forget the depth of that pain if he lived to be a thousand.

Inside the waiting room, he pressed a handkerchief into her hand and sandwiched her between the security of the wall and his body while she cried and his hands moved up and down her back in long, soothing strokes. Dear, sweet God, how could one woman have so many tears, so much hurt inside her?

He'd been keenly attuned to her nervousness from the moment they arrived at the dedication. He'd noted the sudden paleness of her face when they entered the room full of children and marveled as she'd gathered her composure and faced them so bravely. Even when they'd started going into the individual rooms, he'd kept a close eye on her, fearing that her tenuous control would snap and feeling a fierce pride when it held through those first few visits.

It wasn't until they approached the bed of the young girl who had just become a mother that he'd noticed the first cracks in Mallory's self-control. From that point on, her poise deserted her with each additional atrocity they witnessed.

As they'd stood by the last child's bedside, he'd observed Mallory's silent battle with her heartbreak and known there was nothing he could do to ease her pain. It didn't take a genius to know that every time she looked into the faces of the suffering little ones she was reminded that Cassie's days were numbered, too. He could only guess at how that made her feel.

He did know how it made him feel. Helpless. Powerless. Feelings that still held him in a paralyzing grip. All he could do was hold her and try to absorb her anguish into his soul. All he could do was whisper words of reassurance into her ear and offer her kisses of comfort.

It wasn't enough. At that moment, Baron could have strangled Thea Barlow with his bare hands and without a smidgen of remorse.

He didn't know how long Mallory cried, but it seemed like an eternity. When she finally drew away from him, she whispered a shaky "I'm sorry."

Baron shook his head. "You don't have to be sorry for anything. I know how hard that must have been for you."

Surprise flickered in her tear-damp eyes.

"Tom told me about Cassie," he explained.

Her pale face grew even more ashen. "What did he tell you?"

"About Cassie's heart condition and what a hard time you've had. I'm sorry."

"I don't want your pity!" she flared, turning away from him.

Baron reached out and grasped her shoulders, turning her to face him. "And you don't have it," he said, brushing back a strand of tear-soaked hair that clung to her flushed cheek. "What you have is my admiration. I can't imagine coping with the situation with your courage."

His confession brought a sigh that seemed to drain her of her brief burst of anger as well as her small reserve of strength. She sagged against him; his arms circled her once more, fitting her against him like one of Cassie's puzzle pieces.

"And I can't imagine not having it to cope with," she said, her voice cracking. "I've lived for Cassie for so long, it's impossible to imagine a time when I won't have her."

"Isn't there anything they can do?" Baron asked.

"There are different surgical maneuvers, but for one reason or another, the doctors have advised against them. A transplant is the best treatment, and four-year-old hearts that are a match don't come along every day."

There was nothing Baron could say.

Mallory lowered her gaze to his shirt and gave a cry of dismay. "Oh! I've ruined your shirt."

He glanced down. The fabric was streaked with foundation and mascara. "It'll wash out," he told her as she brushed ineffectually at the stains. "It's no big deal."

"What's going on?" The sound of Thea's voice sent both Baron's and Mallory's gazes winging to the doorway.

Thea stood there, a look on her face that could only be described as lethal. Her face flaming, Mallory jerked free of Baron's embrace.

"Seeing those kids was more than I could take," she explained. "I knew I shouldn't come."

Thea shook her head in disbelief. "Well, if you're finished, you can go."

Mallory and Baron started for the door. "Not you," Thea said, halting Baron with a hand in the center of his chest. "I want to talk to you."

"Somehow I figured as much," Baron said. He waved at Mallory, who gave him a halfhearted smile and a perfunctory "thanks" before disappearing through the doorway.

"What did you want to talk to me about?" Baron asked more politely than he felt.

"The little scene I interrupted."

He thrust his hands in his pockets. "What about it?"

"It looked as if the two of you were pretty chummy."

"She has a tender heart, Thea. She was upset." He indicated the tearstain on his shirt.

"She wasn't crying when I walked in."

"Look," Baron said, his patience wearing thin, "why don't you cut to the chase?"

"Fine. I will. Consider this a word of friendly advice. If you're thinking of getting involved with her—don't."

"I've told you I'm not ready for an involvement with anyone."

"So you keep saying, but somehow I don't believe you. I just want to remind you that if you become involved with your cohost, it could mean your job. We do have rules."

Baron's laughter was tinged with bitterness. It had nothing to do with rules and a lot do with Thea's jealousy. "Don't try to tell me WTN has a policy of noninvolvement among employees. First, I know it isn't true, and second, if it were true, I find it very interesting that you'd want to enforce it considering the . . . discussions you and I have had and the flirtations I've seen you carrying on with various other employees."

Thea had the grace to blush, but her tone was still angry. "Don't push me on this, Baron. Leave Mallory Ryan alone."

"Or what? You'll have my job?" Baron shook his head. "I think my success on 'The Edge!' will hold me in good stead."

A cunning light came into Thea's eyes. "Don't be too sure. If Price thinks you're moving in on his woman, he might not have any qualms about letting you go, no matter how good the ratings are."

Baron knew that Thea would have no reservations about telling Price. "You're really a piece of work, you know that?"

"Why thank you, Baron," she said, turning to go. At the doorway, she turned and regarded him with a thoughtful expression. "You know, there could be another ending to this story."

"Yeah? What's that?"

"Price could be so upset about what's going on between you and Mallory that he'd chuck Mallory. Word is out that Delores SanAngelo and NTN never reached an agreement. She's looking for a job. And she *was* Price's first choice."

Baron's conversation with Thea was still playing through his mind later that evening as he sat in front of the television watching a preview for the upcoming *The Grinch Who Stole Christmas.*

Recalling Thea's parting statement, he came to the conclusion that Thea, as well as Cassie, needed a heart transplant. Like the Grinch's, Thea Barlow's heart was two sizes too small.

He wondered if Mallory had recovered from her emotional crash that afternoon. He could call, but he knew her well enough to know that she would say she was fine, whether she was or not.

He could go and see for himself. He could just drop in and see firsthand if she was bouncing back. The idea held definite appeal. Before he could change his mind, Baron zapped the TV screen into darkness and was on his way out the door, scooping up the keys to his pickup as he went. Maybe he'd stop and get a pizza. All kids liked pizza, didn't they?

"I'll get it!" Mallory called to Carmen when the doorbell rang at dusk. Pushing up the sleeves of her lightweight sweater, she peeked through the window and was surprised to see Baron standing on her doorstep. His back was to her, but she would recognize that dark hair and those wide shoulders anywhere.

Instantly, her mouth grew dry and her heart began to thunder in her chest. What was he doing there? She unfastened the chain and pulled the door open. He turned. Smiled. Her heart began to race.

"Hi."

"Hi." Her voice sounded small and breathless, like Cassie's when she'd overexerted herself the slightest bit. Mallory was marginally aware that Baron was holding a pizza box and that he was wearing jeans, a pullover and battered sneakers. She was acutely aware that he looked even more handsome in the casual clothes than he did in his dressy duds.

"What are you doing here?" she asked.

He held the box in his hands aloft. "I thought I'd bring dinner and see how you were doing after this afternoon."

After spending the entire afternoon in the depths of depression, the unexpected kindness was almost her undoing. She longed to tell him that she was tired. And worried. Scared. "I'm okay."

"Liar." The smile of understanding in his eyes belied the accusation. "You'd say that no matter what, wouldn't you?"

"Yeah, I probably would," she said. She tilted her head the direction of the foyer. "Come in. I'd hate for that pizza to get cold."

Baron handed Mallory the box and was shedding his jacket when a small voice said, "I know who you are."

Cassie stood in the hallway, clutching Matilda in a tight embrace.

"You do, do you?"

She nodded. "You're Baron. I've seen you on my mommy's television show. You make her mad."

Mallory felt her face grow hot. "That's Mr. Montgomery to you, Moppet."

Baron only laughed. "Baron's fine," he said. Then, to Cassie, he added, "I know who you are, too."

Cassie's eyes, eyes that had dark circles beneath them, grew wide. "You do?"

Baron nodded. "You're Cassie. I've seen your picture in your mommy's dressing room. And you make her happy."

Cassie smiled, Baron's observation pleasing her. "Would you like to see my pet fish? I have five."

"Sure."

Holding Matilda tightly in one arm, Cassie extended her hand in a trusting gesture. "I wanted a puppy," she said, "but Mommy said she didn't have time to train it not to puddle on the carpet."

"Puppies can be a lot of work," Baron agreed, taking her hand.

"Hold it!" Mallory said. "You can show Mr. Montgomery your fish later. But he brought some pizza, and it's going to get cold if we don't eat it soon."

"Pizza! Goody! What kind?" Cassie asked, her eyes sparkling.

Mallory lifted the box and sniffed.

"Canadian bacon," Baron supplied.

A smile bloomed on Cassie's face. "That's my favorite! How did you know?"

"Every kind is your favorite," Mallory corrected, leading the way through the living room to the cheerful kitchen with its bright blue-and-yellow decor.

Silk sunflowers stood proud and tall in a terra-cotta vase. Baskets of every shape and size cohabited with yellow crockery bowls and bold blue glassware on the space between the tops of the cabinets and the ceiling.

"Nice room," Baron commented, glancing around in appreciation.

The offhand comment pleased Mallory more than she wanted to admit. "Thanks."

"What can I do to help?"

"If you don't mind paper plates, they're in the cabinet over the coffeepot," Mallory said, pointing.

"You're talking to a bachelor, remember? It's guys like me who keep the paper-plate manufacturers in business."

Mallory laughed.

As they stuffed themselves on pizza and soda and Mallory watched and listened to the conversation between Baron and Cassie, she knew that whenever she looked back at that night, she would remember the laughter above all else. She hadn't realized how much she needed it, or how lacking in fun her life had been since Cassie's birth.

She was learning that even though Baron could be cold and hard, he could also be gentle and teasing...nice. His interest in what Cassie had to say appeared genuine. He didn't talk down to her, and he teased her unmercifully. Cassie loved it. She'd missed Price coming around the past couple of weeks and, for tonight at least, Baron was filling that void in her life. In short, Baron was good with her, the way few men are who are seldom around children.

As Cassie took Baron to see her fish and Mallory cleaned up the pizza remains, she realized that void extended into her own life. She needed and missed adult companionship. Other than Price, Carmen was the only grown-up she saw on a regular basis, outside of WTN. She'd been too busy trying to make ends meet to establish any real friendships. Not only did she miss adult companionship, she missed male companionship. Tom was right; she was too young to be alone. But how could she expect to find a man willing to take on her problems when her own husband hadn't been able to stand the pressure?

Mallory fought back the sting of even more tears. She'd succumbed to self-pity too much lately. She had to get a grip, or Cassie would realize that something was wrong.

The sound of childish giggles accompanied by sexy masculine laughter filtered through the house and into the kitchen. Mallory smiled. Maybe it was time for her to go and join the fun. God only knew when there would be another opportunity.

She found Baron—shoeless—lounging against the headboard of Cassie's bed, Cassie sitting cross-legged in the middle while he related some tale about five friends named Flopsie, Mopsie, Cottontail, Peter and Doodles. Careful not to interrupt, Mallory stood leaning against the doorjamb, watching the expression on Cassie's face as the story unfolded.

From what Mallory could tell, the story was a combination of *The Tales of Peter Rabbit, The Little Mermaid* and *The NeverEnding Story.* Whatever else it was, it was funny—at least to Cassie. Mallory wasn't sure when she'd heard her daughter laugh so much.

When Baron ended the tale with the customary "and they all lived happily ever after," Mallory's throat tightened and her eyes stung.

Cassie begged for another story, but Baron told her it was her turn. Cassie told him a riddle—more corny than funny—but Baron laughed as if it were the most hilarious thing he'd ever heard. Pleased with herself, Cassie collapsed into another fit of giggles. Suddenly, gasping for breath, she rolled off the bed and onto the floor, squatting in a way that was all too familiar, a way that kids with Cassie's problem quickly learned helped their breathing.

Baron was beside her in an instant. Mallory lunged away from the door and launched herself across the room, pushing him aside in her anxiety. The memories of the children at the hospital were too fresh to afford her any semblance of aplomb.

"Cassie!" she cried sharply. "Are you all right?"

Cassie looked up at her with wounded eyes that seemed to ask why this had to happen when she was having so much fun. "My chest hurts," she said, even though Mallory knew that went without saying.

"Okay, Moppet, okay," she soothed, smoothing back Cassie's hair. "Just stay there a minute. It'll be okay."

Cassie nodded. Still squatting, she looked up at Baron and offered him a wobbly smile of encouragement. The bravery in that smile broke Mallory's heart, and if it didn't move Baron's he was a hard man, indeed.

But he was moved, Mallory thought, meeting his gaze over Cassie's head. Anyone could see that. The look in his eyes asked what he could do to help. Mallory's transmitted back the answer: *Nothing. Wait.*

Finally, Cassie stood, and Mallory picked her up into a close embrace. "Feel better?"

Cassie nodded. "But my head is going around and around."

"Then let's get your jammies on so you can get some rest," Mallory suggested, putting her on the bed.

"I don't want to rest," Cassie said, poking out her bottom lip in a pout. "I want to play with Baron."

"You'd better do what Mom says," Baron told her, speaking for the first time since Cassie had dived off of the bed. "I'll come back another time, when you're feeling better."

"Promise?"

Baron sketched an X over his heart. "Promise."

Cassie nodded in agreement and relaxed against the pillows.

"Why don't I go fix us some coffee?" Baron suggested. Mallory nodded. "I'll be there in a little while. As soon as Cassie says her prayers."

The little while was more like thirty minutes. Baron was well into his second cup of coffee when Mallory entered the kitchen, her face pale and drawn.

"How is she?" he asked, rising and pouring her a cup of the fragrant brew.

"She isn't dizzy anymore and the pain has gone away," Mallory said, scraping back her fall of dark auburn hair.

Baron carried the coffee to her and, taking her cold hand in his, closed her fingers around the warm mug. She looked up at him in thanks.

"And how are you?" he asked.

"I'm . . . fine," she said, her lips quivering.

"Like hell you are!" His voice was rough, sharp.

"Please don't be so gentle with me," she said in a feeble attempt at humor. "I might go to pieces."

Baron leaned his hip against the cabinets and made a close survey of her colorless face, from the dark circles beneath her worried eyes to the tense set of her lips.

"I don't know what's kept you from it," he told her in a voice as gentle as it had been harsh.

"Someone has to maintain the appearance that everything is okay . . . for Cassie's sake. And, since I'm all she has, that someone has to be me."

"Where's your ex?" Baron asked.

"Mark? He moved to San Diego."

"And you never hear from him? He never asks about her?"

Mallory shook her head. "I get a measly two-hundred-fifty dollars a month from him for child support, and only because I got the law after him. He's remarried and has a, quote, 'normal' child now."

Baron swore. "I can't imagine him not wanting to know how she's doing, not wanting to share whatever time she has left."

Mallory put her free hand on Baron's arm. "It's okay," she said. "I appreciate your concern—even your anger—but I don't mind. Really." She offered him a half smile. "I do pretty well most of the time, but when she's really sick I sometimes get caught up in the hopelessness and unfairness of it all."

"That's understandable."

Mallory looked at him with bleak eyes. "And then there are days like today, when I can't ignore the hard cold fact that one day...soon—" her voice cracked and her eyes filled with tears "—my baby is going to be taken away from me."

Baron took the cup from her trembling hands and set it on the countertop.

Her eyes swam with tears. "I don't think I can take it, Baron," she said, shaking her head as he drew her into his arms. "I can't imagine what life will be like without her."

As she had earlier in the day, Mallory put her arms around Baron's waist. "Sometimes I think the hardest part is being by myself. Not because I have all the worry and all the bills, but because I'm so alone in this, so isolated."

"Then why do you isolate yourself?" he breathed against her temple.

She drew back and looked up at him. For the moment, she'd regained her fragile hold of her composure, but moisture still glittered in her eyes. "Because I don't want anyone's pity—not for me or Cassie."

Baron lifted his hands to frame her face. "You're a damn stubborn woman, Mallory Ryan," he said, lowering his head toward hers.

As if she'd been waiting for him to make the first move, as if she needed the closeness he offered, she melted against him in total surrender. Her lips parted for him, and it was all Baron could do to keep from tangling his hands in her hair and devouring her mouth with all the hunger that had built inside him.

She wouldn't have objected. He knew that, just as he knew she wouldn't reject his kiss. But some deep intuitive feeling told him that while she would accept the savageness of his need, her own needs would best be served by gentleness. And maybe his would, too.

Taking her lips in a succession of slow, drugging kisses, Baron's hands cupped her head while his thumbs made feather-light strokes along her cheekbones and the delicate sweep of her eyebrows. His fingertips grazed her cheeks, the firm line of her jaw and then they tracked the curve of her throat that was arched to give him freer access to her lips.

The kisses they shared grew deeper and more abandoned the longer he held her. It was as if the touch of his lips had awakened her from a deep sleep, and once awakened, she found herself faced with a hunger that longed to be assuaged.

Baron felt her hands moving over his back in a caress that was tentative, almost shy. His breath caught and his heartbeats kicked into a higher gear. Sweet, he thought. When had he held anyone so sweet?

"This is crazy," she said, her voice a breathless quiver against his mouth. "I don't do this."

"It's just a kiss," he murmured, taking her lips again. "Just a kiss."

But he wanted it to be more. He clamped his hands over the fullness of her hips and drew her against him, so that she would have no doubt about where this was leading. Her response was a little moan and a reciprocal pressure of her hips against his.

Taking the move as a go-ahead, Baron slid his hands beneath her sweater, molding her more closely to him.

The front clasp of her bra parted with an expert flick of his thumbs, and then the softness of her breasts filled his hands that had ached to touch her. His own body felt full, heavy with the need to ease the pain of his self-imposed celibacy.

His mouth made love to hers, and the slow, deep thrusts of his tongue mimicked the act of love. He could feel the excitement building inside her and knew he was rushing her, but he couldn't seem to help himself. He should take it slow, let Mallory make the next move.

As if she could read his thoughts, her tongue joined with his, timid at first, then growing bolder when she heard his groan of pleasure . . . darting and twining with his in a frenzied dance as old as time.

Throwing caution to the wind, Baron lifted her, planting her bottom squarely on the countertop and wedging himself between her thighs. He never took his mouth from hers. Scooping up the edge of her sweater, he lowered his head and took her into the heat of his mouth.

She gave a little cry that sounded like a sob of pain. He felt her hands winnowing through his hair to the back of his head, holding him against her, while her hips surged against him.

Knowing what she sought, Baron pressed the heel of his free hand against her, cursing the denim that separated his questing fingers from her yielding softness, pushing her without mercy toward the summit she strove to reach.

His breathing grew as harsh as hers. His heart thundered in his chest. There was no mistaking the instant she tripped over the edge. Baron held her tightly and swallowed her sob of pleasure, while he fed her need until the tremors ceased and she was still and quiet in his embrace.

He drew back to look at her. Tears and mascara made tracks down her face.

"What have I done?" she said in an anguished whisper.

"Nothing," Baron said, brushing at the tears with his thumbs.

Her face flamed with color. "I can't believe that I . . . that I let you . . . I mean, I'm sorry, but I can't. It wouldn't be fair to you."

"What wouldn't be fair to me?"

"To have sex with you. To use you to ease my own sexual frustrations."

Baron felt like laughing. He felt like crying. *She* was afraid of using *him?*

"This happened so fast," she said when he didn't answer. "I mean, one day we're arguing, the next we're . . . we're making out in the kitchen. That isn't like me. I don't do what I just did with . . . with relative strangers."

She spoke briskly, as if she felt the need to explain away their actions . . . or the need to keep talking to keep from acting on the electric feelings that still arced between them.

Baron nodded, taking her hand in his. He kissed each finger, letting his tongue lave each sensitive tip. Her quick, indrawn breath was strangely gratifying.

"You're right," he said. "My head tells me you're right, even though the rest of me is putting up a pretty good argument to the contrary."

"And you aren't mad?"

"No," he said, lifting her down from the counter, and pulling her against him in a tight embrace. "I'm not mad. Things happen. What happened between us just now... I'm not sorry. And if I brought you any pleasure at all, then I'm very happy."

The time it took for Baron to drive home was ample for him to think through the consequences of what had just happened between him and Mallory as well as for him to reconsider his feelings for her. He wanted her—there was no doubt about that. Even now, his body was cursing him for a fool while his mind congratulated him for being such a kind, understanding guy.

Mallory had a point, though. This thing between them had happened fast. They hadn't dated. They hadn't flirted. They worked together. The only incident that pointed to any kind of mutual awareness were those few stolen kisses in the cab, and that could be chalked up to opportunity and too much champagne.

Baron wasn't sure when things started to change. Was it when Tom told him that Price's attitude toward Mallory was based on nothing more than his heart being touched by her circumstances, and her attitude toward him was based on the fact that he'd befriended her?

Because of his own changing feelings for Mallory, it was what Baron wanted to believe. It was ironic that the running gag of "The Edge!" was for him to find her a man, when the truth was that she needed someone. She was strong, but the years of worry had taken their toll. If something happened to Cassie, Mallory would need someone there to pick up the pieces, and Baron was beginning to think that he wanted to be that someone.

He thought of Mark Ryan and cursed. How could any man walk away from his responsibilities—hell, how could a father walk away from a kid as cute and sweet as Cassie—without ever looking back? Baron had only been around her for a couple of hours, and he was in love with the child. In love with her bravery, her stoicism, the laughter in her eyes. His parents would be crazy about her, too.

Whoa, Montgomery! You're gettin' the cart way ahead of the horse, here.

Just because Mallory had let him kiss her, touch her in intimate and exciting ways, wasn't any cause to send out wedding invitations.

The thought brought him up short. Wedding invitations implied love. And he wasn't ready yet to call what he felt for Mallory love. If anything did come of what had happened between them, it would come slowly. After everything she'd been through, Mallory was understandably gun-shy about forging another personal relationship. God knew the idea terrified him, too.

Chapter Nine

During the next week, the show revealed the subtle alteration in Baron and Mallory's relationship. The jesting was still as astringent, but there was a difference in the content of their teasing and an awareness in the way they looked at each other that lent a new tension to their repartee.

Now, Mallory confronted Baron about *when* he was going to find her a date and Baron responded he was checking out the applicants personally—after all, he couldn't have her getting involved with some jerk who might break her heart, make her bitter and ruin her already "sunny" disposition for the show.

The audience even got into the act, bringing photos of possible candidates, and on occasion, real people—neighbors, cousins, brothers—they thought would be perfect for Mallory. Of course, either Mallory or Baron nixed everyone for some reason or another, reasons that left the audience laughing and ready for the next day's offering.

Behind a desk, in an office where a multimillion-dollar corporation was run, a man with a heart full of regrets watched the interplay with a sorrowful smile on his face. He'd missed so much in her life, but at least he was able to witness this. His daughter was falling in love. It was plain to anyone with eyes to see. He wiped a lone tear. She deserved this happiness. God knew, he'd caused her enough heartache.

Though Mallory did her utmost to behave as though nothing had transpired between them, she couldn't help wondering what Baron must think of her. She shuddered to think that he might believe she made a habit of moving from one man to the other when things went bad.

And she shuddered when she remembered what had happened between them. There were nights she couldn't sleep for thinking of the depth of the release she'd experienced beneath the assault of his clever hands and lips. And when she did fall into a fitful rest, she awakened with his name on her lips, her body throbbing with a delicious aching need.

She wasn't sure she was ready for a man in her life, especially a man like Baron Montgomery. But ready or not, he had awakened her to the fact that she had needs and that sacrificing those needs for the needs of her daughter wasn't a healthy situation for either her or Cassie.

Knowing she had to pursue her feelings for Baron, no matter how slowly, Mallory invited him to dinner. They learned that they both loved old movies, lasagna and rain. A few nights later, he came bearing a gift for Cassie: the dog she had longed for.

"Baron!" Mallory chided as sternly as she could while watching Cassie roll around on the floor with the short-legged, Jack Russell terrier.

He held up his hands. "I know, I know. You don't have time to housebreak a dog. Well, Maggie is almost two years old and she's already trained to go to the door when she wants out. Carmen will love her."

Mallory regarded the wide smile on her daughter's face. "Well, it's obvious Cassie does."

"I think the feeling is mutual," Baron said, watching as the small white dog burrowed as close to Cassie as possible. "She belonged to a family who had to get rid of her because one of the kids is highly allergic to everything, including dog hair. They gave her to an older couple in my building, who said that every time they took Maggie out for a walk, she went crazy when she saw kids. They didn't think it was fair for her to be shut up with them when she needed a child to love who would love her back."

Mallory looked skeptical. "That's a pretty good story. Guaranteed to win over all but the most hard-hearted mom, which of course, I'm not."

"It's a true story." Sincerity gleamed in his eyes. "Actually," he said, "I don't know how you can deny a dignitary access to your home."

"Dignitary?"

Baron nodded. "Maggie is short for Margaret. Margaret Thatcher. The original owners thought there was a resemblance through the eyes."

That he managed to deliver the explanation with a straight face was a miracle.

As if on cue, Maggie looked up at them and inquisitively cocked her head to the side. "See what I mean?"

"Oh, yeah," Mallory said dryly. "She's a dead ringer, all right."

"Did I mention that she's had all her shots, not to mention that I had her bathed and dipped before I brought her over?" he asked, a look of supreme innocence on his handsome face.

Mallory listened to Cassie's happy laughter and was smart enough to know she'd been snookered. If she'd learned anything through the years, it was how to give in gracefully. She gave a deep sigh and a short nod. "Okay, Maggie stays."

Mallory and Baron were both trying to put what had happened between them in some sort of perspective. Baron decided to play it cool off the air as well as on. He'd come at her in a roundabout way—through Cassie. He didn't want to scare Mallory off, and he'd done enough hunting to recognize the wary look in her eyes. The wrong move would send her running so far and so fast that he might never be able to get close to her again.

Though he appeared to content himself with family dinners and watching movies and playing with Cassie, Baron hadn't forgotten the response he'd wrung from Mallory. He relived every moment, every kiss. He dreamed of the feel and taste of her, and could think of little else but the way she'd cried out in pleasure when he brought her to satisfaction.

And in the darkest hours of night, when sleep eluded him, he fantasized about pleasing her again…and again. The next time he'd do it right, with nothing between their bodies but a sigh and a film of sweat. He cursed his memories, but they didn't go away, not even beneath the sharp sting of a cold shower.

By the end of the week, Maggie had established herself as a permanent fixture. True to Baron's claims, she never had an accident in the house. She was good-natured, obedient and comforting to have around. She was Cassie's constant companion, content to lie next to her new mistress's bed or sleep at her side while she played with her puzzles or drew pictures with her crayons. Maggie even submitted to being decked out in doll dresses and bonnets, whenever Cassie decided it was time for a tea party.

Mallory didn't know how Cassie had ever done without her, and with tears in her eyes and a knot of emotion in her throat, told Baron so. She'd had no idea how much Cassie, who was unable to run and play with the neighborhood children, missed having a friend.

Baron had brushed away her thanks with a smile and the tears with his thumb. And then he'd kissed her on the cheek and left her standing outside her dressing room door, a bemused expression on her face, a quivering, tentative happiness taking shape in her heart.

The only bump in Mallory's road the week following Baron's first visit to the house was her continued estrangement with Price. She'd tried to approach him on several occasions to apologize or try to straighten out their misunderstanding, but he always avoided the issue with the comment that he had a meeting or he'd catch her later.

He had started calling Cassie again, but it was always when he was sure Mallory wasn't at home. Though she missed his visits, the calls went a long way toward satisfying Cassie's—and Mallory's—need for reassurance that Price cared.

Her own attitude toward Price fluctuated from day to day. One moment she missed him; the next, she cursed him for not owning up to his past mistakes and making her and Cassie's presence in his life known to his family.

Mallory knew her feelings were irrational, but she couldn't seem to help herself. She'd got exactly what she asked for, but somehow it felt as if she'd been abandoned again.

The night of the celebrity auction found Baron once again in his tuxedo and Mallory in a long gown encrusted in glittering teal sequins. Though he hated the whole ordeal, he couldn't deny that it was a well-planned, ritzy affair, and there was enough new money present to put a small nation on its feet.

He'd never been big on blind dates, and he couldn't imagine spending the evening with a total stranger and pretending to have a good time, especially since his relationship with Mallory was progressing slowly and positively.

His attitude was one notch off surly when Mallory was "bought" by Michael Connelly, a handsome young man in his mid-thirties, who was making his name as an independent film producer.

It came as something of a shock when Baron realized that Thea was involved in the bidding for his Saturday night, but he wasn't surprised when she came out top bidder. It was ironic that he'd skirted her advances, made excuses, lied and basically worked a miracle holding her off while somehow managing to hang on to his job, only to have everything undermined by a few lousy dollars in less time than it took him to shave every morning.

But life was often ironic, and more often unfair. There was nothing he could do but accept the situation and see if he could keep his integrity, his job and his clothing intact.

As usual, when there was money or beautiful people involved, the media had a field day with the auction results. "Inside Edition" ran a segment about Michael Connelly falling for Mallory the first time he'd seen her face on his TV screen and hinted that the young entrepreneur planned to pull out all the stops for his celebrity date.

The episode didn't do much for Baron's state of mind, which he readily admitted was outright garden-variety jealousy. When "Entertainment Tonight" ran a similar piece on his date with Thea and suggested that there might be something going on behind the scenes at WTN, his mood switched from sullen to hostile.

He felt like going to Thea's apartment and telling her to forget the date, to find a new cohost for the show, that he wouldn't be blackmailed anymore. But he knew he wouldn't. Quitting "The Edge!" would probably mean leaving L.A. and Mallory, and he wasn't ready to do that...at least not yet.

Thea recradled the phone and smiled at the empty room. Everything was set for her date with Baron the following night. She was proud of herself. She'd finally backed the elusive Mr. Montgomery into a corner he couldn't talk his way out of. She supposed she should be ashamed for pursuing him with such unabashed determination, especially since he'd made it clear that he wasn't interested. But *embarrassment* was a word she'd stricken from her vocabulary years ago. Boldness had been the key to her past successes. Set a goal. Strike a course. And don't let anything or anyone get you off track.

Her immediate goal was Baron Montgomery.

She knew Baron's background from his résumé, knew his work ethics and something of his personal values from a phone call to his previous employers. She learned that he was telling the truth about his broken heart and that he'd sold his place in Houston, burned his Texas bridges. She knew he needed this job in more ways than one. She'd also learned that he was the kind of man who refused to use his looks to help him on his way to the top—a rather old-fashioned stance, but charming in its way.

All he needed was time, which she'd given him, and a little push in the right direction, which would happen the following night. She had it all planned. They would have their meal at a new dinner theater that showcased up-and-coming young talent, followed by a late-night dessert at her place, catered by Just Desserts.

If things turned out as she planned, she would get her just desserts before the evening was over. She had yet to meet a man who turned down a bona fide offer of sex when it was put to him in plain words. Baron Montgomery would be no different.

The ringing phone startled Thea from her thoughts of seduction. Irritation laced her voice as she spoke into the receiver.

"Hello, Thea."

Tom. He'd been drinking, and he was angry. She'd heard that hard note often enough in the past to recognize it for what it was. "What can I do for you, Tom?" she asked, taking a cigarette from the antique case on the coffee table and lighting it with a flick of the table lighter.

"You can give up this stupid infatuation you have with Baron Montgomery. It isn't pretty, Thea."

She blew out a stream of smoke. "What makes you think it's infatuation?"

"I know you, remember? As a matter of fact, I know you better than you know yourself. You're only doing this to punish me."

Thea laughed. "Why would I want to punish you?"

"Because dealing out misery is what you do best."

"Oh, come on, Tom. You can do better than that. Be more specific."

"All right. Maybe you want to punish me because I didn't let you have the upper hand in our relationship."

"Our relationship was centuries ago. I've forgotten it."

"Maybe you want to get back at me for trying to foil your pursuit of a man you only want because you know you can't have him. Hell, I don't know. Maybe you want to punish me for caring what happens to you."

In spite of herself, Thea's heart leapt at the confession. It was gratifying to know that Tom still carried the torch after so long. Maybe she should ask him over and see if the old spark was still there.

"I didn't realize you still cared," she said in a husky voice.

"Didn't you?"

"No. After all, it has been a long time. Look, what are you doing tonight? Why don't you come on over and we can . . . talk."

"About what?"

"Old times," she purred. "The future."

"Try honesty for once in your life, Thea. Say what you really mean. Say, 'Tom, I want you to come over so we can see if we're still as good in the sack as we used to be.' Come on, Thea. It'll be therapeutic."

"Come on over, Tommy," she said obligingly. "Let's see if we're still as good together in the sack as we used to be."

"No thanks, Thea," he said in an offhand manner. "I stopped being a substitute for other men the day you walked out on me."

The coldness of his rejection chilled her to the bone. "You bastard! You're going to push me too far one of these days."

"Yeah? Well, you've about pushed me to the wall, and I get really brutal when I'm backed in a corner. Enjoy your dinner tomorrow night, babe. It's almost showdown time for us."

"Having a good time?" Michael Connelly asked the following evening.

Mallory, who had been surveying the crush of rich and famous people assembled for a night on the town, glanced over at him. They had finished a lovely dinner and were waiting for a dessert he'd insisted on sharing with her. After dessert, he was taking her dancing.

It had been years since Mallory had been with a man in any capacity that remotely resembled a date, and the attention of such a good-looking male was a balm to her smarting self-esteem.

"Actually, I *am* having a very good time," she confessed. "I didn't expect to."

Michael placed a hand over his heart, as if her comment wounded him. "A crushing blow to my fragile manly ego," he said.

Mallory smiled. "Don't give me that. A man like you has to have a healthy psyche, or he couldn't do what you do."

"And exactly what is it that I do?"

"Cast your pearls before swine."

"My pearls being my wonderful movies, and swine being the public and critics, I take it," he said, lifting his wineglass to his lips.

"Exactly. You've done some wonderful films, Michael. There's a need for movies that deal with the human experience in a realistic, yet sensitive way, so don't let them get you down." Mallory's voice held undeniable sincerity.

"To mine own self be true, huh?" he asked.

She nodded. "It's the only way any of us will achieve the success we want."

"I'm trying. Actually, we're about to cast a new movie, and I've been looking for someone to play a villainess sort of like Thea Barlow's old role on 'Friends and Lovers.' I don't suppose you'd be interested?"

"I appreciate the offer, Michael. A few months ago, I'd have jumped at it. But I think I'd better stay where I am as long as I can."

Before Michael could reply, Mallory's cellular phone beeped. She reached for her purse, curious but not concerned. Cassie had been fine no more than two hours ago. "My daughter has a heart condition," she explained, "and I try to be available at all times."

Michael nodded as Mallory spoke into the phone. "Hello."

"Mallory," Carmen said, her voice breathless with nerves and something else Mallory couldn't put her finger on.

"Yes, Carmen? What is it?" Mallory heard the reciprocal tension in her own voice. "Is something wrong with Cassie?"

"No!" Carmen hastened to assure her. "Cassie is fine, but Dr. DeBorde just called. They have a heart for her."

"What!" Mallory felt the room whirl and take a dizzying dip. She was torn between wanting to shout with happiness and the urge to cry. A heart for Cassie! The thing that had seemed like such a remote possibility, such a farfetched solution was within grasp. Mallory rested her elbow on the table and rested her whirling head against the coolness of her palm.

"It was some child in Idaho," Carmen said, the explanation bringing reality back with a gut wrenching jolt. "A car accident. They're flying the heart in right now, but you have to get Cassie to the hospital as soon as possible."

"Okay," Mallory said, her head still spinning, her mind racing ahead to all she needed to do. "Okay. I'll be there as soon as I can get a cab. Have you said anything to Cassie?"

"No. I didn't think it was my place, and I didn't know what to say."

"I'll tell her when I get there," Mallory said. "See you soon." She replaced the phone and lifted her gaze to Michael Connelly's. His face wore a look of concern and curiosity. "That was my nanny. The doctor just called. They have a heart for my daughter."

Michael frowned. "A heart?"

"She needs a transplant," Mallory explained, her eyes filling with a rush of unanticipated tears, "but I never expected them to find a match in time." She reached for her purse. "I hate to ruin the evening this way, but they need Cassie at the hospital right away."

"I'll drive you," Michael said, scooting back his chair and rising. "It'll be faster."

"It's been a nice evening, Thea," Baron said with a gracious smile. "The food and entertainment were great. Thank you."

Thea smiled. "It isn't over yet. I've got a whole platter of desserts waiting for us at my place."

Baron's smile faded like someone erasing a smiley face from a chalkboard. He should have known it was too good to be true. "I'm really stuffed. I don't think I can manage dessert."

"A cup of coffee, then," she said. "Surely you can manage a cappuccino. Come on, Baron, the night is young, and I insist."

Baron's lips twisted. "How can I resist an invitation like that?"

She laughed—a throaty sound that was more irritating than it was sexy—and reached for her jeweled evening bag. "Don't sound so enthusiastic. It might go to my head," she said with the barest hint of sarcasm. "I had Just Desserts cater the food, the crème de la crème of their line. Surely there will be something there that takes your fancy."

"Maybe," he said, but he doubted it very much.

Though the time seemed interminable, the traffic wasn't too horrendous, and Michael pulled up at Mallory's house within thirty minutes of the call from Carmen. The Christmas lights strung up around the door twinkled merrily, a symbol of the holiday just two weeks away.

Mallory said a quick but fervent prayer of thanks for the grieving couple who had cared enough to make someone else's season happy by donating their child's heart. She thanked God that it was Cassie who would reap the bounty of the strangers' generosity.

As soon as the car was fully stopped, Mallory turned to Michael with a grateful smile, thanking him and assuring him that they would get together when Cassie was better. Then she brushed her lips against his cheek and was out of the car and up the sidewalk in a flash.

Carmen met her at the door, her face filled with a combination of pleasure and worry. The two women embraced.

"Let me change and talk to Cassie, and we'll go," Mallory said.

Carmen nodded. "I called Dr. DeBorde and told him you were on the way and we'd be there as soon as possible."

"Thank you," Mallory called from the hallway. She was already halfway to her room.

Inside the door, she started stripping off her finery, flinging the dress to the bed, leaving her panty hose on the floor and tossing her jewelry onto the top of the dresser. Knowing she was likely in for a long stretch at the hospital, she dragged on a pair of comfortable jeans, a T-shirt and a pair of worn sneakers. Now wasn't the time to worry about making a fashion statement.

Cassie was in bed, Maggie lying at her feet, a place she'd taken to sleeping despite Carmen's discouragement. They both raised their heads when Mallory entered the room. She turned on the bedside lamp and sat down on the edge of the mattress.

Cassie rubbed at her eyes. "How come you're home so soon?" she asked sleepily.

"I have some good news," Mallory said.

"Is Santa Claus coming early?"

"No," Mallory said with a smile. "Dr. DeBorde called to tell us that he has a new heart for you. We have to go to the hospital, and they'll have to do an operation, but when you wake up, you'll be as good as new."

Cassie thought about that for a moment. "Can Maggie go?"

Mallory smiled. "No, Moppet, I'm afraid not. No dogs allowed in the hospital."

"Will it hurt?" Cassie asked, her bottom lip trembling.

"No," Mallory said with a shake of her head. "You'll be sore for a few days when you wake up, but during the surgery, they'll put you to sleep."

Cassie's eyes were round and wide, filled with innocence and a wisdom beyond her years. "Sometimes when you go to sleep, you might not wake up."

If Mallory hadn't been sitting, the statement would have knocked her to her knees. She forced a smile to her lips. "Now why would you think you might not wake up?" She heard the quaver in her own voice.

"'Cause that's why I say 'Now I lay me down to sleep' at night. So if I die, Jesus will take my soul to heaven with him, won't he?"

Mallory couldn't answer for the lump in her throat. She nodded and blinked furiously at the tears storming the flimsy barrier of her composure.

"Don't cry, Mommy," Cassie said, patting Mallory's hand. "Carmen says nobody is sick in heaven, and we'll all get to walk on the gold streets."

"She's right," Mallory said, struggling to find her voice. Without waiting for Cassie to say anything else, Mallory got to her feet and pulled back the covers, hiding her own fear behind a businesslike mien. "Hop up and put on some jeans, and I'll send Carmen in to get your things together."

Cassie slipped from the bed. "Will Price be there?" she asked, pulling her gown over her head.

The question caught Mallory off guard. She turned in the doorway. "I don't know."

"I want Price to be there when I go to sleep. I want him to sing 'Little Playmate' to me."

"I'll see if I can find him," Mallory said. "You get ready."

Filled with a rising sense of panic, she went back to her room for a jacket. Once inside the door, she just turned in a circle, unable to remember what she'd gone after, unable to focus on anything but the conversation she'd just had with her daughter.

"Sometimes when you go to sleep, you might not wake up."

Reality hit Mallory like a blow to her gut. The euphoria she'd felt on hearing that they had a heart faded beneath the all-too-real possibility that this could be the end, not the beginning. It had taken a child's pragmatism to point out that just because they'd found a heart that was a match and while this was Cassie's one chance to live a relatively normal life, there were no guarantees.

A sob climbed up the back of Mallory's throat. Biting her bottom lip to hold back the tears, she clasped her hands together against her breasts and struggled to calm herself. Her heart was racing so fast, she imagined she could hear her heartbeats pounding in her ears. Her stomach churned sickeningly. She held out a hand and wasn't surprised to see that it shook as if she had some sort of palsy.

Swearing, she clasped her hands together again and sank onto the edge of the bed. She had to pull herself together. Cassie's realistic attitude to the possible repercussions of the surgery was an eye-opener. While Cassie knew she was ill, Mallory had never imagined that Cassie had any inkling of how ill she was. She certainly never imagined that the child understood that she might die during the operation that was the only chance to save her life.

Hysteria rose in Mallory on a dark and threatening tide. A dozen questions, a hundred doubts assailed her. She bit her bottom lip to hold back the fresh surge of tears. Should she do this, or just play out the hand she'd been dealt? Was tampering with Cassie's fate this way tantamount to playing God?

Dear heaven! She wasn't ready to make this decision. She *couldn't* make it alone. Where were the people who were supposed to rally around at a time like this?

Her need to see her mother, to hear Betty Damian's calm, practical voice was like a festering ache inside her. Betty would know just what to say to put things in perspective. She'd been good at that. Mallory was suddenly grateful that she had apologized to her mother for the anger she'd vented toward her when she'd first learned about Price.

Price!

Price was her father. Her family. The knowledge brought a measure of composure. She wasn't in this alone. Even though he was angry with her, Price adored Cassie. He would want to know what was going on, wouldn't he?

Without stopping to give the question more than a cursory consideration, she found Price's phone number in the nightstand drawer and punched it in.

A woman answered; her voice was cultured, pleasant.

"Is Price there, please?" Mallory blurted, focused only on her need to give Cassie what she wanted... maybe the last thing she would ever request.

"I'm sorry, but he's out for the evening. A business meeting." The voice had grown the slightest bit cool... and wary. "May I ask who's calling?"

"This is Mallory."

"Mallory who?"

"Ryan," Mallory supplied. "When do you expect him?"

"I'm not sure, Ms. Ryan. May I ask what this is all about?"

Mallory exhaled the explanation on a rush of breath. "The hospital just called and said they have a heart for Cassie. She'll be going into surgery soon, and she's asking for Price. Will you please tell him I called and tell him to come to the hospital the minute he gets in?"

Carmen poked her head in the doorway. "Let's go, Mallory."

"Look, I have to go, Mrs. Weatherby. Just tell Price to come. Cassie and I need him."

Chapter Ten

"Did Price say he'd come?" Cassie asked when Mallory hung up.

"He wasn't at home. He's having a business meeting with someone."

Cassie hugged Matilda tighter and stuck out her bottom lip. "I want Price."

Mallory felt like crying...and like shaking her daughter. It wasn't like Cassie to be difficult. She must be picking up on Mallory's stress.

"I know, Moppet," she said, doing her best to hold on to her shaky composure, "but I don't know where to find him. I'll call him again later, okay? Now pick up that bottom lip, and let's go. Dr. DeBorde is waiting for us."

Cassie dragged her feet, but she moved.

They were getting into the car when Mallory realized that Thea might know where Price was. It was worth a try. Mallory instructed Carmen to get Cassie buckled in, told her she wouldn't be a minute, and rushed back inside to make the call.

"How was it?" Thea asked, a sultry smile on her face.

"Definitely decadent," Baron said as he finished the last bite of his chocolate brownie topped with fudge frosting, ice cream, whipped cream and a sprinkling of pecans. He set down his dessert plate and leaned against the sofa back, his arms extended along the top. "It was excellent, actually."

Thea set down her coffee cup and reached for the silver pot, an excuse to scoot closer to him. "I knew you'd like it if you just gave it a chance," she said, pouring more steaming liquid into her cup.

Baron had the distinct impression she was talking about more than their dessert.

"Maybe you ought to take some out to your friend," he suggested, recalling the sullen expression on the young doorman's face when he realized that Baron was with Thea and that she was taking him to her place.

"Who? Lance?" Thea asked.

"If Lance is the kid wearing the doorman's uniform and the scowl, then, yes, Lance. He seemed a little upset that we were together."

Thea shrugged off the idea of Lance's jealousy with a brittle smile and a toss of her head. "I talk to him as I come and go, and I lent him a CD once. I think he's flattered that I pay attention to him."

"I think he's infatuated with you, and you bruised his ego by bringing me here," Baron commented. "Maybe I ought to watch my back when I leave."

"He's just a pretty, harmless boy." Thea turned toward Baron, and their knees touched.

He tensed.

"How's your heart?" she asked.

"I beg your pardon?"

"Your broken heart," she said, reaching out and placing her hand on his chest where his heart beat strong and steady. "Have you recovered?"

"I'm getting there," he evaded.

"With Mallory Ryan's help?"

Baron circled her wrist with his fingers and pushed her hand away. "I plead the fifth," he said with a half smile.

"Well, she can't have you."

Before Baron realized what she was up to, Thea leaned forward until her breasts pushed against him. She slid her free hand around his neck. For an instant, he was stunned into immobility.

"I've made no secret about wanting you," she said, her lips close to his.

"Thea..." he said, grabbing both her wrists and turning his head to dodge her kiss. "Don't do this. You won't like yourself in the morning."

"Don't tell me what I will and won't like!" She pulled free of his loose grasp and aimed an open-handed blow to his face.

For a stunned moment, they just looked at each other. Thea looked as horrified by her actions as Baron felt.

The phone shrilled into the tomblike quiet of the room. Thea answered it in a voice that was unexpectedly subdued.

"No, Mallory," she said, flicking a glance at Baron, "I don't know where Price is. All I know is that he was meeting Henry Simmons about a new game show."

Baron straightened. Mallory! Why was she looking for Price? he wondered, with a pang of hurt.

The strained look on Thea's face gave way to her usual shrewd expression. "Can I help you with something?" Her gaze met Baron's once more as she repeated what she was hearing on the phone. "Cassie is having her surgery and wants Price there? What kind of surgery?" A look of surprise flickered across her features. "I didn't know about her heart. I'm sorry, I wish I could help."

Her heart? Baron couldn't stop the disappointment that filled him. Had they found a heart for Cassie? If Cassie was having her transplant and Mallory needed some support, why hadn't she asked for him instead of Price? She'd known he would be with Thea to satisfy the celebrity auction agreement.

"Let me talk to her," he said to Thea, holding out his hand for the receiver.

Thea thrust the phone at him.

"Mallory, this is Baron," he said. "What's going on?"

"Oh, Baron!" she said in a rush. "In all the excitement, I forgot you'd be with Thea tonight. I'm sorry to ruin your evening."

"Forget that!" he snapped. "What's this about Cassie having surgery?"

"Dr. DeBorde called while I was out with Michael Connelly," she explained, her voice unnaturally high and breathless. "Some child in Idaho passed away, and the heart is a match for Cassie. I have to take her to the hospital as soon as possible. She wants Price there, and he really should be, but I don't know how to find him."

Baron's first instinct was to calm her down, though a part of him wondered why Cassie was asking for Price and why Mallory felt he should be there. He didn't like the logical reason that registered in his mind. Had he been right about Cassie's parentage?

It didn't matter, Baron reminded himself, recalling the coolness he'd sensed between Price and Mallory the past several weeks. Whatever was between them was in the past. "Take it easy," he soothed. "I'll see what I can do."

"Thanks, Baron. I appreciate it. Look, I've really got to go."

"Wait! What hospital?"

She gave him the name of the hospital and the street, and severed the connection with another hurried thanks and a brief goodbye.

Baron cradled the receiver, a thoughtful look on his face.

"I always suspected that there was something between Price and Ms. Goody Two-Shoes," Thea said. Smug self-righteousness glittered in her eyes. "It seems there was more than even I imagined."

"What are you talking about?"

"I'm talking about Cassie." Thea shook her head. "I can't believe I didn't see the resemblance before. It's uncanny, really."

"Shut up, Thea!" Baron said, rising. He didn't want to give his own nebulous fears validity by hearing them vocalized.

"Oh, come on, Baron!" Thea said, leaping to her feet. "There has to be something there! Looks aside, if Cassie isn't Price's child, then why is Mallory so hell-bent on finding him and why does Cassie want him there so badly?"

Baron was wondering that himself. He had no answers, but he did know that Mallory needed some emotional support. If not Price, then him. Instead of answering Thea, he started toward the door.

"Where are you going?" she demanded, grabbing his arm.

"To see if I can find Price and then to the hospital."

Thea grew deathly pale. "If you walk out that door, I'll have your job. I swear it on my father's grave."

Baron couldn't believe what he was hearing. "Why are you going to have my job? Because I won't sleep with you, or because I'm interested in Mallory?"

Thea cocked her head at a haughty angle. "As far as I'm concerned, the reasons are one and the same."

Baron had enough. He was through compromising his self-worth to keep his job. He was through being a victim of her blackmail. No job was that important. He shook his head in disbelief.

"Why are you so hateful, Thea?" he asked, flinging caution to the wind. "Were you born that way, or is it a learned trait? I'd really like to know." He was surprised to see a glimmer of hurt in her hazel eyes, but he pushed on relentlessly. "Why do you try so damned hard to seduce a man, when it's clear that all you're really out to do is emasculate every man you come into contact with?"

"Shut up!" she cried, clapping her hands over her ears.

Baron dragged her arms down to her sides. "Why, Thea?" he pressed.

Tears slipped down her cheeks. "No man is ever going to get the best of me again," she said, through clenched teeth.

"Okay," Baron said with a nod. "For some reason known only to you, you aren't enamored of the male sex," he stated. "So why do you keep setting yourself up for a fall? You wind up getting hurt, and they wind up despising you."

She pulled free and dashed the tears from her eyes. "Oh, I inflict the pain far more often than I receive it," she said doing her best to maintain her usual air of haughtiness.

"What's so frightening is that inflicting that pain pleases you so much," Baron said. "Maybe it's time you took a good look inside yourself and ask yourself why it's so important for you to try to destroy every man you meet."

"Go to hell, Baron," she said.

He nodded. "I'd offer you the same sentiment, but I have a feeling you're already there." Without another word, he turned and walked out of the apartment.

This time, she let him go.

Mallory paced the floor, wringing her hands and praying intermittently. The waiting room was empty except for battered magazines and the hum of the nearby soft-drink machine. Visiting hours were over; the hospital corridors were silent except for the occasional squeak of a crepe-soled shoe on the shiny vinyl flooring. Carmen sat thumbing through a magazine, but Mallory couldn't shake the feeling that she was alone.

When Mark left, leaving her responsible for her and Cassie's future, her anger had buoyed her up, lessened her feelings of fear and aloneness. But the anger had faded long ago, and since the death of her mother, Mallory had been acutely aware of the fact that she had no family, no one close that she could count on.

She rubbed her upper arms to ward off a sudden chill. They'd taken Cassie to God knows where. Something about X rays and blood tests—all the necessary preparations before surgery. Mallory wondered if Cassie was scared, or if she was taking all the tests and all the strangers in stride, the way she usually did the medical trappings connected to her illness.

They had been pulling into the emergency room parking lot when Mallory realized she had broken her promise and called Price at his home. She had told Mrs. Weatherby that she and Cassie *needed* Price, and the poor woman had no idea what was going on. Mallory rubbed at her throbbing temples. How could she have betrayed Price's confidence that way? What had she been thinking?

That was the problem. She hadn't thought. She'd reacted. To her fears, her insecurities. To Cassie's wants and needs. She'd acted without giving consideration to the consequences of her actions, and sooner or later, she'd have to pay for her careless behavior. Was Price even now calling someone to take her place on "The Edge!"?

She could throw herself on his mercy and claim the stress of the moment, but remembering how adamant he'd been about keeping her and Cassie's existence a secret, it was doubtful that he would forgive her.

Would he fire her? The thought that she might lose the first secure job she'd held in years sent a shiver of apprehension through her. She pushed it away. She wouldn't—couldn't—worry about that until she knew Cassie was going to be okay.

Thea paced the floor, alternately cursing Baron for being so frank about her behavior and crying because she was ashamed to admit he was right. She was ashamed of a lot of things that didn't bear thinking about.

She was wiping her eyes on a tissue when she heard a light tapping on her door. She spun toward the sound, her heart hammering in surprise. Had Baron come back to apologize? She looked through the peephole. Lance stood there looking as dejected as she felt. She really didn't want to deal with his hurt feelings now, but there was no sense putting it off. With a sigh, she opened the door.

"Hi, Lance. What can I do for you?"

He gave her a level look. Smiled. "More to the point, what can I do for you? I saw your boyfriend leave, and he didn't look like he was in a very good mood." He touched the tearstain on her cheek. "He made you cry."

His tenderness brought back the lump to her throat and the tears to her eyes. Except for Tom, no one had been gentle with her since her father died when she was twelve. She felt Lance's arms go around her and she relaxed against him. She didn't stop him when he lowered his head to kiss her; she just closed her eyes and let the pleasant sensations wipe away all her misery.

She heard the door shut, felt Lance pull her closer. She didn't know how long they kissed, gentle kisses that were a balm to her aching spirit. It felt nice to be comforted.

Lance's hands moved to her hips and dragged her closer. "I want you," he said against her mouth before taking her lips in a kiss that bore little resemblance to those that had preceded it.

He wanted her? Of course he did. But she wasn't in the mood for sex, no matter how handsome Lance might be, or how much he wanted her.

"No, Lance," she said, trying to put some distance between them.

"Yes." His voice was hoarse, filled with need and urgency. "I'm tired of you putting me off. Sick of your teasing."

There was an ugly light in his eyes Thea had never seen before. Feeling more than a little uneasy, she braced her hands against his shoulders and pushed. "I wasn't teasing! I was just . . . flirting a little."

"Flirting. Teasing. Same thing." Despite her struggles, Lance maneuvered Thea toward the sofa she and Baron had recently vacated. He flung her onto its softness and fell on top of her, pinning her there with his body.

Thea took his weight with a grunt of pain. An ancient memory surfaced. Another man. Another man she'd trusted, pressing her into the feather mattress. . . .

"Shut up! Shut up or you'll be sorry. I'm not gonna hurt you. I'm just gonna make you feel real good."

Thea bucked beneath Lance's weight and moaned against the unwanted recollection.

Lance captured her chin in one hand. This time there was no pretense of tenderness. Like the hands that pinned her against her will, the kiss was brutal . . . like those hateful kisses so long ago. Fear rose in her on dark wings of desperation.

"Stop!" Thea gasped, fighting his hold and the old feelings of helplessness and alarm. She managed to free one hand and struck out at him, scoring his cheek with her nails.

Howling with pain, he slapped his hand to his bleeding face. With fury radiating from his eyes, Lance grabbed the front of her dress. Using every available bit of strength, Thea threw her body to the left. The sound of the fabric tearing was loud over their harsh breathing. Thea felt the coolness of air as it hit her body, almost bared to the waist.

Lance fell on her vulnerable flesh like a starved person. Sobbing, knowing that she had to do something to save what was left of her dignity and self-worth—not to mention her sanity—Thea stretched out a hand toward the heavy silver coffeepot she'd used to serve Baron not ten minutes earlier. Her fingers encountered the heat of the urn and inched upward until they closed around the handle. Even though her prone position prevented her from making a good swing, she sank her teeth into her bottom lip and swept the heavy pot from the silver tray and toward Lance's head with all the force she could muster.

He must have seen it coming; he turned just as the vessel connected with a satisfying thump. His cry of agony punctuated the air. Thea wasn't sure if it was from surprise or pain from the scalding liquid that cascaded all over his face and neck and spattered her bare breasts and stomach. She was too frightened to feel more than peripheral discomfort.

Desperately, she struck another blow to the side of his head. The footed bottom smashed against his temple. Blood poured from his ear. Swearing, he rolled off her and dropped to his knees beside the sofa, cradling his head in his hands.

With tears streaming down her cheeks, Thea scrambled from the couch and ran to the desk on the opposite wall where she kept a small caliber revolver. She grabbed the weapon from the drawer and pointed it at Lance. Some still-calm portion of her brain noted that her hands were shaking.

Quaking like a sail in a ragged wind, she reached for the cordless phone with her free hand and turned it on. She had to call someone. The police. Or 911. *Tom.*

A feeling of relief swept through her at the thought of Tom. She closed her eyes and imagined him there, taking care of things, taking care of her the way he used to.

A sound sent her eyes flying open. Lance was looking at her, a look of hatred in his eyes. With a feral growl, he started to his feet.

Thea gave a sharp cry of dismay, and took a step backward. Then, knowing she couldn't let him see her fear, she aimed the gun at his head. "Move," she threatened in a voice far calmer than she felt, "and you're a dead man."

The plane carrying the heart had landed, and an ambulance carrying its precious burden safe in an ice chest was on the way from LAX. Mallory was sitting in Cassie's room waiting. It seemed like hours since she'd received the call from Carmen.

Cassie had received an injection and fallen asleep. Mallory supposed it was necessary, but it was far past Cassie's bedtime, and the excitement had taken its toll. She would have slept anyway. It was just as well, Mallory thought. Sleeping, Cassie wouldn't see her mother's tears of uncertainty.

Wiping at her eyes with a tissue, Mallory got up and went out into the hallway. Maybe she could find a cup of coffee somewhere. She was passing the elevators on the way to the snack bar when a bell sounded and the doors slid open.

She turned to see who it was. Price stood near the back wall, his salt-and-pepper hair tousled, his handsome, craggy face a study in weariness and worry.

The moment he stepped off the elevator, Mallory's last bit of composure crumbled like a stale cookie. He was here. Mrs. Weatherby had told him about her call, and he was here. Mallory was too relieved to even think about the possibility that he might fire her.

"I'm sorry," she said, her voice cracking and her eyes brimming with more of those damnable tears. "I shouldn't have called, but I was so scared, and Cassie wanted you...." Her voice trailed away, and a sob clawed its way up her throat. "She...she wanted you to sing to her."

Without a word, Price gathered her into a close embrace. "Shh" he said, rocking her back and forth and patting her awkwardly on the back. "I'm the one who owes you an apology."

"But I called your house, and I promised I wouldn't."

Price took her shoulders in a gentle grip. "Under the circumstances, I think the breach of promise was justified."

"But what did your wife say?"

His smile was a sardonic twist of his lips. "She had quite a lot of questions, which I answered... truthfully." He drew a deep breath. "It was a shock, of course, but I should have told her a long time ago."

"I'm sorry," Mallory said again.

Price released her shoulders and gave her a real smile. "Can we talk about this after I see my granddaughter?"

Mallory smiled back. "Sure," she said, turning and retracing her way back to Cassie's room.

Cassie hadn't moved. Mallory went to one side of the bed, Price to the other. She shook her daughter's shoulder gently. "Cassie...Cassie, honey, Grampa Price is here."

Cassie's eyelids fluttered and she managed to force them into sleepy slits. When she saw Price, her mouth curved sweetly. "I knew you'd come," she said in a slow, languid voice.

"I wouldn't have missed being here for anything or anybody," he said, taking her hand in both of his. Mallory felt the prickling of tears again. Did he mean it? Had his coming caused more trouble between him and his wife than he let on? Had he risked angering her to come and be at Cassie's side?

"Can I get you anything, Punkin?" Price asked.

"I wanted you to sing to me," Cassie said on a sigh. "I wanted you to sing 'Little Playmate.'"

Price cast an embarrassed glance at Mallory. "Okay," he said, drawing a chair closer to the bed. "Here goes..."

He barely made it through the first line of the old song before Cassie dropped off to sleep again. Seeing the even rise and fall of her chest, he bent over and kissed her soft cheek. When he straightened, there was a suspicious gleam in his green eyes. "She's a little trooper."

Mallory nodded.

Price cleared his throat and squared his shoulders. "How about a cup of coffee?"

"I was just about to get some when I ran in to you," Mallory said with a nod. "I think it's going to be a long night."

"I think you're right." He stopped on the way to the door to give Mallory's shoulder an encouraging squeeze. "Be back in a minute."

When he was gone, Mallory closed her eyes and murmured a short prayer of thanksgiving that he had come and that he wasn't angry with her.

She heard a noise and opened her eyes. Baron stood in the doorway wearing a blue suit and pale gray shirt. There was no hint of a smile of greeting on his face, and his blue eyes were shadowed with worry. She wondered why he was so dressed up and remembered that she'd interrupted his dinner date with Thea.

He stepped into the room, and Mallory leapt to her feet. "Baron! What are you doing here?"

"I came to be with you."

The simple statement was accompanied by a look that made Mallory feel warm and somehow comforted. She tried to smile, and the attempt died a sudden death when the tears started again. Would she ever be free of them?

Without a word, Baron pulled her into his arms. She buried her face against his chest. "I'm glad you're here," she whispered.

"So am I," he said against her hair. "How is she?"

She drew back to look at him. "Good. The heart is on its way from the airport."

"I guess it would be silly for me to ask if you're worried."

"Yes," she said with a feeble smile, "it would."

"It'll be okay," he said.

Instead of acknowledging the statement, Mallory lifted herself to her tiptoes, drawn by the tenderness in his eyes. Their lips met in a kiss so tender, so pure, it brought an ache to her heart. Baron held her so tightly, it felt as if he'd never let her go. And Mallory knew she didn't want him to.

She loved him, she thought with a bit of wonder. She didn't know how it had happened; she certainly hadn't planned it. She didn't need the complication of a man in her life, not now, but it didn't matter. She loved him.

"Ahem!"

Both Mallory and Baron turned toward the sound. Price stood in the doorway, two cups of coffee in his hands. Mallory stepped out of Baron's arms, but he kept one arm firmly around her shoulders. The two men eyed each other like boxers sizing up the competition.

She could feel the tension in Baron's body, could see it in the set of his jaw and the wariness of his eyes. Price looked thoughtful rather than angry.

"I'm a little surprised to see you here," he said at last. "I didn't know you were so close to Mallory and Cassie."

"Really?" Baron replied. "I could say the same about you."

The straightforward comment took Price aback. Mallory couldn't bear any more. She was sick of living a lie. Tired of deception. No matter what the consequences, she was finished with that part of her life.

She looked at Price and hoped that he could see that she was sorry. Then she lifted her gaze to Baron's.

"I had a personal reason for asking Price to come," she said. The expression in Baron's eyes was bleak, resigned. Mallory drew a fortifying breath and spoke before her courage deserted her.

"I asked Price to come because he's my father."

Chapter Eleven

Tom had been fixing himself a late meal when the phone rang and Thea had given him a hysterical and garbled account of what had happened to her. Tom instructed her to call 911 and said he was on his way. Though a part of him had seen the possibility of something like this happening, he couldn't deny the ripple of anxiety that coursed through him.

When he pulled up outside Thea's building, the police were loading Lance into a patrol car. Tom resisted the urge to push his way through the uniformed policemen, drag the young doorman from the car and smash in his pretty face. He settled for directing a chilling stare at the younger man before taking the marble steps two at a time.

Showing his WTN identification, Tom had no problem getting past the burly doorman on shift and glanced around with interest. The marble-and-glass entrance was as upscale and slick as any he'd seen. A towering Douglas fir decorated in white and gold soared upward opposite the bank of elevators to the left. "Joy to the World" wafted through the air from hidden speakers, making a mockery of what had transpired in Thea's condo just moments before. Tom took the elevator up, chiding himself for the negative thought.

Tom smiled at the female detective standing outside Thea's door. "Hi. I'm Tom Madsen."

The woman looked at him with eyes that had seen far too much and been impressed with very little. "And I'm Joan Benedict." Her attitude added the silent, "So what?"

"I'm here to see Ms. Barlow. She called me."

The pronouncement elicited the slightest bit of softening in the policewoman's eyes. "I'll tell her you're here."

Tom watched the detective disappear through the door and leaned one shoulder against the far wall while he waited. Joan Benedict returned a couple of minutes later and jerked her chin toward the gaping door.

"Go on in."

Another woman sat on the sofa, a spiral notebook on her lap. Thea, who was wearing a bulky cardigan over her evening attire, stood across the room looking at him with wide, uncertain eyes, twisting her hands together.

Tom's heart lurched. He wasn't sure he'd ever seen that look on Thea's face. While he wasn't a fan of her aggressive, I-can-do-anything-you-can-do-and-probably-better look, he wasn't sure he ever wanted to see her this vulnerable again.

"I got here as soon as I could."

The woman on the couch rose to shake his hand, introducing herself as Lieutenant Masters, a rape counselor with the LAPD. She must have seen the horror he felt at her announcement, because she was quick to allay his fears.

"No. He didn't rape her, but only because she fought so hard and used her head."

"Thank God."

The counselor smiled at Thea. "I'll be going, but if you want to talk some more about what you told me, just give me a call. You have my card?"

Thea nodded and held up the card that was sandwiched between her index and middle finger.

"Great," the woman said with another smile. "See you later, and have a Merry Christmas."

"Thank you," Thea said.

When the door shut behind the policewoman, Thea's spine seemed to lose its starch. Tom crossed the room and draped his arm around her shoulders. "Come on. What you need is a nice, long bath to help you unwind. Which way to the bathroom?"

Thea pointed, and Tom led her through her elegant white-and-taupe bedroom to the master bath that was equipped with a small television and a CD player. He picked out a disc, and soon the tender strains of Yanni's "Felitsa" wafted in aching softness throughout the room. Tom turned on the brass handles, tested the water temperature and squeezed in a lavish dollop of expensive foaming bath gel.

"Go ahead and get in," he said, rising. "I'll fix us a pot of coffee."

As he started past Thea, she grabbed his arm. Their eyes met—Thea's dull, weary; Tom's curious, cautious.

"Thanks for coming."

He nodded. "Sure." The soft sobbing of the violins accompanied him from the room.

When Thea emerged from the bathroom thirty minutes later, she was wearing a pair of old sweats that looked as if they belonged in the rag bag instead of on the usually elegant television executive. Though he could barely discern the UCLA logo on the front, Tom recognized the sweats as a pair of his, a remnant of the time they'd spent together. He was surprised that she owned anything so old, much less that she'd hung on to anything that would remind her of him.

She had scrubbed off every trace of makeup and slicked her wet hair away from her face. The severity of the style accentuated the square line of her jaw and her distinctive cheekbones as well as the patrician line of her nose and the elegant sweep of her eyebrows. She'd never seemed more beautiful.

"Coffee?" he asked, as she seated herself at the bar.

"Please."

Tom poured two mugs of the fragrant brew and laced one liberally with sugar and cream.

"I take mine black, remember?" she said, when he set the cup in front of her.

"Not tonight, you don't. You need something to give you a boost."

"Did anyone ever tell you that you're bossy?" Thea asked, wrapping her hands around the mug.

Still standing, Tom rested both forearms on the top of the bar and leaned toward her. "Now that's what I'd call the pot calling the kettle black."

She took a sip of the coffee and thought about that a second. "I guess you're right," she admitted. A ghost of a smile hovered on her lips. "Actually, this tastes pretty good."

"I thought it might." Silence reigned a moment, before he asked, "Do you want to tell me about it?"

"Not really, but Lieutenant Masters said I should tell you...everything." She looked down at her hands, took a deep breath and raised tormented eyes to his. "First, I want you to know that I owe you an apology. You and Baron and a lot of other people."

Silent, Tom regarded her over the rim of his mug.

Over the course of the next few minutes, Thea told him about her date with Baron, the call from Mallory and how she'd threatened Baron with the loss of his job if he left. There were tears in Thea's eyes when she relayed word for word what Baron had said about her and her ways and means.

"I was thinking about what he said—and he's right—then Lance came."

"Why did you let him in?" Tom asked.

"He'd been here before. I don't deny that I flirted with him, but that's as far as it went. We like some of the same music..." Her voice trailed away. "He seemed angry that Baron had made me cry, and he put his arms around me and—" she exhaled harshly and met Tom's eyes with disconcerting directness "—it felt good to be held and comforted. But then he made it clear that he wanted more, and I told him no, and he...didn't want to take no for an answer."

"Go on."

She brushed the wetness from her cheeks with an impatient gesture. "We struggled, and he threw me down onto the couch. I knew I couldn't let it happen again, and I managed to—"

Thea rambled on, but Tom hardly heard. His mind zeroed in on what she'd just said. A sick feeling settled in his gut.

"What do you mean, you couldn't let it happen again?" he asked, interrupting the outpouring of words.

"What?" Thea asked, staring at him with a blank look.

"What did you mean about not letting it happen again?" Tom repeated.

Thea's face grew parchment white. She looked down at her coffee, as if it were a crystal ball and she hoped to find the answers to her predicament in the dark depths.

She was silent for so long that Tom thought he was going to have to prompt her again. When she finally spoke, her voice was low, strained, thick with emotion.

"My daddy died when I was twelve," she said, "and Mama started seeing a man the next year. Gib Jefferson was handsome and laughed a lot, and everyone loved him. Daddy had always been sour and strict, so none of us kids were too upset when they got married."

"The son of a bitch molested you!" Tom spat, going straight to the heart of the matter. Thea flinched as if he'd struck her. She seemed to shrink before his eyes. She refused to look at him.

"He said if I told Mama, she wouldn't believe me, and if she did, he'd just say that I started it, that I was always flirting with him and parading around the house in my short shorts and halters. Mama and I didn't get along real well, and she was so crazy about him, I figured she would believe him."

Tom noticed that Thea's usually cultured voice had taken on the cadence and phraseology of the Ozark mountain region she'd been born and raised in. She paused, as if she were trying to find the words, or maybe the courage to go on. Tears fell unimpeded to the countertop, and still, she refused to look at him.

"I was fifteen and a half when I got pregnant. Mama was dead by then."

Tom bit back a violent curse.

"He took me to one of his cousins way back in the hills. She—" a sob ripped its way from her throat, and Thea buried her face in her hands "—she did an abortion. I thought I was gonna die, and I've wished a thousand times I had."

"Stop it!" Tom said, rounding the bar and putting his arms around her from behind, curving his body protectively over hers. He felt the resistance in her, but held on tightly while she cried out the tears that were more than twenty years overdue.

While she cried, Tom cursed Thea's stepfather, damning him to an eternal hell. Giving vent to his anger helped keep his own tears from falling. When the tears were gone, Thea straightened and leaned back against him, limp and empty.

When she spoke again, she directed her comments to the opposite wall. A weary tonelessness underscored her pain.

"I ran away when I was sixteen. I made myself a promise that Thea Barlow would be someone to be reckoned with someday. And I swore that I'd never let a man take advantage of me again, that I'd never let one hurt me. I guess that's why I always had to have the upper hand, always had to call the shots—you know, the old 'do unto others before they do it to you' mentality."

She laughed, but the sound held no humor. "It didn't work, Tom. I still got hurt."

"You reap what you sow," he said, his heart raw and bleeding for all that she'd gone through.

"Do you know why I sabotaged our relationship?" she said after a while.

"No."

"Because you were the one man I couldn't control, the one man I couldn't figure out. On one hand, you were so good to me, I figured it was all just some sort of scam. And then you'd rake me over the coals for something I'd done, and I'd know that you were right, and that guilt made me feel small and insignificant and angry—at myself and at you. It was easier to let it go, to drive you away than it was to look inside myself and see why I behaved the way I did."

"Facing our faults is never easy."

"No." She tilted her head back and looked up at him over her shoulder, meeting his eyes for the first time since she'd started her story. Hers were awash with tears. "I've missed you."

He could tell the confession was a hard one. "I've missed you, too."

"Does it matter?" she asked, a measure of apprehension in her eyes.

"Do you mean, does what he did to you change how I feel about you?" He shook his head. "No."

She bit her bottom lip to control its trembling and let out a long sigh. "I'm going to get some professional help, Tom."

"I think that's a smart move."

She dropped her head forward and rested her forearms over his, hugging them against her. "I'm really, really tired."

"Why don't you go to bed?" he suggested, pressing a kiss to the vulnerable spot at the nape of her neck.

"I think I will." She swiveled around on the stool and looked at him. "Will you come with me?"

Tom knew the invitation for what it was. Thea was ready and willing to pick up the threads of their old relationship. "No." Tom shook his head. "If I do ever get back in your bed, I'm never leaving."

"I wouldn't want you to."

"No? Well, I'm not going to let you run our relationship, either."

"A dictatorship, Tom?" She said it with a hint of her old scorn.

"A partnership, Thea. A full partnership." He leaned forward and kissed her lightly. Her arms went around his neck, and she held him tightly. Fiercely. Possessively.

When Tom pulled free, he saw that her eyes were filled again with tears. "Go to bed," he commanded with soft urgency. "I'll take the sofa. You're worn-out, and we both need to do some thinking."

"There's one other thing I haven't told you," she said, slipping from the stool. "And you'll need to do a lot of thinking about it."

"What's that?" he asked with a frown.

"Because of what Gib had done to me, I can never have any children," she said, and, without waiting for him to comment, she turned and left the room, her usually straight shoulders slumped in weariness and dejection.

For some reason, Tom wasn't as surprised as he might have expected to be. He thought about her Saturday forays to the park, her indefatigable energy when it came to entertaining the kids at play. Her visits to the hospitals. All those years he'd wondered why she'd done something that seemed so out of character.

Now, with her confession, it all made sense.

He sat down on the sofa and cradled his head in his hands. He'd dreamed of a family. Dreamed of having a family with Thea. As she said, it would require a lot of thinking for both of them.

Mallory paced the waiting room floor, aware that both Baron and Price were watching her with unconcealed concern. Realizing there was no sense in everyone staying, Carmen had gone home to bed so that she could come later, while Mallory rested. But Mallory wasn't sure she would ever rest again. Her thoughts churned round and round, interwoven with prayers for Cassie's safekeeping.

She glanced at Price and Baron. Neither of them was talking much. Mallory assumed they were both thinking about the bomb she'd dropped that evening. Though Price had insisted that the call she'd made to his wife was unimportant under the circumstances, she couldn't forget the look on his face when she told Baron the truth.

Baron had been stunned at the news, too. Just seconds after her announcement, the nurses had come to take Cassie away, and there had been no time for discussion. The night had passed; dawn ushered in a new day.

"Come sit down," Baron urged when she passed him for the umpteenth time in the past hour. "Try to rest."

"I can't."

"Try."

She had no more than sat down when a voice said, "Ms. Ryan."

The sound of her name sent three pairs of eyes looking toward the doorway. Dr. DeBorde stood just inside the room, his face drawn with exhaustion, a weary smile of greeting on his face. She hadn't heard him enter the room.

Mallory leapt to her feet, mentally preparing herself for whatever news he might impart. Baron rose, too, drawing her close to his side.

Dr. DeBorde smiled. "Cassie is out of surgery, and things look good."

Mallory heaved a sigh of relief. Beside her, Baron and Price both breathed a simultaneous "Thank God."

"She'll be in ICU for several days, but if all goes well, you should have a very merry Christmas. For now, I suggest that you all go home and get some rest. Come back this afternoon and I'll let Mallory go in and see Cassie for a few minutes."

"I'll stay," Price said. "What if something—"

"If something happens, your being here won't change things. I'll have the nurse get Mallory a beeper." He smiled kindly. "Go home. I'm pretty good at what I do, and that little girl in there is a fighter."

Holding back tears of relief, Mallory nodded and tried to smile. "Thank you, Dr. DeBorde."

When the doctor left, Mallory, Baron and Price started wearily down the hall. Outside the hospital, Price put his arms around Mallory and gave her a comforting hug—only the second hug they'd shared in Mallory's twenty-seven years of existence.

It felt strange. It felt right. It brought tears to her eyes. Tears of thankfulness that they'd found each other, tears of sorrow for all they'd missed.

"I'm sorry I screwed everything up," she apologized again.

"Don't worry about anything but Cassie," Price instructed gruffly. "I'll take care of everything on my end. It'll be okay, I promise. And don't bother coming in for the show. We'll make do without you."

Too choked up to speak, Mallory nodded. He released her and started to go, but she grabbed his hand. There was a question in his eyes. "Thank you," she said.

Price nodded and walked away.

Mallory felt Baron's arm go around her, and she sagged against him. "I can't remember where I parked," she said, looking out toward the vast parking lot.

"It doesn't matter," Baron told her. "I'm driving you home. You can pick up your car tomorrow."

She was too exhausted to argue, and it was nice to have someone take over for a change.

As Baron put her in his truck, her thoughts turned from Cassie to Price and Mark and Kevin and Baron. Of the love she'd lost and how it had affected her, and of the love she'd found and how it would affect her future.

Her mother had loved Price, and he was a good man by anyone's standards. His coming tonight told her that he was committed to his new role as father and grandfather, despite the problems it might cause at home. She was fiercely glad he cared, even though she was sorry for the pain his family would no doubt suffer.

She could see that her feelings for Mark had been a young girl's love, an immature feeling based on passion and a pocketful of dreams. The problem was, that when the dream didn't materialize, Mark couldn't take the reality. Instead of facing their problem with Cassie, he had run from it. Somehow, Mallory knew he'd be running until the day he died.

After suffering from Mark's defection, she felt she understood Kevin Damian's feelings of hurt and betrayal when he'd found out that Betty had tricked him. At seventeen, Mallory had been devastated that he'd let his bitterness and anger flow over into their relationship. As an adult, she understood his anger and could empathize with his pain. She wasn't sure she'd ever understand how he could cut her out of his life the way he had Betty, but she'd forgiven him.

Now there was Baron and a whole new set of worries. Would he return her feelings? Was she ready to trust her heart again?

By the time she fell asleep, just two short blocks from the hospital, she'd come to the conclusion that life was just too uncertain and too short to miss having the love of any person, even for a while.

"C'mon, sleepyhead," Baron said, leaning over her and kissing her lightly on the lips. Mallory opened her eyes a slit and saw that she was home. All throughout the neighborhood, Christmas lights twinkled, giving the California neighborhood a seasonal ambience it lacked the rest of the year. It was the most wonderful time of the year, she thought with a sleepy smile.

She put her hand against Baron's cheek and felt the roughness of his whiskers against her palm. She heard his sudden indrawn breath and marveled that she could have such an effect on him. Her own breathing grew shallow, tortured, as she lifted her arms and twined them around his neck.

She loved him. She wanted him. She was glad it was Christmastime, glad to be alive, to have what she had. It was a good life, lacking nothing but the love of a good man. She had a feeling that man was sitting beside her, but even if it turned out that he didn't feel the same, she knew she needed what he could give her, even if it was only for a while.

Drawing his head down, she fused her mouth to his.

Baron's response didn't disappoint her. His arms dragged her close and his mouth ravaged hers with a hunger that sent her desire spiraling. In the close confines of the car and the warmth of his arms, she felt secure in a way she hadn't felt in years.

He drew back and slid one hand beneath her sweater, sliding his hand inside the lacy cup of her bra. She felt the rough abrasion of his thumb against the aching tip and opened her eyes. He was looking at her, gauging her reaction.

Christmas lights chased each other along the eaves and down the porch supports, dappling the sculpted, savage planes of his face in a changing kaleidoscope of color. The look in his eyes was as primal as the Mayan masks that adorned the walls of Price's office; it kindled the smoldering, dormant passion that lay deep inside her.

She groaned, a sharp burst of sound as the desire exploded into hot flames that licked throughout her body, enveloping it in a spreading heat that burned its brightest and hottest at the very core of her womanhood.

Unsure that she'd ever felt this degree of desire for a man, Mallory gave Baron her mouth, pulling at his shirt and fumbling with the buttons with trembling, frenzied hands, wanting, needing to feel the warmth of his flesh against hers.

She didn't know how he got her sweater and bra off, wasn't sure when he shed his shirt, but when her bare breasts came into contact with the crisp hair on his chest, an exquisite need began to unfurl inside her like a ribbon of smoke.

She made a sound in her throat, something low and feral and totally unlike her. Her hands molded the muscles of his back, her mouth savaged his. The part of her mind that could still form conscious thought told her that this behavior was unlike her, that her actions were out of character... wild... crazy....

She didn't care. All she cared about was quenching the fire, of filling the emptiness inside her. She felt the clasp of her jeans give and heard the grinding of her zipper...and his. Somehow she kicked them off, along with her underwear.

Baron slid to the middle of the seat and turned her to face him, easing one of her thighs over his. Locking her fingers in the thickness of his hair, she touched her mouth to his in a kiss as gentle as the others had been rough. Then with slow, seductive movements, he began to stoke the fire.

Mallory woke up in slow increments, filled with well-being...and a touch of embarrassment. Had she and Baron really made out in his pickup like a couple of teenagers? Had she really behaved so wantonly? And had she really brought him inside with her afterward? Almost on cue, she heard the softness of his breathing. With a smile, she turned to her side.

He lay there, big and masculine and rumpled—the shadow of his beard giving him a tough look. It was nice waking to find a man sleeping beside her.

Mallory raised her head and glanced at the bedside clock. Quarter till six. She should get up and call about Cassie, and she would. But right now, she just wanted to lie there and look at Baron sleep and think about how lucky she was.

But her excitement was mixed with a healthy dose of uncertainty. Could she ask him to take on the problems of her life? She wasn't sure. All she was sure of was that her feelings for him far eclipsed what she'd felt for Mark during the best days of their marriage.

Beside her, Baron stirred and opened his eyes. The lazy smile that curved his lips sent a shiver of desire through her.

"Hi."

"Hi," she said with a tremulous smile.

He reached out and drew her against the hard, warm length of him. The hand that skimmed over the curve of her hip and up to her breast robbed her of breath and stole her thoughts; the touch of his mouth threatened to rob her of her mind.

"I should call and see about Cassie," she said, between kisses.

"Cassie is fine, or the hospital would have beeped you," Baron murmured against her lips.

Mallory nodded. He was right. Dr. DeBorde had promised to let her know if there was the slightest change in Cassie's condition for the worse.

With the night of worry and desperation behind them, with their first urgent bout of lovemaking tickling their memories, Baron made love to her slowly, sweetly, thoroughly.

Later, when they lay spent in the tangle of sheets, Mallory sighed in complete satisfaction. She didn't know how this had all come about—Price, her job, Baron, Cassie's second chance—but she knew that she'd be forever thankful for whatever guardian angel was watching over her.

"I have to get up and go home so I can get ready for work," Baron said. "See if I still have a job."

Mallory raised her head from his chest to look at him. "What do you mean?"

"Thea wasn't thrilled when I left her last night. As a matter of fact, I imagine she'll be at Price's door first thing this morning, telling him how insubordinate I was."

"What did you say to her?" Mallory asked, frowning.

"A lot of things, including my feeling that she needs some serious help for her problems, which appear to be many and deep-rooted."

Mallory grimaced. "Not a good move, Montgomery. I've known Thea for years, and she can be very vindictive."

"Well, she'll just have to fire me, then. I'm sick of her trying to get me into her bed, and I just wasn't in the mood to have her pawing me last night."

"Pawing you?"

"Couldn't you tell she was putting the make on me? You even walked in on us that day in my dressing room."

Mallory's fingers toyed with the crisp hair on his hard stomach. "I assumed I'd walked in on what poets call a tender moment."

Baron shook his head. "You walked in at the right moment. If I recollect right, she was implying that I should do what she wanted if I hoped to hang on to my job."

"She threatened to have you fired if you didn't . . . return her advances?" Mallory asked, aghast.

"On several occasions."

"I can't believe it!" Mallory said with a shake of her head. "She told me to keep away from you, and I thought that was just her jealousy. But threatening you with the loss of your job is blackmail—not to mention sexual harassment. Why didn't you say something to Price?"

"What was I supposed to say?"

Mallory smiled wryly. "I guess a sexual harassment charge wouldn't hold much water, would it?"

"Considering the gender element, I didn't think so. I tried a dozen times to tell her in a nice way that I wasn't interested, but she's a very determined lady.'' His chest lifted with a sigh. ''I hoped I could salvage my job, but after last night, I don't care about that as much as I care about getting her off my back.''

Mallory sighed. ''You'll know soon.''

''Yeah,'' Baron agreed. He nuzzled her neck. ''So tell me about Price. I guess you knew I thought you two were having an affair.''

''I suspected as much.''

''The first day I came to work, the day we found out about Delores, Thea hinted that there was something going on between the two of you.''

''I should have known Thea was behind the gossip,'' Mallory said. ''I knew I got a few speculative looks, but I didn't realize what everyone thought until the day Price offered me the contract. When I saw the expression in your and Thea's eyes, I knew what everyone was saying behind our backs. But I needed the job, so I signed.''

''Tell me how you came to be Price Weatherby's daughter.''

Mallory told him about her marriage to Mark, about their moving to Vegas so he could run one of the casinos and how Cassie's illness had affected their marriage. She told him about her uphill financial struggle after Mark left, about her moving back to L.A. so that Betty could help with Cassie.

She detailed her mother's deathbed confession about her affair with Price and about her mother's marriage and ugly divorce from Kevin Damian, including the way he'd turned his back on the child he'd raised as a daughter.

''I guess it's crazy, but I still miss him,'' she said. ''A lot.''

"Damian?"

Mallory nodded. "In spite of everything, he was a good father. The best. And I've learned the hard way that you can't turn off love just because someone hurts you."

Baron threaded his fingers through her hair and forced her to look at him. "Speaking of love...I do, you know."

Her eyes widened the slightest bit. "Do what?"

"Love you."

"Oh, Baron!" Tears filled her eyes and she clamped her lips together to still their trembling.

"Marry me, Mallory," he said, his voice low and urgent.

"Baron, I..."

"Do you love me?"

"Yes." There was conviction and defiance in her tone.

"Then that's all I need to know. I want to marry you, to be a part of every day of your life."

"My life isn't always so wonderful," she said. "What about Cassie?"

"What about her? Surely you know I love her, too."

"I know you do, and she's getting very attached to you, but what if this transplant doesn't work? What if her condition gets worse and—"

Baron stilled her worries with his fingers. "If she gets worse, you won't have to go through it alone. I'll be there for you."

"You have no idea how trying the stress of an illness like Cassie's can be to a relationship," she said, determined that he be aware of all the negatives up front.

"I'm sure it can, but I want to be your husband and Cassie's father. I want us to have a child of our own. I may drive you crazy in other ways, so crazy you might want to leave me, but I swear to you, that I'll never let you down the way the other men in your life have.''

Mallory searched his eyes, looking for the truth of his feelings. What she saw was his very soul.

"What do you say?" he asked with a grin. "Shall I announce our engagement on the show this morning, and put an end to everyone's misery?"

"The show! If we get married, what will that do for the show?"

"Is that a yes?"

"It's a maybe," she said. "Seriously, Baron. WTN has invested a lot in the concept of this show."

Baron raised himself up on one elbow. "Yeah, well, the question might be moot. Like I said, I may not have a job when I get there this morning. You may have to support me until I find another job."

"That goes for me, too. Mrs. Weatherby might be so upset about me and Cassie that she might demand that Price keep his distance from us." She sighed. "We may as well get dressed and find out."

"Price said you didn't have to go in for the show."

Mallory got up and slipped into a robe that was draped across the foot of the bed. "I know what he said, but I'm going by the hospital to see how Cassie is doing. If she's okay, I'll see you at the station."

"And are you going to marry me or not?" he asked her retreating figure.

Just inside the bathroom door, she stopped and faced him. She cocked her head to the side in a considering way. "I think I am, Mr. Montgomery. Job or no job."

"Good," he said with a nod.

When the door closed behind her, Baron reached for the telephone and asked the operator for Information, jotting down the number he requested on a scrap of paper he pulled from the pocket of his jacket.

It was amazing just how much information was at a person's fingertips, he thought with a satisfied smile.

Chapter Twelve

Tom and Thea woke before the sun. Over coffee, he begged her to let him call Price and tell him what had happened. "You're too upset to work," he said.

"I'm body sore, but to tell you the truth, I feel better than I have in ages," she said. "Besides, I'd rather no one know what happened."

"You aren't pressing charges?" Tom asked.

"I am, but I'm going to try and keep it as quiet as possible. I don't want or need anyone's pity."

"Okay," Tom said. "It's your life."

"You're darn right it is," Thea said with a nod. "I did a lot of thinking last night, Tom, and I decided that I'm not letting what Gib Jefferson did to me ruin any more of my life than it already has."

Tom smiled. "Good girl."

"I made another decision."

"What?"

"I'm turning in my resignation to Price today."

"What! Why?"

"I think that's obvious. I don't think there's any way I can redeem myself—not at WTN, anyway. It's time to move on, start over."

"I see your point, but I hate to see you give up a good job."

"There are a lot of good jobs out there."

"Okay," Tom said. "Whatever you think."

When Tom left thirty minutes later, giving her a brief kiss on the cheek and telling her he'd see her at the station, Thea dressed and headed for the hospital, stopping by an all-night market and buying a handful of colorful Mylar balloons and a stack of Little Golden Books for Cassie. She had an idea she would find Mallory at her daughter's side, and there was a lot Thea needed to say to Mallory.

Mallory was surprised to see Thea waiting to make the trip down to the main floor when she stepped off the elevator onto Cassie's floor at quarter till seven. There was a haunted expression in Thea's eyes. She looked as if she'd aged ten years overnight.

"Thea!" Mallory said, unable to hide her surprise. "What are you doing here?"

"I came to bring Cassie a gift, and to talk to you."

Mallory wondered if it was her imagination or if there was really a diffidence in Thea's attitude. She stepped off the elevator and gestured to the nearby waiting room. "We can talk in here."

Thea sat in a powder blue chair; Mallory seated herself in its nearby companion, upholstered in navy.

Thea clasped her hands together in her lap. "I spoke with the nurses. I'm glad Cassie is doing so well."

"So am I."

"I didn't know her condition was so serious," Thea said. "But then, there was no way I could know, since I went out of my way to make myself your enemy, not your friend."

Unsure what was on Thea's mind or where the conversation was going, Mallory only said, "I never knew exactly what I'd done to earn your dislike."

"It wasn't you," Thea was quick to correct. "It was me. I've had some problems the last several years, and I took it out on everyone around me. I want you to know I'm sorry."

The shock of Thea's apology ranked right up there with the shock of learning that Price Weatherby was her biological father.

Thea's lips curved up at the corners in a sarcastic smile. "You don't have to say anything. I know you're wondering what's going on, if this is some sort of trick, but I assure you, it isn't. When Baron left my place last night, he said some things that made me step back and take a hard look at myself." She paused and drew in a deep breath. "And then something else happened that hit me even harder."

Mallory sensed the tension in Thea, could feel the waves of nervousness radiating from her. Whatever had happened had truly shaken her up.

"I'm not saying I'm going to be a saint from here on out," Thea said. "And, I won't change overnight, but I am going to try to be a more considerate person."

"Do you want to talk about it?" Mallory said, baffled by this new Thea Barlow.

Thea shook her head. "Suffice it to say that my actions were linked to my low opinion of myself. Being an actress leaves you vulnerable to the vagaries of the audience and the writers. You understand that.''

Mallory nodded. She understood all too well.

''Well, I wanted to end all that. When I started my corporate climb, it was partly because I felt that an executive position carried more clout, more prestige than being a soap actress. I don't deny I wanted the power as well as the position, and I didn't care who got hurt on my climb to the top.''

''But none of it has made you happy.'' Mallory made the statement with an inborn certainty.

''No,'' Thea said, ''it hasn't. Until recently, I never realized that responsibility goes hand in hand with power—and I'm not talking about the responsibility of doing a job well.''

''Why are you telling me this?'' Mallory asked.

''Because I've made your life miserable from time to time, and I want you to know that I regret it. Even if we can't be friends, I hope we can at least reach a place of mutual respect.''

''I've always respected your work as an actress and your ability as an executive,'' Mallory told her truthfully.

Thea tried to smile and looked as if she might cry instead. She took a deep breath. ''I'm handing in my resignation this morning.''

''What!''

Thea nodded. ''I've stepped on too many toes at WTN to ever change the way people feel about me. It's time to move on.''

''But . . . what will you do? Where will you go?''

''I don't know,'' Thea said with a shrug, ''but I have a lot of skills, and there's bound to be someone out there who needs them. I may even go back into acting. It has its ups and downs, but it's a lot more satisfying."

"That's because you were so good at it," Mallory said.

"Thanks." Thea rose to go. "I left some books and balloons at the nurses' station for Cassie. I hope she enjoys them, and I sincerely hope she has a speedy recovery."

"Thank you." Thea turned to go, and, with a bemused expression on her face, Mallory watched her walk away. She had a sudden thought and leapt to her feet, hurrying out into the corridor.

"Thea!"

Thea, who stood at the elevators, turned.

"Call Michael Connelly," Mallory urged. "He told me last night he was looking for someone to play the lead in a new movie he's producing. And he specifically said he was looking for someone who could play a villainess the way you used to play Vanessa Brandt on 'Friends and Lovers.'"

Mallory saw the sudden flicker of interest in Thea's eyes. Gratitude followed.

"Thanks, Mallory," she said, as the doors slid open. "I owe you one."

When Mallory arrived at WTN later that morning and told Baron about her talk with Thea, he announced that Thea had apologized to him, too.

After they finished the show, Price asked to speak to Mallory before she left for the hospital.

"Thea turned in her resignation," he said as Mallory sat in the chair across the desk from him. "If she hadn't quit, I was going to fire her."

"You were?"

Price nodded.

"I thought she was good at what she did."

"She was. She was excellent at her job, but I'm not blind. I knew she'd been putting the make on Baron ever since he arrived, and I let it slide. I figured Baron was a big boy—he could put an end to it if he wanted to. But when I saw how you and Baron feel about each other last night, I realized I'd made a mistake in not calling her on the carpet sooner. I've also had some complaints from a couple of other male employees."

"So you'd decided to fire her?"

Price's smile was slow, almost apologetic. "I know you told me to stay out of your life and let you fight your own battles, but I wasn't about to let her come between you and the man you love. Not if it was in my power to stop it."

Mallory couldn't help smiling back. She was touched by his feelings. "If that isn't just like a father!"

Price shrugged. "I do what I can."

"Which is a perfect segue to your coming to the hospital last night. What happened between you and your wife?"

"We had our two sons and daughter over for a long talk over breakfast this morning." He colored slightly. "I couldn't see any sense in telling the tale a half a dozen times."

"And?" she prompted.

"And I told Pamela about Betty, and about Betty's confession before she died. Pamela was hurt, naturally, but she's a wonderful woman and a great believer in forgiveness. And luckily for me, she loves me. The fact that I've been a good husband and faithful to her since that time with Betty, stands me in pretty good stead."

"And your children?"

There was a hint of devilry in Price's eyes. "Your brothers and sister, you mean? They were a little angry—not at you, at me. But they'll come around. They want to meet you. Cassie, too, of course. She'll love playing with her cousins."

Brothers and sisters? Cousins? The thought that she had two brothers and a sister as well as nieces and nephews was something of a shock. She'd never thought about Price's children except in an abstract way, and the thought that they wanted to meet her was thrilling... and frightening.

"They're pretty good kids," he said, and then chuckled. "Kids! Paul is thirty-three, Steven is thirty-one and Lucy is about your age."

Mallory's head whirled. She rose and went to the window. "I don't know about this."

Price came up behind her and put his hands on her shoulders. Their eyes of their reflections met in the glass. "Let's just take it slow and easy, Mallory. Give it some time. It's going to be okay, I promise."

And deep in her heart, Mallory knew he was right.

Cassie improved day by day. Much to Mallory's surprise, Pamela Weatherby, her three children and four grandchildren—two boys and two girls—showed up at the hospital with Price one evening to visit their newest relatives.

Mallory was overwhelmed by the goodwill they all exhibited, a reminder that there were kind, generous and forgiving people in the world if you were lucky enough for their lives to touch yours.

She often thought of how she had felt so alone the night of Cassie's surgery, and how suddenly full her life was with people, people she hoped would grow to love her and Cassie just as she would learn to love them. A family. Her family.

Two days after Thea announced her resignation, Baron saw a small notice in the paper that Thea Barlow had filed assault charges against one Lance Turner. Mallory thought she understood the reason behind Thea's sudden change of heart.

Two days after that, Thea and Tom announced that they planned to be married the first of the year. Tom told Mallory that Thea had contacted Michael Connelly and tried out for the part of Sophie in his new movie. Her new agent said her chances looked very good.

Mallory and Baron's wedding was set for Christmas Eve day and would take place on the set of "The Edge!" Cassie was so thrilled by the prospect of having Baron for her new daddy, she could barely contain herself. All of Mallory's new family would be there, and Price would give her away. Mallory and Baron wouldn't be able to take a real honeymoon until spring, but Price decided to run a special movie Christmas day so Mallory and Baron and Cassie could spend the day together as a family.

As soon as their "I do's" were said, they would go to the hospital and bring Cassie home, along with a round-the-clock nurse who would be a permanent fixture during her recuperation. Mallory would have her daughter home and a new husband. Life couldn't get much better.

"You look gorgeous!" Pamela Weatherby said, adjusting the puff of ivory tulle and beads nestled at the back of the close-fitting hat Mallory wore with her upswept hairdo. Her dress was a long, ivory-tinted, off-the-shoulder cable-knit sweater dress with close-fitting sleeves, plain except for the scattering of faux pearls. A choker of the real thing circled her throat, her "something borrowed" from Pamela. She hadn't wanted anything too fancy or expensive for this second wedding; she'd been practical too long.

Baron was waiting for her on the set. They'd started off the show as usual; the on-the-air wedding was a surprise to both the studio audience and the at-home viewers.

First, Baron left the set on the pretext of some late-breaking story, and when he came back, he was dressed in an elegant black suit that had elicited a few wolf whistles and a murmur from the crowd.

Later, Mallory left to change. All that was left now was to send out the justice of the peace and go back onto the set to gauge the reaction of the audience.

She watched as the justice of the peace was introduced and heard the rumble that came up from the audience. When Baron told them they were about to witness a wedding, the crowd went wild. When he announced that he was marrying Mallory, they almost brought down the house.

"I take it you approve?" he called, over the noise.

Chants of "Baron! Mallory!" filled the studio and the airwaves. Baron motioned for Mallory, and she stepped out under the hot, bright lights and into Baron's arms. He kissed her, a kiss that stole her breath and sent the audience into a frenzy. Laughing, she drew away and waved at the crowd.

Price stepped out of the wings and introduced himself. "I'm Price Weatherby, the owner of the Weatherby Television Network, and I'm glad you could all make it to my daughter's wedding!"

Whistles and cheers threatened to take off the roof. While the crowd applauded, a crew of stagehands whisked away the sofa, the chairs and the coffee table and replaced it with standing candelabra, and an elaborate triple arch of antique wrought iron that was bedecked with fresh ivy and creamy magnolia blossoms.

The stage was set in a matter of minutes, and Mallory, Baron and Price took their places before the justice of the peace. A sudden hush fell over the audience, and somehow, Mallory was able to block out the fact that she was about to say her wedding vows before several million people.

She heard the justice of the peace ask who was giving her away, and heard Price's response. She felt Baron take her hand in his. When she looked up at his handsome face, she felt a thrill of pride that he was hers, and a thrill of fear that he was hers.

He must have recognized the sudden burst of apprehension reflected in her eyes, because he gave her a quick wink and a smile that sent her heart soaring.

In turn, they said the traditional vows that would bind them together for a lifetime, but even as they spoke the words, Mallory knew they were unnecessary. She was bound to Baron in ways that went beyond words. She was tied to him by her heartstrings that thrummed and sang every time he looked at her, every time he touched her. She was constrained by the tender cords of love and need she both gave and received. And she was secured by the promise of joy and hope for a life filled with bright tomorrows she saw in his eyes every time she looked at him.

They exchanged rings that symbolized the continuity of their love, and then she was in his arms, and the crowd was roaring again, and she heard the justice of the peace introduce them as Mr. and Mrs. Montgomery.

She heard the familiar theme music start, and before she knew what he had in mind, Baron swept her up into his arms and, facing the camera, grinned and said, "Remember, you saw it first on 'The Edge!',—the show that's on the cutting edge of what's happening in your world—right now!"

At seven that evening, Mallory and Baron were more or less alone for the first time since they'd become man and wife in front of a goodly portion of America.

Carmen had been given a couple of weeks off to stay with her daughter, and Cassie, worn out from the excitement of being at home and seeing her beloved Maggie, had fallen asleep, hoping her early retirement would hurry Santa's visit.

Mrs. Huffman, the R.N. Price had hired, was in the bedroom adjoining Cassie's, ready to assist the child however she could if the necessity arose. After they'd wrapped up the show and been feted by Price and her new family and the whole crowd at WTN, they'd brought Cassie home and spent the afternoon entertaining her and reveling in the fact that she was at home and doing so well.

Now it was their time. Mallory and Baron lay on the carpet in front of a roaring fire, necking and petting like two oversexed teenagers. It had become a matter of principle to see who could hold out the longest. They were both breathing heavily; they were both trembling. They were both hotter than Fourth of July firecrackers.

"Calfrope," Baron groaned against Mallory's lips as she worked some particularly clever magic with her hands.

She drew away from him a few inches, her brow furrowed in question, her hands still busy. "Calfrope?"

"It's an old Texas saying," he wheezed.

"How many times do I have to tell you I don't speak foreign languages?" Mallory chided in a soft voice.

"Uncle, then," Baron said huskily, his eyes full of love and desire. "I give. Go ahead, have your way with me. I can't take anymore."

Mallory shook her head. "You have no stamina, Mr. Montgomery. And the only way to build stamina is to keep doing the exercise over and over."

"Gladly, Mrs. Montgomery. Every day if you want. Every night, too. But please—just put me out of my misery."

Mallory's lips quivered, and she leaned over to kiss him. The doorbell rang, shattering the stillness and the mood. Both she and Baron froze.

"Are we expecting someone?" Baron asked, not bothering to hide his frustration. "'Cause if we're not, and that's some carolers or someone looking for someone's house—they're dead."

"No one that I know of," Mallory said, straightening her clothes. "You get it. I'm a mess."

Baron rolled to his back. "Look at me. I can't go to the door like this."

She glanced at him and grinned naughtily. "I guess not." The doorbell chimed again. "Coming!" she called, leaping to her feet and smoothing her hair as she headed for the foyer.

She looked through the wavy glass of the leaded window, but she couldn't tell anything about the man on the doorstep except that he was big and burly. Unfastening the dead bolt, she opened the door a few inches. "May I help you?"

The man turned, and Mallory felt her world go spinning wildly out of control. She grabbed the doorjamb to steady herself.

"Daddy?" she said, the ten years since she'd learned that he *wasn't* her father forgotten as if they'd never been.

The man on the doorstep actually staggered back a step when she called him by the familiar name.

"Hello, Mallory," Kevin Damian said, his voice somber, his eyes filled with shame and apprehension and the slightest sheen of tears. "I came to offer you my congratulations and wish you a Merry Christmas."

Without the slightest hesitation, Mallory unhooked the chain and flung the door wide. Kevin Damian stepped into the warmth of the house and her arms, and the love that neither time nor pain could erase.

Later, when the tears had run their course and Mallory, Baron and Kevin were sitting in the kitchen drinking hot chocolate and munching on Christmas cookies, Mallory absorbed the sight of her dad's beloved face while he and Baron talked.

Kevin looked good. Older, heavier, but still handsome, still the man who had been her friend, her champion, the only man she'd thought she would ever love.

Though she'd been stunned to see him on her doorstep, it never occurred to her not to accept his apology. How could she claim to love him and not forgive him? His coming back into her life now, when she'd been blessed with so many other wonderful things—Cassie's continuing good health, a whole new family, Baron— was just the icing on her cake.

Kevin glanced over at her and, smiling, reached across the table. Mallory placed her hand in his.

"God, I've missed you, baby," he said in a strangled voice. "I've wanted to contact you—started to—a hundred, maybe a thousand times, but I was afraid you'd reject me the same way I did you all those years ago." He shook his head. "If Baron hadn't called me, I might never have made the move."

Mallory looked across the table at her new husband. "When did you call?"

"The morning after Cassie's surgery. There was such misery in your voice when you spoke of Kevin, I thought he deserved to know how you felt, and maybe he even deserved a piece of my mind for the way he'd hurt you."

"What Baron didn't know is that I'd wanted to get in touch with you, but was afraid to. By the time I was able to separate my feelings for Betty from my feelings for you back when your mom and I split up, you were in college at Arizona State. You don't know how much I've regretted the way I treated you."

"How did you know where I went to school?"

Kevin smiled. "I read about you winning that scholarship in the paper. I tried to keep up with what was happening with you as best I could. I remarried a couple of years after Betty and I divorced, a young woman who wanted a career more than she did a family, and she told me time and again that if she were you, she'd never forgive me. So, whenever I got the urge to call, I remembered what she said, and didn't."

"So you're married?"

"No," Kevin said. "We divorced after a couple of years. I read about your marrying Mark, and then when you moved away, I lost touch completely. I didn't know about Cassie or your divorce or that you'd moved back to L.A. when your marriage broke up. I didn't know where you were until I read Betty's obituary and saw that you were working on that soap opera."

"I came back here because there was no money, and I needed Mama's help with Cassie."

Kevin scrubbed a thick hand down his ruddy face with its neatly trimmed gray beard. "When I think of you scrimping and doing without, I could kick myself. It was all so unnecessary."

"Stop it!" Mallory said. "We're not going to beat ourselves up for the past. If there's one thing Cassie has taught me, it's to live each day to its fullest, because we aren't guaranteed any tomorrows."

He squeezed her hand. "I don't deserve your forgiveness, but I'm thankful that you're a bigger person than I was."

"Anger just eats you up from the inside out," Mallory said.

"Believe me, I know. All I got by cutting you out of my life was a lot of empty years. That's what really hit me when I heard Betty had died. All the wasted years. I realized then, that it didn't matter who planted the seed, I was your real dad."

Mallory nodded. "Price is a wonderful man, and I know we're going to get closer the more we get to know about each other. But you were the one who rocked me to sleep and who sat up with me when I was sick and went to my dance recitals and waited for me to get home from my dates. You're my real dad, and nothing will ever change that."

"I hope that someday Cassie will be able to say the same thing about me," said Baron, who had been listening in silence.

Mallory offered him her other hand. "She will."

From the living room, Betty's antique clock chimed midnight.

"It's Christmas Day," Mallory said with a smile. "We'd better get some sleep. Cassie is notorious for waking up at the crack of dawn on Christmas, and I don't think her surgery will change that."

"Yeah," Kevin said. "I'd better get going. I have some gifts in the car, though. Some things for you and Cassie, and a wedding gift."

Mallory started to tell him he didn't have to do that, but knew that he did. "If you don't have any plans for tomorrow, why don't you stay the night?" she said suddenly. "I don't have any spare beds, but you're welcome to the sofa. It's pretty comfortable."

She could see the indecision on Kevin's face—the worry that his staying would be an imposition on the newlyweds warring with his loneliness.

"Are you sure you don't mind?" he asked at last.

"We'll be disappointed if you don't stay," Baron said.

"But you just got married this afternoon."

"So we'll be very, very quiet," Baron said with a wicked grin.

"Baron!"

He laughed, then turned serious. "We've got the rest of our lives for a honeymoon, Kevin. We'd really like for you to stay."

There was a suspicious glitter in Kevin Damian's eyes as he nodded.

Twenty minutes later, Kevin was ensconced on the sofa and Santa had placed Cassie's long-wished-for toys beneath the tree. Baron and Mallory were snuggled together in her double bed.

"Thank you for giving me back my dad for Christmas."

"It was nothing any wonderful, considerate, kind and loving husband wouldn't have done," Baron said, pulling her closer against him.

"That's what I love about you, Montgomery," Mallory said, rubbing her lips against his chest. "You're such a humble sort of guy."

Laughing, Baron rolled her over onto her back and pressed his lips to hers in a long, slow kiss.

It was a long, long time before either of them was able to utter anything but a moan.

"Mommy! Baron! Wake up! Come quick!" Cassie's excited voice was punctuated by Maggie's sharp bark.

Mallory forced her leaden eyelids upward and saw that it was barely light in the room. Cassie stood by the bed, her nurse hovered in the doorway in case she was needed.

"Morning, Moppet," Mallory said around a yawn. "Merry Christmas."

"Get up, Mommy!" Cassie urged, taking Mallory's hand. "Come see what's in the living room."

A rumpled Baron raised himself on one elbow. "Hey, Short Stuff! Did Santa come?"

Cassie's eyes were wide and filled with wonder. "He came, but he must have got tired 'cause he fell asleep on our couch."

Kevin! In the semidarkness, with his girth and his beard, it was understandable that Cassie might mistake him for the jolly old elf himself. Mallory and Baron exchanged amused smiles.

"That isn't Santa Claus," Mallory said. "That's the man who was my daddy when I was growing up. He's your grandfather."

Cassie's forehead puckered in puzzlement. "I thought Grandpa Price was your daddy."

"He is." Mallory chucked Cassie beneath the chin. "You'll understand it better when you get older."

"So I have *two* grandpas?"

Mallory nodded. "Isn't it great?"

"Actually, you have three," Baron corrected. "You haven't met my dad yet. He'll be your grandpa, too."

Cassie rolled her eyes in a typical four-year-old's expression. "Three grandpas! That's too many!"

"Oh, honey," Mallory said. "You can never have too many. The more family you have, the more love you have."

"And presents?" Cassie asked with a sly smile.

"And presents," Mallory said with a nod. "But you need to remember that gifts get old and broken, but love lasts forever."

Responding to the seriousness in Mallory's eyes, Cassie nodded. Then she grinned. "Can we go open our presents now?"

Baron laughed. Mallory sighed. "By all means."

"Goody!" Cassie left the room with her nurse, still with that sedate walk. Maggie was close on her heels.

Baron and Mallory got up, donned robes and followed Cassie into the living room. The R.N. had plugged in the chiming Christmas bells that were ringing out the "The Twelve Days of Christmas." The lights on the tree twinkled merrily, and the Christmas angel on top cast down a serene smile. Kevin sat on the sofa, watching Cassie's excitement with a look in his eyes that could only be described as ecstasy.

Mallory's throat tightened. How could anyone wish for anything more than what she had in this very room? She gripped Baron's hand tighter and he brought her hand to his lips.

"Merry Christmas, Mallory," he said, the look in his eyes telling Mallory that he loved her.

"Merry Christmas to you, too."

Kevin turned and smiled, and her heart filled to overflowing. For a person who'd been alone and unloved for so long, her life was now filled with a surfeit of the emotion.

She'd been blessed with the greatest gift of all.

* * * * *

COMING NEXT MONTH

#925 FOR THE BABY'S SAKE—Christine Rimmer
That Special Woman!
Andrea McCreary had decided to raise her unborn baby on her own.
Clay Barrett had generously offered a proposal of marriage, and soon
realized their arrangement would not be without passion....

#926 C IS FOR COWBOY—Lisa Jackson
Love Letters
Only the promise of a reward convinced Sloan Redhawk to rescue
headstrong, spoiled Casey McKee. He despised women like her—yet
once he rescued her, he was unable to let her go!

#927 ONE STEP AWAY—Sherryl Woods
Only one thing was missing from Ken Hutchinson's life: the woman of
his dreams. Now he'd found Beth Callahan, but convincing her to join
his ready-made family wouldn't be so easy....

#928 ONLY ST. NICK KNEW—Nikki Benjamin
Alison Kent was eager to escape the holiday hustle and bustle. Meeting
Frank Bradford—and his adorable twin sons—suddenly showed her this
could indeed be the most wonderful time of the year!

#929 JAKE RYKER'S BACK IN TOWN—Jennifer Mikels
Hellion Jake Ryker had stormed out of town, leaving behind a broken
heart. Stunned to discover he had returned, Leigh McCall struggled with
stormy memories—and with Jake's renewed passionate presence.

#930 ABIGAIL AND MISTLETOE—Karen Rose Smith
Abigail Fox's generous nature never allowed her to think of herself.
Her heart needed the kind of mending only Brady Crawford could
provide—and their kiss under the mistletoe was just the beginning....

MILLION DOLLAR SWEEPSTAKES (III)

No purchase necessary. To enter, follow the directions published. Method of entry may vary. For eligibility, entries must be received no later than March 31, 1996. No liability is assumed for printing errors, lost, late or misdirected entries. Odds of winning are determined by the number of eligible entries distributed and received. Prizewinners will be determined no later than June 30, 1996.

Sweepstakes open to residents of the U.S. (except Puerto Rico), Canada, Europe and Taiwan who are 18 years of age or older. All applicable laws and regulations apply. Sweepstakes offer void wherever prohibited by law. Values of all prizes are in U.S. currency. This sweepstakes is presented by Torstar Corp., its subsidiaries and affiliates, in conjunction with book, merchandise and/or product offerings. For a copy of the Official Rules governing this sweepstakes offer, send a self-addressed, stamped envelope (WA residents need not affix return postage) to: MILLION DOLLAR SWEEPSTAKES (III) Rules, P.O. Box 4573, Blair, NE 68009, USA.

SWP-TS94

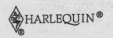 HARLEQUIN®  Silhouette®

The movie event of the season can be the reading event of the year!

Lights… The lights go on in October when CBS presents Harlequin/Silhouette Sunday Matinee Movies. These four movies are based on bestselling Harlequin and Silhouette novels.

Camera… As the cameras roll, be the first to read the original novels the movies are based on!

Action… Through this offer, you can have these books sent directly to you! Just fill in the order form below and you could be reading the books…before the movie!

48288-4	Treacherous Beauties by Cheryl Emerson	
	$3.99 U.S./$4.50 CAN.	☐
83305-9	Fantasy Man by Sharon Green	
	$3.99 U.S./$4.50 CAN.	☐
48289-2	A Change of Place by Tracy Sinclair	
	$3.99 U.S./$4.50CAN.	☐
83306-7	Another Woman by Margot Dalton	
	$3.99 U.S./$4.50 CAN.	☐

TOTAL AMOUNT	$	
POSTAGE & HANDLING	$	
($1.00 for one book, 50¢ for each additional)		
APPLICABLE TAXES*	$	_____
TOTAL PAYABLE	$	_____
(check or money order—please do not send cash)		

To order, complete this form and send it, along with a check or money order for the total above, payable to Harlequin Books, to: **In the U.S.:** 3010 Walden Avenue, P.O. Box 9047, Buffalo, NY 14269-9047; **In Canada:** P.O. Box 613, Fort Erie, Ontario, L2A 5X3.

Name: _____

Address: _____ City: _____

State/Prov.: _____ Zip/Postal Code: _____

*New York residents remit applicable sales taxes.
 Canadian residents remit applicable GST and provincial taxes.

CBSPR

"HOORAY FOR HOLLYWOOD" SWEEPSTAKES

HERE'S HOW THE SWEEPSTAKES WORKS

OFFICIAL RULES — NO PURCHASE NECESSARY

To enter, complete an Official Entry Form or hand print on a 3" x 5" card the words "HOORAY FOR HOLLYWOOD", your name and address and mail your entry in the pre-addressed envelope (if provided) or to: "Hooray for Hollywood" Sweepstakes, P.O. Box 9076, Buffalo, NY 14269-9076 or "Hooray for Hollywood" Sweepstakes, P.O. Box 637, Fort Erie, Ontario L2A 5X3. Entries must be sent via First Class Mail and be received no later than 12/31/94. No liability is assumed for lost, late or misdirected mail.

Winners will be selected in random drawings to be conducted no later than January 31, 1995 from all eligible entries received.

Grand Prize: A 7-day/6-night trip for 2 to Los Angeles, CA including round trip air transportation from commercial airport nearest winner's residence, accommodations at the Regent Beverly Wilshire Hotel, free rental car, and $1,000 spending money. (Approximate prize value which will vary dependent upon winner's residence: $5,400.00 U.S.); 500 Second Prizes: A pair of "Hollywood Star" sunglasses (prize value: $9.95 U.S. each). Winner selection is under the supervision of D.L. Blair, Inc., an independent judging organization, whose decisions are final. Grand Prize travelers must sign and return a release of liability prior to traveling. Trip must be taken by 2/1/96 and is subject to airline schedules and accommodations availability.

Sweepstakes offer is open to residents of the U.S. (except Puerto Rico) and Canada who are 18 years of age or older, except employees and immediate family members of Harlequin Enterprises, Ltd., its affiliates, subsidiaries, and all agencies, entities or persons connected with the use, marketing or conduct of this sweepstakes. All federal, state, provincial, municipal and local laws apply. Offer void wherever prohibited by law. Taxes and/or duties are the sole responsibility of the winners. Any litigation within the province of Quebec respecting the conduct and awarding of prizes may be submitted to the Regie des loteries et courses du Quebec. All prizes will be awarded; winners will be notified by mail. No substitution of prizes are permitted. Odds of winning are dependent upon the number of eligible entries received.

Potential grand prize winner must sign and return an Affidavit of Eligibility within 30 days of notification. In the event of non-compliance within this time period, prize may be awarded to an alternate winner. Prize notification returned as undeliverable may result in the awarding of prize to an alternate winner. By acceptance of their prize, winners consent to use of their names, photographs, or likenesses for purpose of advertising, trade and promotion on behalf of Harlequin Enterprises, Ltd., without further compensation unless prohibited by law. A Canadian winner must correctly answer an arithmetical skill-testing question in order to be awarded the prize.

For a list of winners (available after 2/28/95), send a separate stamped, self-addressed envelope to: Hooray for Hollywood Sweepstakes 3252 Winners, P.O. Box 4200, Blair, NE 68009.

CBSRLS

OFFICIAL ENTRY COUPON

"Hooray for Hollywood"
SWEEPSTAKES!

Yes, I'd love to win the Grand Prize — a vacation in Hollywood —
or one of 500 pairs of "sunglasses of the stars"! Please enter me
in the sweepstakes!

This entry must be received by December 31, 1994.
Winners will be notified by January 31, 1995.

Name _____

Address _____ Apt. _____

City _____

State/Prov. _____ Zip/Postal Code _____

Daytime phone number _____
(area code)

Mail all entries to: Hooray for Hollywood Sweepstakes,
P.O. Box 9076, Buffalo, NY 14269-9076.
In Canada, mail to: Hooray for Hollywood Sweepstakes,
P.O. Box 637, Fort Erie, ON L2A 5X3.

KCH

OFFICIAL ENTRY COUPON

"Hooray for Hollywood"
SWEEPSTAKES!

Yes, I'd love to win the Grand Prize — a vacation in Hollywood —
or one of 500 pairs of "sunglasses of the stars"! Please enter me
in the sweepstakes!

This entry must be received by December 31, 1994.
Winners will be notified by January 31, 1995.

Name _____

Address _____ Apt. _____

City _____

State/Prov. _____ Zip/Postal Code _____

Daytime phone number _____
(area code)

Mail all entries to: Hooray for Hollywood Sweepstakes,
P.O. Box 9076, Buffalo, NY 14269-9076.
In Canada, mail to: Hooray for Hollywood Sweepstakes,
P.O. Box 637, Fort Erie, ON L2A 5X3.

KCH